**Also available from Julie Moffett
and Carina Press**

The Lexi Carmichael Series

Suggested reading order

No One Lives Twice
No One to Trust
No Money Down (novella)
No Place Like Rome
No Biz Like Showbiz
No Test for the Wicked
No Woman Left Behind
No Room for Error
No Strings Attached
No Living Soul
No Regrets
No Stone Unturned

**Stay tuned for the next book in the
Lexi Carmichael Mystery series from Julie Moffett**

No Questions Asked

Coming Winter 2019

Also from Carina Press and Julie Moffett

Scottish Historical Romance

The Thorn and the Thistle
Her Kilt-Clad Rogue (novella)

Also from Julie Moffett

Historical Paranormal Romance

The Fireweaver
The Healer
A Double-Edged Blade
Across a Moonswept Moor

Young Adult

White Knights
Knight Moves

S0-BIW-596

NO BIZ
LIKE SHOWBIZ

Julie Moffett

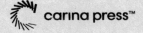

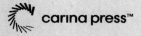

ISBN-13: 978-1-335-08015-8

No Biz Like Showbiz

Recycling programs
for this product may
not exist in your area.

www.CarinaPress.com

Printed in U.S.A.

"A good friend knows all your best stories.
A best friend has lived them with you."

This is for you, my girlfriends, old and new.
Much love now and always!

Donna B. Moffett
Sandra Moffett Parks
Elizabeth Craig Moffett
Katy Moffett
Kit Greening Daniel
Cathy Vida Malik
Maria Kieslich
Diane Bennett
Joyce Wallen
Laura Demas Petrosian
Cathy Telles Witschger
Liz Baldin McCarty
Elizabeth Byrne Burley

NO BIZ
LIKE SHOWBIZ

Chapter One

My name is Lexi Carmichael and I have a problem with most of today's television programming. Not because of the sheer implausibility of a majority of the shows—although that does factor—but because too many programs seem to feature a tech genius who can solve the problems of the world with one stroke of a keyboard.

Here's how it happens…a tech head is desperately trying to hack into a system. Death, the collapse of the free world, or the apocalypse is imminent if he fails. (Yes, tech heroes *always* seem to be guys, since I guess in Hollywood a woman doesn't know her way around a keyboard.) *He* types commands frantically as the clock ticks down to doomsday. As the scenario continues, our frazzled hero takes a moment to run his fingers through his perfectly styled hair before he types just one more command and bingo, he's in. He'll then have a whole millisecond to navigate a completely unfamiliar system, find the magic switch, and shut down the entire system in time to save the day, world, girl, whatever, with one stroke. All of this while the super-expensive, cutting-edge government system or expensive black-market technology used by the show's villain will aid our intrepid hero by providing helpful visual prompts like Access Denied or Access Granted in big bold letters across the screen as he works his hacking magic.

Just shoot me.

I'm a *real* hacker and yes, I'm female. I double-majored in mathematics and computer science at Georgetown University and have spent most of my twenty-five years learning how to bypass cryptographic protocols, exploit system vulnerabilities, and finesse distributed denial of service attacks. I've never had to avert an apocalypse, but if I did, I'm pretty sure it would take more than one freaking minute, and I wouldn't be worried about my hair while doing it. My first successful hack on a relatively simple system took five hours. It might have taken four, but my mom kept distracting me by yelling through my bedroom door that if I gave ballet class just one more try she'd give me a hundred dollars to spend however I wanted. So, watching these types of shows and movies is hard on both my nerves and stomach.

Despite this, I still have a television and occasionally go to the movies. Although I never did learn to dance ballet, I did create a place of solitude for myself in a small apartment in Jessup, Maryland, which is near the National Security Agency, where I used to work. Now I'm the Director of Information Security for a hot new cyber intelligence firm in the DC area called X-Corp. The job title sounds impressive, but I'm still the same girl I've always been, except I've been trying hard for the past several months to expand my social horizons outside my safe virtual cocoon. That means I'll watch television once in a while just so I can have something to talk about if the conversation lags, which it inevitably does if I'm involved.

On Mondays, I generally eat dinner in front of my laptop while gaming and watching *Repercussions*, a sci-fi cable series about a group of young adults who discover they're the prodigies of a race of super aliens. However, I'd seen this episode, "The Savant Within," so I'd muted it to concentrate on my game.

My game is "Hollow Realm," an online real-time strategy scenario where players command magical armies in massive and complicated battles against each other. My best buddies, Elvis and Xavier Zimmerman, genius twins and excellent strategists at "Realm," were remotely supporting my current struggle against a bunch of demon-controlled ogres. It wasn't going well.

I ate another spoonful of my dinner—Cheerios—and tried a couple of virtual maneuvers with my army of Glimmers—shimmery forms that could use light to destroy an enemy. Mistake. A group of frenzied ogres with light-deflecting shadow shields called murks crushed me.

"Crap. Total failure."

Dejected, I pushed my chair back from my monitor. I'd have to try to recoup my losses another day.

My computer pinged me. I glanced down at the message.

Better luck next time, Lexi.

I typed back.

Thanks, Elvis. You and Xavier rock. Appreciate the support. Let me know if you need help with the zombies on Zeroth.

Will do. Hoping for pizza and Quake with you soon. How are you feeling?

I'm good. Going back to work tomorrow. I look forward to that pizza and more gaming soon. Miss seeing you.

Me too. A lot. Bye.

Bye.

I stared at the message for a moment. Just a few years ago I never would have imagined one of my best friends would be a guy, let alone one of the few people in the universe who could beat me at most online fantasy role-playing games. But now, Elvis probably knows me better than anyone. We're mirror images—two awkward geek rulers within the world's new cyber-universe, while we remain outsiders in the real world. It's a nice feeling to know he always has my back in both worlds.

I drank the rest of the milk from my bowl and carried it out of the bedroom. I'd taken one step into the kitchen when I saw a man dressed in jeans, a dark sweater and a short black leather jacket leaning against my counter.

"*Slash!*"

I jumped a good foot straight up and lost control of my bowl. Slash caught it and the spoon with one hand.

"Easy there, *cara*." He put the bowl in the sink, then turned to face me.

Slash is one of the most fascinating and complex people I've ever met. He's Italian-American and probably the sexiest überhacker in the universe. He works for the National Security Agency in some top-secret capacity, and his knowledge is so important and integrated with the security of the United States that a team of FBI agents follows him around the clock.

Slash and I had just returned from what had turned out to be a dangerous case in Rome. Typically, hunting hackers doesn't involve bodily harm, but this case had been an unusual one and we'd both nearly died. I'd been shot in the left hand and was still rocking a line of stitches across my back.

He grinned. "How are you doing?"

His black hair was shorter on the side of his head that had been injured and he also had a walking cast on one leg. All of that only served to make him look even sexier and more mysterious than usual.

I pressed my hand to my chest. "Well, not counting the five years you just took off my life by showing up unannounced in my kitchen, okay, I guess."

It's kind of a running joke between Slash and me. No matter what kind of alarm I buy or how I set it, he gets into my apartment. I don't think he's ever once knocked on my door. It used to freak me out, but now it's just part of our game.

"How about you, Slash? You feeling any better?"

He carefully rotated his shoulder. "The doctor took the sling off two days ago. It's feeling pretty good. I've got some physical therapy ahead of me to get it back to full strength."

"That's great."

He took a step across the kitchen and gave me a kiss on the cheek. He smelled good. He *always* smelled good. "I've been thinking about you, *cara*."

He took my left hand in his and turned my palm up. "You got the bandage off. How does it feel?"

I flexed my hand. "It hurts, but it's better. I'm so used

to the twinges I barely notice it. I have to squeeze a therapy ball thirty minutes a day. I'm going back to work
tomorrow." I glanced down at his leg. "How's the cast?"

He leaned over and tapped his leg. A hollow thump
sounded. "It's uncomfortable. I must wear it for another two weeks."

I sighed. "Jeez. We're a couple of wrecks."

"*Si.*" He put his arm around me. "But it's better than
the alternative."

"True. Well, since you're here, do you want to sit
down?"

He smiled and I led him to the couch. As he sat
down, I saw a shoulder holster and gun peek out from
beneath his jacket. I helped him prop the leg with the
cast on the coffee table before sitting next to him and
leaning back against the cushions. I put my feet on the
table next to his.

Slash is another anomaly in my life. I'd met him
when we both got mixed up in an international case
while we working at the NSA. At some point, over the
past few months, our relationship had evolved. It happened so subtly I couldn't put my finger on when or
how exactly it occurred. But something had definitely
changed between us in Rome, so now I had to calculate
what it meant in terms of everyday interaction with him.

"Slash, there's something I've been meaning to ask
you."

"Ask away."

"We're friends, right?"

"Absolutely."

"Is that all?"

He shifted slightly on the couch, studying my face.
"What's on your mind, *cara?*"

"Well, back in the crypt in Rome, you said…you said you loved me."

My cheeks heated. Why was I embarrassed? I wasn't the one who had said it. Slash had uttered those three words, throwing them down like some kind of gauntlet between us. Unfortunately, we'd been running from an armed bomb at the time, so I couldn't ask for clarification. Now that we were home, was I supposed to do something—say something—in response? If so, what?

"Ah, *si*, I did say that."

Holy cow. Slash *loved* me. My stomach felt funny and fluttery at the same time. "So, did you say that for a reason, or was it a turn-of-phrase-because-we-are-in-serious-peril kind of thing? You know, in case we bought the farm."

"Bought the farm?"

"Died."

He chuckled. "No. I said it because I meant it. I *am* in love with you. Quite desperately, actually."

I searched his face for signs that he was teasing. But he met my eyes with a calm, even gaze. "Define what you mean by love."

He touched my hair. "Italians do not define love. We show it. It became clear to me in Rome—actually, *you* became clear to me. I realized that you had become the most important thing in my life."

"I had? How?"

He sighed. "Where to begin? I think you've surprised me in ways I never expected. In addition to your intelligence, you are one of the most genuine, open and courageous people I've ever met. There is no pretense with you. No hidden agenda in the relationship."

"Why would anyone have a hidden agenda?"

"Why, indeed?" He fell silent.

I hesitated and then plunged on. "Well, I feel it's important to point out that you've omitted any mention of my lack of social graces."

He shrugged. "They are overrated. I haven't always got it figured out either."

I blinked. "You haven't?"

He chuckled. "I haven't. *Cara*, I've faced my share of social bullying, even as an adult."

Slash, bullied? The man who seemed to handle people and complex situations with effortless grace? The same man who attracted women like electrons attracted protons?

"You, Slash? That's…impossible."

"Why? I was overweight and oversmart when I was young, and kids can be quite cruel."

"I'm sorry. I understand the trauma of bullying quite well. But you seem so confident now."

"At some point, I lost the baby fat and eventually figured how to use my intelligence to my advantage in social situations. But I was still more comfortable with computers than with most people, even girls."

"Wait. *You* had problems with girls, too? Really?"

He laughed. "*Il mio Dio*, I adore you even more. *Si*, really."

I held up my hand. "Well, at least you've had relationships. I can count the number of friends I have on one hand, and I've never been in an, um, romantic relationship with anyone on a boyfriend-girlfriend level."

He took my hand. "Good."

"Why is that good?"

"Because I like the idea of being your first significant other."

"You want to be my significant other?"

He raised an eyebrow. "Would you like me to be?"

I considered his words. "I… I don't know. What about Finn?"

Slash sighed, dropped my hand, then crossed his arms against his chest. "What about him?"

Finn Shaughnessy is my boss and a guy who still wants to have a talk with me about a relationship that we may or may not be having. I'm having mixed feelings about Finn. I'm physically attracted to him, but I've been slowly coming the conclusion that I am not going to be able to date him—if that's even what he wants—mostly because I don't think I can handle the complexity of dating my boss.

"I'm not certain of my relationship status with him."

Slash's voice hardened. "Finn is not my concern. How *you* feel is what matters to me."

"Fair enough. But how do you sort it all out? How do you ascertain you've accumulated enough information to decide whether or not you're going to enter into a romantic relationship with someone?"

"When you want to be *with* someone, you'll know."

I'd know? Who was he kidding? I never knew about stuff like that. *Never.*

"We're talking beyond just the physical attraction, right, Slash?"

"*Si*, that's right."

I paused, thinking about what it would be like to have sex with Slash. Okay, I'll admit I'd thought about it before, but now his declaration of love had really put it on the table. No question I was attracted to him and, based on the number of intimate touches and kisses he'd given me in the past, it seemed clear I appealed to him. I still couldn't fathom why. A guy as hot and accomplished as Slash could easily have his pick of any woman on Earth. So, why he liked me remained a bit of mystery. For me, the easy part was my attraction to him—both physically and intellectually. The hard part was the emotional attraction and how to define or even sustain that so that it equaled love or at the very least, an intimate relationship on more levels than just the physical.

"It just doesn't seem logical to rely on what might be the heat of the moment or an intangible concept like love to enter into something as important as a relationship."

Slash's jaw tightened. "You'll figure out what you want from Finn. I cannot do that for you. All the same, I want you to know I'm here and I'm not holding back any more. You opened the door to me in Rome and I stepped through. I'm not going to back off, Finn or any other man notwithstanding. But you should know, if I enter the game, I play to win, especially if the reward is something particularly valuable to me."

This statement seemed significant. I remembered something my best friend Basia had told me once about Slash being a player. She said guys like him enjoyed the thrill of the chase, but lost interest after the win.

"Is love a game to you?"

Slash linked fingers with me again. "I admit that it has been for me in the past. But with you, no." He pressed his lips to my palm. "Never. Believe me, if it was just a game, I would have had you in my bed long ago."

I didn't want to ask, but I knew I'd regret it if I didn't. "So, is that the end game? You know, sex?"

He looked surprised at the question and then chuckled. "Sex is not the end, *cara*. It can be the *beginning* of an intimate connection. But in our situation, there are so many aspects that are completely out of my control. Sex isn't going to resolve those. Only you can, when you're ready."

"Wait. We have a *situation?*"

"I'm afraid we do."

I studied him. "You're actually worried. What could you possibly be worried about?"

"*Tu mi hai rapito il cuore.*"

"What did you say?"

"I said you have stolen my heart."

"I did?"

He pressed my palm against his chest. "*Si*, you have. As a result, the power of this relationship belongs to you. Perhaps it has from the first moment I saw you in your bedroom in that ridiculous T-shirt, boldly testing my hacking skills. Then, when you kissed me in Rome, I knew for certain."

"How?"

He shook his head. "I don't know. I just did. Because of that, I'm not going to make you, trick you, or even seduce you into choosing me, as much as I'm tempted. And you should know I'm tempted very much. I want you to come to me willingly, with an open heart, because then it *will* matter. Not only to me, but to you and your heart."

My pulse quickened. "Define willingly."

He laughed and kissed the top of my head. "See, that is exactly why my heart is yours. I'll define nothing more. You'll know when you know. Just inform me, at some point, if you consider Finn, or anyone else, your boyfriend so I can figure out how to manage that. Deal?"

"You could manage that?"

"I could. Just promise me you'll keep me informed."

He made it sound easy, like I could figure things out just like that. But he was Slash and things like that always seemed to come easy for him, despite what he'd said about his past.

I sighed and put my head on his shoulder. "Okay, I promise."

Chapter Two

I got into work early the next day after my routine swing through Dunkin' Donuts for two chocolate glazed, a large coffee and a large Diet Coke. There was no one in the reception area when I came in, so I strolled into my office and set my laptop on the desk. I took a sip of my coffee and sat down in my chair, enjoying the quiet. I would've been more excited to be back in the office if I wasn't so worried about talking to Finn.

I like working at X-Corp. I enjoy the challenge, the work and even the people, which surprised me. It used to be that all social interactions made me nervous. I think I'm improving, though. Now I get anxious primarily when something happens that involves potential romantic interaction, or when I've injured or maimed someone, which seems to happen on a regular basis.

I haven't had to worry much about romantic interaction until recently. At age twenty-five, I've never had a boyfriend and I've had sex exactly one time. The encounter took place with a fellow geek after we both imbibed too much mystery punch at a nanotronics lecture at the university. After our liaison, he realized he liked men. I try not to be too worried about that, but it lingers in the back of my mind.

Basia had convinced me that I needed to expand my really, *really* small horizon and explore the possibility of romance. She's been guiding me with mixed results, but at least I'm trying.

The problem is that my love life is now a royal mess. I may, or may not, be dating my boss, and Slash just said he loves me. Somehow I've gone from the Sahara Desert of dating to the revolving door of men. It was not at all the slow, modest exposure to dating and interaction with the opposite sex that I'd hoped for.

I was pondering that peculiarity when Basia bounded into the office with her usual enthusiasm and perkiness. It never ceases to amaze me that we managed to share a college dorm room, let alone become best friends.

"Hey, Lexi. I can't tell you how wonderful it is to see you behind your desk again. I've missed having you here." She planted herself in my visitor chair and crossed her legs, flipping her fingers through her dark bob. "You're here early this morning. How are you feeling?"

I dug the small therapy ball out of my purse and began squeezing it. "I have to do this for at least thirty minutes a day. But it doesn't hurt too much anymore."

"I'm glad. What about your back?"

"Better. The stitches itch a lot."

"That's okay. It means it's healing."

"I know. The doctor said the scar would barely show."

She grinned. "I bet it's sexy. Think of the stories you can tell your grandchildren." Then her smile faded and I knew she was remembering how close I had come to dying.

"Why did you come back to work so soon? Finn told everyone you'd be out for two weeks."

I sighed. "My mom."

My mother, well-known model and former beauty queen Clarissa Carmichael, had visited me every day since I had returned from Rome. In addition to fussing over me like a baby, she kept offering to set me up with her best friend's son who was doing his medical internship at a nearby hospital. Her goal in life is to see me married off to a rich, preferably politically connected husband, who can provide for my every need. She consistently ignores the fact that I already have two degrees, a decent paying job, and the ability to support myself just fine. Instead she likes to pretend I'm a bubbly young woman who loves clothes, make-up and talking about boys. I love my mom, but she exhausts me more than most people.

"Well, that explains it. Anyway, I'm glad you're back and feeling better. Have you heard about the client meeting today?"

"No. I haven't seen Finn yet. Do we have a new client?"

"Potentially. It's a Hollywood production company—SWM. I totally love their new cable show, *Milkmaids and Models*. They take rural, farm-raised girls to Hollywood and turn them into models."

I stared at her.

"It's a great show. Really. It's on tomorrow. I'll come over and introduce it to you, if you'll promise to make some popcorn."

"I'd rather have twenty-six pap smears than watch that. Give me *Doctor Who*, *Repercussions* or *Star Trek* any day of the week."

She rolled her eyes. "You don't know what you're missing."

"Thank goodness."

She laughed and came behind the desk, perching on the edge. "This is exactly why I've missed you."

"At least someone missed me. So, are you going to the meeting?"

"Not unless they need X-Corp's translator there. Are you?"

I hadn't seen anything from Finn about a meeting in my email. "I'm not sure."

"Okay. Anything else going on in your life that I should know about?"

I considered a moment. "No. All's well."

"Cool. Let me know how it goes if you're in on the SWM meeting."

"Will do."

She bounced out of my office.

I watched her go, wondering why I hadn't told her about Slash. I told Basia *everything*. I had to. She was my social navigator.

Except this morning, I'd hesitated. She'd warned me away from Slash more than once. I knew she'd disapprove of whatever I said about him, even if I wasn't doing anything about it. She'd almost had a heart attack when I'd mentioned that Slash had given me a bottle of wine a few months ago and told me we'd open it on the day we first made love. Now he'd said he loved me…as more than a friend. I wasn't sure Basia's heart would survive a development like that. Especially since I wasn't sure how my *own* heart was handling it.

It wasn't that Basia didn't like Slash—she did. She just thought Finn was a safer bet for me. It's hard not to agree. Finn never shows up unannounced at my apartment, doesn't carry a gun, and isn't followed around by the FBI. Finn and I have had a couple of dinners and shared a few passionate kisses. I stopped as far as taking a shower with him, but I'm not exactly sure why. It just didn't feel right. I think that having worked for Finn these past couple of months has somehow changed the dynamic between us. I'm having an increasingly hard time thinking romantically about the man who signs my paycheck.

I started to get a headache just thinking about it, so I pushed aside my anxiety and shot Finn an e-mail asking if he wanted me in on the morning meeting with SWM. He shot me one back telling me he'd prefer me to go home and rest. When I threatened to fill his inbox with spam, he relented.

Conference
room
two
in
ten
minutes.

That gave me time to refill my coffee cup, grab my laptop and make my way to the conference room. When I got there, Finn was standing with his hands on the back of a chair, talking to two men. The middle-aged man closest to me wore a Dodgers baseball cap and had a bulging stomach hanging over his belted jeans. He glanced at me when I walked in, and I almost recoiled. He had the hairiest eyebrows I'd ever seen. They formed a black caterpillar bridge over his blue eyes. I tried not to stare.

Finn smiled when he saw me. "Hello, Lexi." He motioned for me to come over. "This is John Cartwright from SWM Productions and his PA, Tony Rabbin."

Tony was blond and my age, dressed in a pressed pair of khakis and a button-down pink shirt. He was really, *really* tan.

I looked at Finn blankly. "PA?"

"Personal assistant."

I wasn't sure what exactly a personal assistant did, but Tony stuck out his hand, so I shook it. Eyebrow Guy passed up my offer of a handshake and waved at me instead. "Sorry. I have a thing about handshakes. Never know where someone else's hands may have been. And please, call me Cartwright."

I looked down at my hand, thinking he had a pretty good point. "Okay, Cartwright."

"Lexi is our Director of Information Security." Finn pulled out a chair for me. "She's solved most of our most difficult cases."

Since we'd technically only had a few real cases, it wasn't a big vote of confidence. But Cartwright didn't have to know that.

I sat and the men followed suit. I opened my laptop as Finn asked, "So, gentlemen, what can X-Corp do for you?"

Cartwright leaned forward, putting his elbows on the table. "We've got a computer issue on one of our most popular shows."

Finn nodded. "Okay. What kind of computer issue?"

"A bad one. Someone is hacking into our system and skewing our results show."

I peered around the laptop lid, my interest piqued. "Hacking?"

Cartwright shrugged. "Hacking, smacking. I don't know what it's called. All I know is some yo-yo is messing with my show. It's got to stop before we end up down the entertainment toilet."

Finn leaned back in his chair. "Can you give us some background on the show and a bit more detail on what's happening?"

Cartwright removed his ball cap and set it on the table. He was balding on top and what stringy hair he had left was plastered against his scalp. He rubbed at the bald spot. "You've heard of SWM Productions, right?"

Unlike me, Finn apparently had done his homework, so he got to answer. "Of course. You produce mostly game shows."

"No, not games shows. Reality television. There is a big difference, you know."

"I stand corrected."

"Yeah, well, we're running a half dozen shows right now, with our most popular one being at risk because someone is screwing up the voting."

Finn nodded as he jotted something down on a pad of paper. "Okay. Tell us more about the show."

"It's one of those reality dating shows. You know, people seeking their soul mates. This show features nerd kids, the ones who couldn't figure out how to French kiss if a pair of lips hit them in the pie hole."

I erupted in a fit of coughing and everyone looked my way.

Finn asked, "You okay, Lexi? Need some water?"

I thumped my chest and shook my head, trying to clear my throat. "No, sorry. I'm good."

Cartwright cracked one of his knuckles and I flinched. "Anyway, geek is the new chic, so we were among the first to jump on that bandwagon. Fifteen geek guys vie for the attention of one geek girl. People enjoy watching these smart kids trying to figure out how to get some. It's been our most popular show for two years running. The revenue it generates is more than double our other shows combined."

I swallowed my distaste. "Ah, you said something about hacking."

Cartwright waved a meaty hand. "Yeah, yeah, I'm getting there. Anyway, in the spirit of all this geeky crap, a couple of the company bigwigs got the bright idea to have all our voting online. So, the girl doesn't get to choose which dork she wants to date—as if she could anyway—so, the audience does it for her. The girl has to abide by the audience decision."

I nearly leapt from my chair. "*What?*"

Finn gave me a warning glance. Perhaps to prevent me from leaping across the table to strangle Cartwright, he spread his hands and leaned forward. "So, the online voting is the problem?"

Cartwright shrugged. "Exactly. Dumb idea, in my opinion. I told the suits we needed judges on stage. Three judges with at least one of them easy on the eyes. You know, some chick with big hair, big knockers. That's always a draw. But I was overruled. Audience participation was considered key."

If I had the fantasy power of blasting light like the Glimmers, I'd have knocked Cartwright flat on his back in a white hot flash of blinding brightness. Unfortunately, he was a potential client and X-Corp needed the business, so I swallowed the distaste.

"So, Mr. Cartwright, does SWM have an IT staff that set up this voting system or do you outsource?"

Cartwright looked at me blankly. "IT?"

"Information Technology. You know, computer experts."

Tony spoke up. "Oh, we do all that in house. We've got four dedicated IT employees to handle it."

Cartwright waved his hand. "Dedicated employees, my ass. Apparently we have a bunch of idiots. No matter what they do, they can't stop this idiot from wrecking the show."

Tony looked at me apologetically. "This hacker has been able to compromise our system on a regular basis, no matter what precautions we take. Worse, he's skewed the voting so that it's impossible to determine which votes are legitimate and which aren't. The way he's slanted things has not gone over well with our audience, not to mention our star. She's furious and we're at our wits end."

Cartwright thumped his fist on the table. "Ratings are in the toilet and this hacker is driving us crazy with his stupid demand."

I stopped trying to take notes and closed my laptop. "Demand? You mean he does more than just manipulate the data? He actually communicates with you?"

Tony nodded. "He's claiming to be some kind of hacker god. He wants us to cancel the show or else."

"Or else…what?"

"Or else he'll take it down for us."

I sympathized with the hacker. "How does this guy communicate with you?"

"So far, just by email. He issued a so-called social manifesto." Tony nervously wound his fingers together in his lap.

A hacker with a social cause?

Intrigued, I crossed my arms on top of my laptop. "A manifesto? What does it say?"

Tony glanced nervously at Cartwright. "It seems he doesn't agree with the portrayal of the geeks on the show."

"Who cares whether he agrees or not?" Cartwright smashed his Dodgers cap back on his head. "Shutting him down is why we are here. We just want it to stop as soon as possible."

Finn tapped his pen on his pad of paper. "Have you at least contacted the authorities?"

Cartwright rolled his eyes. "You do realize this is the L.A. police force you are talking about. They patted our hands and told us they'd look into it. Like hell they will. We don't have time to wait for them to get their heads out of their asses. The show is sinking. We want someone on the premises now, working 24/7 to catch this idiot. Can you help or not?"

Finn nodded. "Of course we can help. Why doesn't Tony answer any other questions Lexi might have while we talk pricing?"

I motioned to Tony for us to step out in the hall. I tucked my laptop under one arm and held my coffee cup in the other hand. We walked out to the reception area and sat in a couple of the oversized chairs.

Tony still seemed nervous and perched on the edge of his seat, his leg twitching. "Look, I don't know what else I can tell you. I'm not a computer kind of guy."

"That's okay." I tried to reassure him, knowing that some people got anxious when asked anything technical. I felt the same way when required to engage in social niceties. "I just have a few more general questions. Does the audience know that the votes are being skewed?"

"Oh, my God, no. But I think they're beginning to suspect something isn't right."

"Not surprising seeing as how you're lying to them."

"It's not lying. Well, not exactly. Withholding the truth is not the same as lying. Besides, it's all in the name of entertainment, according to Mr. Cartwright."

I began to like Cartwright even less. "Do the contestants know something is amiss?"

"Not officially, but hello, these are geeks we're talking about. It's not like we can fool them for long. Look, we just need someone to shut that hacker down or keep him out. Either way, we don't care. It would be a big blow to SWM if this show were to shut down because of some unhinged nutcase."

"Hopefully we'll be able to help you catch this guy."

I looked up as Finn and Cartwright walked out of the conference room. He pointed a stubby finger and me and waggled his eyebrows. "I understand you're the best, so we want you."

Finn stepped between us. "I already told you, Mr. Cartwright, I'm not sure Lexi is well enough to—"

"I'll do it. I'm fine."

Cartwright narrowed his eyes at me. "So you'll catch this jerk and shut him down?"

"I'll give it my best shot."

"I don't want a best shot. I want definite."

"Nothing in life is definite but death."

He glared at me. "Can you catch him or not?"

"I'm pretty good. That's all I can promise."

"I'll hold you to that promise. Got it?"

"Got it."

"Good. Then make it happen."

He gave me a final glare and stalked off to the elevator with Tony trailing behind like a puppy.

Finn motioned for me to follow him back to the conference room. Once inside, he put his hands on the back of the chair. "Are you sure about this, Lexi? You aren't even recovered from Rome and you're going to travel to Hollywood?"

"I'm good, Finn, really. Focusing on something other than the fact I nearly died will actually help my recovery. Trust me. There is nothing like a good hack to make me feel better."

He reached out and took my hand. "Does it still hurt?"

I wiggled my fingers. "A little. The physical therapist gave me exercises to strengthen the muscles. I can do them in Hollywood just as well as I can do them here."

"What about the rest of your injures?"

"Are healed or healing. I'm fine, Finn. Really."

He sighed. "I can't dissuade you?"

"Not even if you employ all of your lawyerly skill, which is quite considerable, I might add."

"Well, there is no question this would be a big step for X-Corp and open up a potentially untapped market for us. Cartwright saw you on the news, you know, as a result of the case in Rome. He asked for you specifically."

I grinned. "Good thing I was discreet in Rome." My smile faded. "If he asked for me specifically, then why did you want to keep me out of the meeting?"

He exhaled. "Because I really do want you to stay home and recover. I'm not just talking physically, Lexi."

I appreciated his concern, perhaps more than he knew. "I know. It was a scary situation. But I'm okay,

Finn. Besides, I'm better when I'm working and my mind is busy."

He touched my cheek. "I never would have agreed to let you go if I thought it put you in harm's way."

"You shouldn't feel guilty."

"Yet, I do."

I nodded. "I understand. I'm feeling that way a bit myself."

He studied my face. "Why are you feeling guilty about Rome?"

"I don't feel guilty about Rome. I feel guilty about you. You're too many things to me, Finn. A friend, a co-worker and my boss. I almost shared a shower with you. I don't understand if you're supposed to be my boyfriend, or even if you want to be. I'm not sure how to handle it all."

"Why don't we continue getting to know each other in our personal time outside of work?"

"But taking a shower with you or having sex with you is *too* personal for me."

"Then we don't have to go there. Yet."

"But I don't know that we'll *ever* get there. It's too much for me, Finn. The truth is, I can't manage the complexity of a relationship with you right now. I didn't invite you into the shower with me because I wasn't ready for that. Now that you write my paycheck, I'm not sure I'd *ever* be comfortable with it. I'm sorry. I just don't think I can be your girlfriend—if having sex with you means that—as well as being your co-worker."

He looked surprised. "You…you want to leave X-Corp?"

I blew out a breath. "No, Finn. I really like my job.

I want to stay. But I think I may need a breather from this thing between us."

He blinked and then pulled out a chair and sat down in it. "Well, bloody hell. I didn't see that coming."

I pulled out a chair and joined him. "See, I'm handling this all wrong. You are going to fire me."

He laughed hoarsely. "No. Oh, God, no. You are my best employee and X-Corp's most valuable resource. But even if you weren't, I wouldn't fire you because you didn't want to date me. It would be reprehensible, not to mention illegal."

"I'm doing a bad job of explaining myself."

He shook his head. "No, no. You're doing fine. This is on me. I should have realized the uncomfortable position I've put you in. I didn't think too hard about it because I really, really enjoy your company. I wanted… well, I know what I wanted."

I remained silent. I wasn't sure what else I could add.

He ran his fingers through his hair. "Well, bugger it. I'm not sure how to handle this myself. But I understand your dilemma. I really do."

"Thank you, Finn. I hope you'll still consider being my friend. Seeing as how I have so few."

He smiled and reached across the table, taking my non-injured hand. "That is non-negotiable."

"I knew there was a reason I liked you."

He smiled back and a weight lifted from my heart. I still had my job and a friend…at least for the time being.

I let out a breath I hadn't realized I was holding. "So, what's our plan for SWM?"

He released my hand and leaned back in the chair. "I told him I couldn't guarantee you for the job. But Cartwright is willing to pay us more than double if you'll be on the case personally."

"I'm more than willing to earn my paycheck, Finn."

"I don't doubt that. But after this, I may have to give you a raise."

"You might. But only because I have to deal with a jerk like Cartwright."

"I figured you didn't like the crack about geeks and their pie holes."

"You think?"

"I didn't much like that crack myself."

I tapped my fingertips against the lid of my laptop. "Well, I guess I'll go home and pack."

"Are you sure you're up for heading out tomorrow? I'm still on the fence about this."

I thought of my mother. "I'm sure I can handle this. In fact, the sooner I go, the better. Trust me on this."

He sighed. "Okay, then. I'll have Glinda get you a ticket."

"Perfect."

My mother would be beyond upset if she knew I was leaving again especially when she thought I was still on my deathbed. Guess I would play dumb if she came by tonight and call her from Hollywood after it would be too late to stop me.

Finn frowned. "Oh, Lexi. There's one more thing I think you should know before you arrive in Hollywood."

I cocked my head. "And that would be?"

"It's the name of Cartwright's show. It's...well, let's just say more than a bit offensive."

"Wow. I'm *really* going to despise this guy now, right?"

"I'm betting yes, and it's okay if you despise him as long as you also remember he's a client. A well-paying client."

"Okay."

"Are you ready?"

"As ready as I can be. What is it?"

"Better that I show you. Open up your laptop to your browser."

I opened it up, typed in my password and clicked on my browser. He angled it away from me, and typed something.

"Here goes. Brace yourself."

"Jeez. What's the big freaking deal?"

"This." Finn punched a key and turned the laptop screen toward me, sliding it my way. I watched as an embedded video began with flashing lights and dramatic music led by a percussion section making a repetitive noise that sounded suspiciously like the staccato of someone typing on a keyboard. Then an announcer's voice boomed, "Welcome to our show where beauty is traded for brains and brawn is replaced with brevity. Tune in tonight and see how…" There was a long drumroll and extensive red, yellow and purples flashing lights, "…*Geeks Get Some.*"

Chapter Three

The one nice thing about Southern California in late November is that the weather is fantastic. Palm trees swayed in a light breeze and the sun was bright. I wore jeans, sunglasses and a light sweater and was warm and comfortable. Tony Rabbin picked me up at the airport, looking even tanner than he had the day before. He drove me to an upscale hotel a few blocks from the studio, then gallantly removed my suitcase from the trunk and gave it to the bellhop.

Tony slammed the car trunk shut. "I'll wait for you. Go check in and drop off your luggage. The results show is tonight and we want you on hand. You should have some time to get a tour and meet the IT team before the show starts."

I didn't have a clue what he meant by results show, but I nodded. "Okay, I'll be back in a few minutes."

I checked in and left my luggage in the room but brought my laptop with me. I came right back down without unpacking.

"That was quick."

"You told me drop off my luggage and come back."

"Yes, but you were just a few minutes."

I looked at him puzzled. "That's what I told you. I'd be back in a few minutes."

"Yes, but a few minutes in Hollywood is not a *few* minutes."

"Okay, that made absolutely no sense."

He laughed. "I'm just not used to punctuality. People are never on time in Hollywood. On purpose."

"Why would anyone be late on purpose?"

He laughed, his blond surfer hair blowing around his head. "What a great question."

"Really? Why?"

"Oh, my God. Why? Did you really just ask why?"

"Was that some kind of a social blunder?"

He laughed. "Not for you. People are fashionably late in Hollywood, I suppose, to make it seem like they are more important. You know, my time is more valuable than yours."

"What's fashionable about that?"

"Nothing at all. Lexi, I think I'm going to like you. The studio is up ahead."

It was so close I could have walked the distance from the hotel in ten minutes. When I mentioned it to Tony, he nearly had a heart attack.

"Hollywood rule number two, after the fashionably late one, is you do *not* walk anywhere in L.A. You must drive or be driven."

"Will I commit another social faux pas if I ask why?"

"Most certainly. It's just the way it is."

I kept my mouth shut as we pulled up to a black gate with a guardhouse.

The guard stepped out. "Hey, Tony. She with you?"

"She sure is, Manny. This is Lexi Carmichael."

I gave him a small wave. He looked at his clipboard,

checked something and then stepped back inside. The gate opened slowly. Tony drove inside and I marveled at the huge complex of buildings flanked by a couple of hangar-sized structures. I saw a coffee shop, a yoga studio, a dry cleaner and an urgent care medical facility all within one strip of buildings. There were dozens of costumed people walking around or being driven by golf carts from one building to another. I watched as three people dressed in what looked like astronaut outfits walk out of one building and into a parking lot holding their helmets under their hands, drinking water and laughing loudly.

"It's like a mini-city in here."

"Yeah, it's pretty self-sustaining." Tony took two sharp right turns and pulled into a parking lot. "Here we are. Studio 27."

I got out of the car and Tony motioned for me to follow him. A uniformed security guard stood at the door. He waved us forward when he saw Tony.

He smiled at me when I passed him. "Welcome to *Geeks Get Some.*"

I cringed. "Jeez."

We walked into a large open area with people running all about. Some guy ran past and nearly brained me with an oversized microphone.

"Sorry." He shouted it over his shoulder without even slowing down.

I looked around. "What's all the rush?"

"Results show in two hours. Come on and I'll introduce you to the IT team."

He led me past a group of three guys all wearing headsets. They huddled around a large camera on a dolly, discussing something about angles.

We took a right down a corridor and into a back room. Tony stopped at a door and opened it for me.

"After you."

I stepped into a large, cold room, blinking when I noticed an entire wall held three enormously large television monitors. The rest of the room was crowded with computer clusters. One corner held a couple of cubicles scattered with papers and a phone. I counted one interior office, which I presumed would be for the IT Director. Four people were visible, one of them a woman, but all were focused on their tasks and none of them noticed us.

Tony made a beeline for one of the men, a tall young guy with white blond hair. He turned as Tony tapped him on the shoulder.

"She's here." Tony motioned to me.

I saw a flash of annoyance in the other guy's eyes and recognized it at once. We had interrupted him in mid-thought. I hated that kind of interruption as well.

He strode over to meet me, his ID badge clipped to the pocket on his shirt. Before I could read it, he held out a hand. "I'm Kyle Mansfield. This is my shop."

I nodded, understanding the need to define the territorial tech boundaries. This was social interaction I understood. I stood in *his* domain. How I acted from this moment on would determine what kind of welcome I'd get.

"I'm Lexi Carmichael. I understand you've got an unwelcome repeat visitor."

Kyle nodded. "A cracker."

Tony looked at him, alarmed. "A cracker? What's that? I thought we had a hacker."

I patted him on the shoulder. "It's okay, Tony. A cracker *is* what you think of as a hacker. We're talking tech lingo now. A cracker is just a hacker with malicious intent."

He looked relieved. "Oh, thank God. I did *not* want to have to explain a new problem to Cartwright. Well, as it's painfully clear I'm out of my league here, I'm going to split. Have fun, kids."

Tony hightailed it out of the room and Kyle motioned to me. "Come on. I'll show you our set-up."

He led me over to a computer cluster. "These are our servers."

"Are they dedicated to the show only?"

"Yes."

"Are you running the voting system off these servers?"

"We are."

He turned stiffly and said nothing more. I got the message loud and clear, as only one geek to another would. He was pissed. Probably because Cartwright or some other bonehead had told him they were bringing in an outsider because he couldn't do his job right. That wasn't fair in the slightest because not all tech heads are also experts in cybersecurity. It's an entirely different field altogether. For example, I could be a fantastic doctor, but it didn't mean I had the unique abilities of a skilled neurosurgeon.

I decided to keep it straightforward, which is how I'd like it if our roles were reversed. "Look, Kyle, just so you know, I'm not on any warpath here. I'm not assigning blame. I have one goal, to help you catch this cracker. I've got no hidden agenda and I'd prefer to be seen as being on your team, not in charge of your team. Okay?"

I could see the relief on his face. "Yeah, good. Okay. That's good to know."

Now that the air was clear, we could get down to business. A twinge of pride swept through me that I'd handled the situation so well. If only non-tech interaction could go so well.

I leaned forward. "What programming language and systems database are you using?"

"We're using PHP with a MySQL database."

That was a bit more troublesome. There are tens of thousands of common programming mistakes that novice programmers make using this combination, especially when implementing very large public systems. It meant the system was quite vulnerable to penetration if someone was determined and inclined. Not that any of it was Kyle's fault. He might not even be responsible for those choices in the first place. Embedded mistakes could have been made long before he even arrived on the scene.

I tried to be optimistic. "How long have you been working here?"

"Eleven months."

"When did the trouble start?"

Without another word, he led me to his office and sat down behind a desk. The room was no bigger than a large bathroom with no outside windows and floor-to-ceiling glass partitions between him and the control room. Although it was small, it was meticulously ordered with the books on a single bookshelf arranged by size and topic, a single chair for visitors, and an iron file cabinet angled in one corner. His desk was clean with a separate cup for pens, pencils, highlighters and markers. Every loose piece of paper sat safely inside an inbox, and four different stacks of different-colored sticky note pads sat nearby for emergency utilization.

I appreciated the order as I parked my behind in the visitor's chair.

Kyle placed his hands on his desk. "The trouble started about eight weeks ago. The votes came in and were tallied. The results were a bit of a surprise, I guess, because everyone thought the guy who got booted was a fan favorite. But I didn't really pay attention to that part of it. I don't typically watch television. It's not my thing."

"At least we're on the same page with that."

He gave me a little smile. "Didn't even raise any suspicions until the same thing happened the next week. The new fan favorite was voted off. Fans were not happy and Lucy was pissed. Right on screen for everyone to see."

"Lucy?"

"Lucy Shoemaker. She's the catch."

"The catch?"

"The prize, the geek babe, the date the guys all want to get."

"Oh." I wrinkled my nose. "What's the deal with that again? I'm a little fuzzy on how this whole show works."

"The show started with fifteen guys. They all tried to get the attention of the girl and get her to pass them on to the next level. They go on dates, have talks, get social skills lessons from some so-called experts, and do stupid stuff like that. Then the fans vote on which guy they think Lucy should hook up with. The guy with the lowest amounts of votes each week is dropped from the show."

"Lucy has no say in this."

"None, whatsoever. She's reportedly a geek herself,

so the audience is supposed to guide her. But she can try to influence the vote."

"So, let me get this straight. Lucy comes on a television show to date some guys, but she has no say in who she goes out with or who sticks around."

"Finding true love the intelligent way."

"How intelligent is it if someone is voting for them because, apparently, they are too stupid to make the decision for themselves?"

"Don't mess with a winning formula, as Cartwright would say."

I shook my head. "So, the fans, who don't even know Lucy, decide who she should date by doing all the voting."

"Correct."

"Essentially they are saying that Lucy and all the guys on the show are too dumb to make their own dating choices."

"That about sums it up."

"Un-freaking-believable. Then what?"

Kyle shrugged. "Well, when it gets down to the last guy, Lucy can propose to him."

I jumped out of my chair. "Propose? Are you kidding?"

"No kidding whatsoever. It's all done for drama, of course. The two poor, clueless geek souls have found their soul mate, as decided by the far more intelligent audience-at-large. But the system doesn't work so well if it's clear the guys who are fan favorites are getting systematically booted off the show."

I frowned. "How do you know who is a fan favorite other than the voting?"

Kyle rubbed his forehead. "Mail. Snail mail, chat

boards, the show blog, as well as electronic mail. Fans want their favorites to know they're cheering for them."

"That system could be corrupted, too."

"Yes, it's possible, but I didn't see any evidence of it and Noah, who is in charge of tech aspects of the show's social media, hasn't been able to find any irregularities either. I'll introduce you to him and the whole team in a few minutes. The overall problem is we've started getting crucified in the press and our ratings are dropping. If people think their votes don't count, they won't watch."

I considered for a moment. "If I'm completely honest with you, I'm at a loss for something to say about a show that is so inane."

He shrugged. "There's nothing intelligent you *can* say about it. That's what I tell myself, at least. For me, it's just a job. End of story. What's important is that this cracker has to be stopped."

"So the insanity can continue."

"Exactly."

I let out a deep breath and sank back into my chair. "Okay. Fair enough. Let's get back to the nitty-gritty. When the fan favorite got booted a second week in a row, I take it you sat up and took notice."

Kyle's cheeks reddened. "Not just me, everyone. Technically, I should have been onto it after the first time, but I wasn't following the results shows like I should have been. Honestly, I didn't give a flying leap which guy was favored. Didn't see how it mattered to my job performance. My mistake. Everyone, myself included, thought it an anomaly when Kevin got booted. He was clearly Lucy's favorite of the entire show. I thought it was no big deal. So what? The fans had diverged. But after the second irregularity in a row, the voting system became suspect, and by extension, me."

"You?"

"I'm in charge of the voting system, after all."

"Had the system been compromised?"

He leaned forward. "Yeah, it had."

"How did you determine it for sure?"

"Pretty simple, actually. The webserver statistics reported that the voting-acknowledgement page was loaded fifty million times during the voting period, but the vote database had fifty-two million votes."

I stared at him in shock. "Whoa. Back up, dude. Fifty *million* votes? Did you say million?"

"I did."

"For a dumb show about geeks getting some? Really?"

"You'd be surprised. It's a popular show."

"Actually I've moved beyond surprised. I'm significantly concerned about the future well-being of this country. Perhaps the entire human race."

He snorted. "Look, just between you and me, I'm in total agreement with you about this show. It's the dumbest concept on Earth. That being said, we have to stop this guy or my team and I are out on the street looking for new jobs."

I appreciated his concern for his staff. "Okay, so we have two million votes unaccounted for. Can't you just eliminate them?"

"Don't know to which person the votes were cast. We could knock off the last two million votes, but I don't have any way of determining which of those two million were legitimate and which ones weren't."

"Seriously? Legitimacy is important in this farce?"

"Apparently to a certain extent."

"Is it a standard one vote from one IP address type of deal?"

"Yes."

I exhaled, tapping my finger on my chin. "The votes are already in for tonight?"

"Yes, and our cracker buddy added another two million votes, skewing the results again."

"Crap. Well, we can't worry about that now. Let's go back to the beginning. What do you know about the hacker so far?"

"Not a lot. He's a nutcase obsessed with the show obviously."

"Tony said he sent an email with a manifesto."

"Yeah. To me and Lucy."

"You?"

He nodded. "So far, we're the only two he's targeted."

I considered. "Well, it is interesting he's targeting the head of the IT team."

"Not really. We're the *real* geeks here after all."

I looked at him thoughtfully. "You think he's mocking you?"

Kyle's pale cheeks flushed. "Actually, I do."

"Why?"

"Most likely because I'm going along with this farce."

"Alright, tell me what happened after you found the email in your inbox."

Kyle rubbed his temples. "Actually Lucy saw hers first and took it to Cartwright. He went through the ceiling. That's when I found mine."

"Was the content of your email different than Lucy's?"

"No. It's the same rambling manifesto about how

he is some techno-god and that the show offends him. He issues the ultimatum of either take it off the air or he'll do it for us."

I considered it problematic that I was actually starting to like this cracker. "You trace the email?"

"I tried. The trail went nowhere. Sorry."

"It's okay. I'll take a look on my own. Do you have a copy of his manifesto?"

He picked up a folder on his desk and pulled out a single sheet of paper. He passed it over to me.

"Here it is. Brace yourself."

Chapter Four

I looked at Kyle and then down at the sheet of paper.

The Manifesto

Who am I? You think I'm a criminal, but I'm not. I'm a techno-god, a wizard, and an explorer of a whole new digital world. I can find you wherever you may be because I've created the very things that you now cannot live without. I walk past you on the street and you don't know me. You sit next to me on the bus, and you don't see me. Yet, now I rule your world. Ever wonder what makes someone like me tick? Follow me down the rabbit hole—choose the red pill.

Who am I? I'm a cracker. Code, numbers, and electrons flow through my veins like heroin to a junkie.

Who am I? I'm the kid who was always smarter than you, the kid you denigrated or ignored, the kid on the outside looking in. Now I'm the one on the inside and I know more about you than the person you sleep next to at night. I know your credit card number, the details of your latest performance review, and your deepest desires. Your most private information is mine for the taking whenever and however I want.

Who am I? I'm the one giving you a warning about shutting down the television travesty, Geeks Get Some. End this show or I will take it down for you. I'm already running the show, but it needs to be finished. I will no longer take your denigration of my kind because I am no longer powerless. I am still smarter than you and now the power is in my hands.

This is my manifesto.

I looked up from the paper. Kyle watched me.

"So, what do you think?" he asked.

I handed him the paper. "Truthfully, I think he made some good points. He says he's running the show, which is interesting. He also references *The Matrix*, calls himself a cracker, and has an axe to grind. You a cracker, Kyle?"

He blinked in surprise. "Huh?"

"You ever do any cracking?"

He shook his head vigorously. "No. Never. Well, okay. I may have done some hacks that bordered on cracks in my younger years. But I'm not doing this. I swear. You don't think this is me, do you?"

I shrugged. "Honestly, I don't. But you know I'm going to have to check you out. Lots of avenues coming back to you."

He swallowed hard, looking shaken. "I know and it's okay. I've got nothing to hide."

"Believe me, you're the first person I want to clear. I need to know we're on the same side."

"We are."

"Then it should be quick."

Kyle seemed steadier as he slid the paper back into the folder. "Agreed. So, what's your plan?"

I stood. "I need a secure terminal and all the passwords. Set me up an internal account, please. Email me a copy of the manifesto. I'll dissect your account first to see if I can trace the email. I'm sorry about the privacy intrusion, but once you're cleared, you'll be a valuable help to me. I'm going to have to clear your team one by one, as well. Then we can get down to the business of hunting this guy."

"I understand and it's okay. I appreciate you being straight with me. You're just different than what I expected."

I looked at him in surprise. "What did you expect?"

"Some jerk who'd tell me I'm an idiot for not being able to catch this guy and then shove it down my throat."

"Luckily, that is *so* not me. Look, crackers are good at what they do. I haven't seen your security setup yet, but I sincerely doubt it could be all your fault."

"Thanks, I appreciate that."

"No problem. I'd also like to meet the rest of your IT staff. Then I'm going to talk to Lucy."

"Sure, follow me."

Kyle walked me over to where a young woman with shoulder-length brown hair sat facing a double monitor, typing some commands. "Hey, Melinda, I want you to meet Lexi Carmichael. She's coming on board for a while to help us catch the cracker."

Melinda turned around in the swivel chair. Her hair swung loose and half covered her face. "Hi, Lexi, nice to meet you."

She held out a hand and I shook it. Her fingers were cold and clammy.

Kyle spread out his hands. "Melinda is our network expert. Keeping everyone connected."

I nodded. "A most important job."

She smiled shyly. She shifted in the chair and when the curtain of hair finally parted a bit, I saw she had a bad case of acne.

"Melinda went to UCLA."

"Good school."

She nodded. "I liked it."

Kyle moved away. "Well, I'll let you guys get to know each other. I'll set you up a terminal and a place to work, Lexi. Okay?"

"Great. Thanks." I pulled over another swivel chair. "So, Melinda, how long have you worked here?"

She clasped her hands in her lap and finally met my gaze. "About eight months. This is my first job."

"You like it?"

"My friends think it's cool that I work on a popular television show."

"Is it cool?"

"Yes, I suppose it is. The work, that is. Not the show."

"You don't like the show?"

She shook her head. "Not much. Have you seen it?"

"No, but I think the title sucks."

She laughed softly. "It truly does."

I crossed my legs. "I take it you're up to speed on what is going on with this nutcase manipulating the votes. You notice anything unusual?"

"My networks are secure."

"You sure?"

Her hair swung away from her face. "Of course, I'm sure. I check the configurations daily. No irregularities. Kyle has checked it, too."

"Yet a cracker is getting in."

"I don't know how."

"So what's your theory on how he's managed to manipulate the votes?"

"I don't have a clue. Maybe he's using a new method or some kind of trick. After all, new cracks develop every day. But I swear my networks are safe."

"Apparently not safe enough."

"Look, I don't know how he's getting in. He's either being let in, he has the passwords, or he's developed some new magic trick I've never come across. I just don't see it."

I rose. "Okay. Thanks for the insights. If you see anything unusual, alert me right away."

She nodded and turned back to her monitor. I walked over to two young guys who were arguing about something. The guy to my left was tall, thin and had curly brown hair and glasses. The guy on my right was shorter, muscular, and had a dark olive complexion, black hair and brown eyes.

"What are you guys arguing about?" I asked.

The guy with the curly hair stared at me suspiciously. "Who are you?" He pushed his glasses up on his nose.

"Lexi Carmichael. I've been brought on board to help find the cracker who is manipulating the votes."

"*You're* the hotshot from Washington?"

I lifted an eyebrow. "You expecting someone else?"

"Yeah, like a guy."

"Only guys can hunt crackers?"

"Unless you can prove yourself."

"You know, that's about the stupidest sexist comment I've ever heard. And I've heard plenty."

"It is what it is."

The shorter guy put a hand on his shoulder. "Noah, dude, back off. You are way out of line."

I narrowed my eyes. "No, it's okay. I'm up to the challenge. Just how am I supposed to prove my worth to you, Noah?"

He smiled. "Answer some questions, and answer them well. I need to see how much hot is in hotshot."

"Don't make me hurl before we even start."

"Nervous?"

"Not in the slightest."

"Good. Here is the first question. What does the x stand for in AGP 8x?"

"Times the PCI speed."

"QBE stands for…"

"Query by Example."

"What were the first female computer programmers called?"

"Programmers. That's a stupid sexist question."

He raised an eyebrow. "Don't know the answer?"

"Of course I know the answer, but the question remains sexist. Rosies, as in ring around. Look, if you're going to test me, at least make it worthy of my time."

He pursed his lips. "What is the WEP protocol?"

"Wired Equivalent Privacy. It uses an RC4 stream to encrypt data and has a single secret key of a length of 104 bit."

Before he could open his mouth again, I lifted a hand. "Now, let me turn this around, so I can see if you know *your* job. What would be the most efficient method to use if you were trying to crack a WEP?"

He thought. "That's tricky. I'm going to say the PTW technique."

I nodded. "Acceptable."

He smiled and stuck out a hand. "Okay, hotshot, you pass."

"That's hotshot *girl* to you." I shook his hand. "You pass, too, although you need to seriously lose the attitude about women."

"Okay, sorry about the sexist stuff. It's mostly a defensive reaction born from years of difficult interactions with women. Besides, I can't be sure about anyone these days. Things have been kind of tense around here. It's got everyone on edge. Don't know who to trust, you know what I mean?"

"Possibly."

The shorter guy stuck out his hand. "Hey, Lexi, I'm Carlos Ramierez. Just for the record, I'm not sexist in any way."

"Noted." I shook his hand as well. "Can you guys bring me up to speed?"

Carlos frowned, dipping his head toward Kyle, who was sitting at a cubicle working on what I hoped would be my computer. "Didn't he already do it?"

"Sure, I got his version. I want to get yours. Sometimes what the boss sees isn't always what the guys in the trenches see."

Noah laughed. "Not bad, girl boss. Hey, it's okay if I call you that, right? I don't mean it in a sexist way. Really."

"Sure, I guess."

"Cool."

I gestured toward the monitor. "Noah, you also deal with the social media for the show?"

"Yeah, it's one of my minor duties. Someone in media affairs for SWM actually does the posting and tweeting stuff. Technically, I'm the support analyst. I do the installation, testing, maintenance, repair and troubleshooting and resolving tech problems for the staff on premises and long distance."

"You the software specialist as well?"

"Yep, that's mostly me, too."

Carlos nervously twirled a pencil. "I'm a support analyst like Noah. I'm a jack-of-all trades, but I focus more on the hardware. We heard you were coming and weren't sure what to think. Our jobs are on the line. In fact, we were just arguing about whether to run VDAS."

I frowned. "Vulnerability Detection and Assessment System?"

Carlos nodded. "I thought it might be worth a shot."

Noah sighed. "Look, I've already run it. Twice. We've got *nada*. However this guys is getting in, he's good, not to mention ghostly. No trace of him. It's my not-so-humble opinion that another run of VDAS would be a royal waste of time. But if you want to do it, girl boss, be my guest."

I tried not to roll my eyes. "Okay, any gut feeling as to who is doing this or how he's getting in?"

Carlos shook his head. "No freaking idea, man. Noah is right. He's like a phantom. No trail anywhere. He's burned our asses on this."

Noah nodded. "Yeah, he's a master."

"Either of you sympathetic to his cause?"

Carlos laughed. "Dang straight we are. Look, this show is a joke. They picked the most unstable guys out there. These guys aren't geeks—they're freaks. Seriously. It makes us look bad. But this show is my bread and butter until I can get enough experience to move somewhere else."

Noah shrugged. "Who really cares in the big scheme of things? Everything in Hollywood is fake anyway."

I nodded. "Okay, I've got a few hours before the results show. Where do I find this Lucy girl?"

Noah stuck a pencil behind his ear. "I'll take you to her."

Chapter Five

We stopped outside a dressing room where a young woman with brown hair streaked with pink highlights was curling the ponytail of a woman sitting in a black chair in front of a mirror.

Noah pointed. "Lucy's the blonde in the chair."

I examined Lucy's reflection. She wore a pair of purple yoga pants, and a clingy, low-cut silver top. She was stacked. She had a pretty face, but you could hardly see it behind a funky pair of oversized black-rimmed glasses that seemed completely at odds with the rest of her appearance.

"What's her deal?" I asked.

"She's a geophysics major from the University of Penn I think."

"You think?"

"It's her official bio, but…"

"But what?"

"I'll let you come to your own conclusions, girl boss." He turned and strode down the hall whistling.

I shook my head and stepped into the dressing room, passing the young woman with the pink-streaked hair on her way out.

Lucy removed her oversized glasses and shook her

head left and right, watching the ponytail swing back and forth. She saw me in the mirror and frowned.

"Who are you?"

I walked around to the side of the chair. "I'm Lexi Carmichael. I'm here to help SWM catch the guy who has been manipulating all the votes."

"Thank God. It's about time Cartwright stood up to that jerk. He's been messing up everything."

"I understand he sent you an email."

"Not just me. That computer guy, Kyle, got the same creepy email. Some rambling sob story about how he got bullied when he was younger and how he's going to mess up the show. What a sap."

"Any idea why he targeted you and Kyle specifically?"

"How would I know? I get all kinds of freaky fan mail. I don't pay attention. But he's messing with the natural rhythm of the show, and *that* I care about."

"How exactly is he messing with the natural rhythm?"

"He's rigging the voting and consistently sticks me with the guy I obviously don't like. It's a travesty. Even the fans can't be that stupid."

She peered at the mirror, tugged on her eyelashes. "It's not working." She stood up and yelled. "Mandy, get in here and fix my mascara. I've got clumpy lashes."

The girl with the pink-streaked hair rushed in with a towel on her shoulder. "I've got to help the guys. What's the problem?"

"The mascara is the problem. It sucks."

"You didn't like the waterproof, remember? You said it made your lashes clump."

"Well, I changed my mind. Give me the waterproof."

I stared hard at Lucy. I'd never heard a geek girl worry about clumpy lashes.

Mandy rolled her eyes. "I'll bring it in a minute."

Lucy looked back at me. "Why exactly are you still here?"

I considered her for a moment. "Trying to get to the bottom of this hacker problem, remember?"

"Well, why are you wasting your time with me? Go back to your computer, keyboard, or whatever tech crap you use and do something useful."

I crossed my arms across my chest. "I have another question first."

"What question?"

"What you think of the new technology for the multi-beam echo sounders?"

She stared at me. "Huh?"

"Echo sounders. I read about some new technical developments in the software on NOAA's NGDC website."

"The NOAA *what*?"

"NOAA's NGDC. The National Ocean and Atmospheric Administration's National Geophysical Data Center."

She glared at me. "What is wrong with you? There aren't any cameras rolling."

I crossed my arms. "Let me take a wild guess. You are *not* a geophysics major."

"No kidding, sherlock."

"Then why are you pretending you are?"

"Are you for freaking real? This is reality television. Nothing is real."

"Wait a minute. You're *faking* being a geek?"

"Of course I'm faking it. No one would act this way on purpose."

"None of the guys have noticed?"

"Why should they? They aren't trying to talk to me on their level. They're all too busy trying to figure out how to get some of this." She leaned forward and squished her boobs together. "Besides, if they ask me a stupid question like you just did, the producers simply cut it."

"Cut it?"

"God. Don't you know anything? They don't actually air our *real* conversations on the show. It would bore everyone to death. The producers make up whatever conversations they want. Cut and paste excerpts so people say something interesting or create drama. It's called frankenbiting. It makes for great television."

"So, there is absolutely nothing real about this show?"

"Duh. And you're supposed to be the smart one."

I shook my head. "There is something seriously wrong with you people."

"Me? That's a laugh. Because when it comes right down to it, girlfriend, this show sure as hell isn't making fun of my type."

Her laughter trailed after me as I left her to her clumpy lashes. I called Finn as soon as I could find a quiet corner.

"It's all a fake. The entire freaking show."

Finn exhaled. "It's reality television."

"Look, I understand that Hollywood gets to make stuff up and call it reality. I really do get that. However, in regards to this particular so-called reality show, suspension of disbelief is one thing. But this is a gross misrepresentation. It's wrong on so many levels I don't know where to start."

"I understand this is difficult, Lexi. Don't take it personally. It's just a television show."

"Don't take it personally? They're portraying geeks in the worst possible light for laughs. It's cruel. It's inhumane. But worse, it's inaccurate."

"Trust me, I'm in full agreement. Regardless, there is that pesky little matter called freedom of expression."

I growled. "Don't start with me. Am I talking to Finn the cyber intelligence guru or Finn the lawyer?"

He sighed. "Both. Look, don't misinterpret me, Lexi. I'm not defending reality television."

"Then explain it to me. Why in the world do people watch something like this?"

He paused. "It's like a train wreck, I guess. No one wants to watch, but people can't seem to look away."

Basia had said the same thing, but I *still* didn't get how train wrecks made good television. "You do realize that was *not* a useful explanation."

"Fine." His accent started to slip and the Irish appeared, which usually happened when he got mad. "You want me to tell you it's all a big cluster farce? Well, it is."

I thought about that for a moment. "No, it's worse than that. It's offensive, petty and dumb. Even the girl is a fake."

"What girl?"

"Lucy." I shouted in the phone. "The so-called babe prize. She's not even a geek. She's *pretending* to be a geek. It's beyond insulting."

Finn made a strange, strangled sound and then cleared his throat. "Just try to focus, Lexi. Ignore the extraneous. It's not important. *She's* not important. Find the bloody hacker and come home."

I tried to calm myself. Finn was right. This was a job,

a paycheck and not a moral stance. I needed to find the hacker. Not expose a fake show that apparently everyone on the planet liked, except for me and the hacker I had been sent to bring down.

Jeez.

"Okay, okay. Fine. I got it covered."

"That's my girl. You need any help?"

"No. I think it's a fairly simple solution. But first I need to meet the guys on the show. They may have some insights I'm missing."

Chapter Six

I headed over to Tony's office and asked him where I could find the guys. He walked me through the studio to what he referred to as the Red Room, a staging area for the guys to relax before the show started.

"The guys should be out of hair and makeup by now."

"The guys wear makeup?"

He laughed. "God, the look on your face. Yes, they wear makeup. Trust me, the camera is not kind. But it's not what you're thinking. Mandy, our makeup technician, just smoothes things out for the guys as needed."

"Define *smoothes*."

"Hides the blemishes, acne and occasionally plays up their other features a bit. They look much better for it, trust me."

"Actually, I feel kind of sick thinking about it."

He laughed again. We found the guys sitting in a totally red room, hence the name Red Room. It had several red overstuffed chairs, a circular red couch and a red table. A mahogany bar stood in the back corner flanked by red barstools and a flashing red neon light that said *Geeks Get Some*. It gave me a headache the second I walked in.

I counted seven contestants. Tony had told me they

started with fifteen, so they were down more than half. He'd also told me that Cartwright had chosen the most extreme examples of a geek, whatever that meant. He'd gone on about some of their quirks, but none of it sounded overly relevant, so I'd tuned him out about halfway through his spiel. I figured I'd just have to size them up on my own.

One of the contestants stood up when he saw me. He was dressed in a flannel red and brown checked shirt tucked into a pair of khaki pants. His wiry brown hair looked like he had just stuck his finger in an electrical socket.

"Are you helping out Mandy?" He started walking toward me. "I need my hair fixed again."

Another guy with short red hair and a pudgy face snorted. "Yeah, you need some gel to lock it in place, Anson."

I shook my head. "Me? Ah, no. I'm Lexi Carmichael. I'm here helping the IT staff out with some technical issues."

His face broke into a big smile. "A techie. Thank God. It's great to meet a like mind. I'm Anson Oxlong. I'm a professional gamer for Wicked Fish Games."

"Nice. Done any work on 'Temporal Labyrinth'?"

"You know 'Temporal'?" He looked surprised.

"Of course. Got to Level 16, but couldn't get past the Seismic Sorcerer."

"Ha! That was partially my creation. I hate to say it, but I'm missing my job right now. A lot."

The redheaded guy stood up. "I'm Truman Clark. I'm a paranormal investigator for Black of Night. It's my own investigative company. But I also have a Ph.D. in Cognitive and Computer Science, so I'm tech friendly.

What kind of issues have you got? Maybe I can help. God, please give me something useful to do."

I looked around at the other guys. "I just might. Actually, I came here specifically because I'd like to pick your brains. The show has a follower who is, let's say, a bit of a stalker and it's got the television suits worried. I'd like to track him down. Maybe you have an idea or any thoughts as to who might want to bring the show down?"

Anson's eyes lit up. "A stalker?"

"Of sorts."

Truman slapped his knee. "Sweet. This is right up my alley. Is this about the guy who's been manipulating the votes on the show?"

"You know about that?"

"Of course, we know about that. We aren't idiots, although I'll admit coming on this show certainly makes us suspect."

"Lucy's been talking." A tall, good-looking black guy stood up. "I'm Ray Ferris. All of Lucy's favorites have been getting systematically booted off the show over the past couple of weeks. We've suspected something is up and Lucy, well, discreet isn't a word that leaps to mind when you describe her. She told us she got a creepy email from this guy. He's sticking her with who he wants, regardless of her wishes."

"Any of you think you may know him? Did you read his manifesto?"

"Yeah, Lucy shared it with us." Ray shrugged. "Not like we could do anything about it."

"Did the wording sound familiar to any of you? Could it be a family member or friend trying to help you out?"

Another of the guys stood up. He was unusually tall and skeletal-looking with long thin fingers and sharply pointed bones in his face. His shaggy brown hair seemed barely connected to his scalp and he had either a tiny mustache or a fuzzy bug sitting over his lips. He wore a white shirt that hung on his frame, a pair of black slacks held up by a pair of ridiculous-looking red suspenders and a red bow tie.

"I don't need anyone to help me out, babe. I already got what it takes."

Ray sighed. "Uh, oh."

The guy hitched his pants up and swaggered toward me. He jerked his head with a spastic motion, and to my dismay, he winked. Either that or something flew into his eye. I couldn't be sure.

"Who are you?" I asked.

"The name's Gregg Magnum. You got a problem? I'm your man."

Truman rolled his eyes. "You're nobody's man, dude."

"Don't be hating on me because of my ability with the ladies."

"What ability? You're a master at crash and burn."

I held up a hand. "Gregg, you know anything about what's going on here?"

"Not really. However, you're lucky I have a razor-sharp mind and a photographic memory. How about we have dinner, wine, and some great conversation, illuminated by the glow of soft candlelight?"

"How about not."

"Are you playing hard to get?"

"I'm not playing at all."

Truman made an airplane with his hand and simulated a crash, complete with a booming sound effect.

Gregg frowned at Truman. "Buzz off, loser."

Truman laughed. "I am *so* not the loser, dude."

"We'll see about that." He returned to the couch, a dejected look on his face.

I let out a breath. "So, do any of you know why some guy would issue a manifesto and try to wreck the show?"

"He's not trying to wreck the show." A thin young man dressed in tan khakis and a light blue shirt stood up. His dark hair fell over one eye. "He's trying to manipulate it."

I took a step closer. "And you are…?"

"Eldrick Faston. I don't think he's trying to ruin it or he would have made his initial hack a lot more malicious. He's getting his kicks by controlling us like a bunch of puppets."

I considered him. "Know anyone who would get off on that kind of activity?"

Eldrick shrugged. "Yeah, just about everyone I know. But, hey, it's like the dude said in the manifesto. He's looking for revenge."

Anson nodded. "Yeah, guess he got bullied a lot. Like most of us."

We were all quiet for a moment, before I spoke up. "Look, I'm still not getting it. If he's been bullied, why would he manipulate you—guys in the same family, theoretically speaking?"

"Because we're an extension of the show." Ray rubbed his hand over his forehead. "I don't think he's trying to hurt us directly, he's just trying to control the show. Eldrick is right. He could have shut down this show with one seriously decent hack."

Truman sniffed. "I disagree. His actions are too pedestrian."

"What?" Eldrick glared at him. "A manifesto is *not* pedestrian. Dramatic, even over the top, I'll give you, but not pedestrian."

"It's neither. It's bureaucratic."

One of the guys who had been sitting on the couch abruptly stood. He was short with blond curly hair, gray-tinged glasses and chubby cheeks. "'Bureaucracy is the slime created by the void fermented in the ruins of a revolt.' That was Kirk Masters to Ab'Jona in the episode 'Road to Revolution.'"

I stared at him for a moment. "Okay. And the significance of that comment to this conversation is…?"

Anson rolled his eyes. "Don't you know who he is?"

"Should I?"

"That's Barnaby Knipple."

"Okay. Is that supposed to mean something to me?"

"Don't you ever watch the show?"

"No."

Anson sighed. "Lucky you. Well, Barnaby kind of talks in riddles."

"What?"

Ray interrupted. "No, he doesn't speak in riddles. Quotes. *Repercussions* quotes, to be exact."

"*What?*"

"Surely you've heard of the television show *Repercussions.*"

"Of course I've heard of it. It's one of my favorite shows."

I shifted my gaze back to Barnaby and he lifted a blond eyebrow. "'May Shangra guide you and lead you into everlasting enlightenment.'"

Ray lifted his hands. "See?"

I blew out a breath. "Okay...well, just okay." I glanced over to the last guy sitting in one of the oversized red lounge chairs with his legs crossed. He had short reddish brown hair and watched me with an amused look.

"Who are you?" I asked.

He didn't get up. "Apparently I'm the last of the group to introduce myself. I'm Max Sheffield. I'm the guy who's hoping to God I get voted off this bloody freak show tonight." He spoke in a short, clipped British accent.

"So, Max, you got any theories on the show's stalker?"

"None, except if I ever meet him, I shall lift a glass to him filled with fine Scotch. I only wish he'd do the manly thing and put us all out of our misery sooner than later."

"You agree with his manifesto?"

"Wholeheartedly. I agree this show is a travesty and should be shut down immediately. Nonetheless, I have no one to blame but myself for becoming involved. Now that I've had my fifteen minutes of fame, I'm more than happy to relinquish Lucy to any or all of my admirable fellow contestants. May one of you be so lucky."

"You're her favorite," Anson pointed out.

"For now. Which, thanks to our stalker, hopefully means I'll be the next to go. God Almighty, I wish this room had a stocked bar. I'm going to need a drink to get through the show tonight."

"I'm nervous, too." Truman wrung his hands together. "Really nervous. I wish the show wasn't live. They can't call cut if I have to go to the bathroom."

"Dude, did you take your Pepto Bismol?" Anson sat down on the red couch.

"No. Oh, God, I might be sick."

We all took a step back from Truman.

Max laughed. "Well, welcome to the show, Lexi Carmichael. I sincerely wish you the utmost luck in finding your cyber criminal."

Chapter Seven

Show time was in less than thirty minutes. I itched to get a look at the IT setup and security layout, but I wouldn't have enough time before the show to do it properly. Besides, Kyle wanted me to meet the host of the show, Stone O'Hara.

"Stone?" I shook my head. "That's a first name? Makes him sound like a blockhead."

He laughed. "Just wait until you meet him."

I followed Kyle over to stage right where Cartwright, Tony, two cameramen and a tall guy with brown hair in a navy blue suit were talking. They stopped talking when they saw us coming.

Kyle pushed me forward. "I wanted Lexi to meet Stone."

The guy in the blue suit turned to face me. He had wavy light brown hair that he'd swept to one side, a very square and chiseled jaw, and brown eyes. He was even tanner than Tony, except the color seemed slightly off. I couldn't put my finger on it until I realized it was too even, too perfect. Probably the result of a tanning bed. Ugh.

He smiled and I blinked at the dazzling white teeth. Dentists in Hollywood must make a fortune.

"Welcome to the show, Lexi. I hear you are going to catch our hacker. Good luck with that."

I don't know if it was something in the tone of his voice or the way he looked right through me, as if I weren't there, but I disliked him on sight. Then, without waiting for me to reply, he summarily dismissed me, as if I wasn't worthy of a second more of his time.

Kyle shrugged. "Come on. Let's watch the show from the IT room. You can check out our systems after the show."

I followed him to where Melinda, Carlos and Noah were already sitting in front of the three large television screens hanging on the wall. After a moment, I realized we were seeing three different camera angles. One camera covered the Red Room, where Mandy and another woman were arranging the guys' hair and clothes. Another angle showed Lucy in her dressing room, walking around in a shimmery low-cut white dress and those weird black glasses, as if those would make her a geek. I frowned, shaking my head. The final view was of the main stage where I had just seen Stone minutes ago.

"The show is live?" I asked. "Why?"

"Beats me. Guess it adds to the drama." Kyle plucked a headset off a nearby desk and put it on. "We can hear Cartwright through here in case he needs to direct us or anyone in the stage crew to do something. A live show can get dicey on occasion."

I wasn't sure I wanted to know Kyle's definition of dicey, so I didn't ask.

The crew adjusted things around on the stage for a few more minutes, and then all fell quiet. A short time later, the show finally started.

Music sounded and garish purple and yellow lighting flashed across the stage. "Welcome to *Geeks Get Some*," Stone said in a booming voice. "We are thrilled to invite you to tonight's exciting results show."

He chatted for a bit about the show and the contestants and then introduced a series of clips from the previous night's show. First up were several humiliating scenes of a few of the guys in a hot tub with Lucy. Lucy barely fit into her bikini and kept leaning over at strategic angles to give the guys an eyeful, while continuing to wear the dumb glasses that kept getting steamed up.

It was the stupidest thing I'd ever seen, and I've seen plenty of stupid things in my twenty-five years on the planet.

Gregg, the tall, almost skeletal, guy who thought he was God's gift to women, made a pathetic, painful play for Lucy.

"I'm so hot, baby." He grinned and scooted over closer to her in the hot tub.

Lucy fanned herself. "You're right. It is hot in here."

"No, *it's* not hot. *You're* the one who is hot and I bet I can make you even hotter."

One of the other guys moved closer to her from the other side. "You like alpha males, right? I could do that. Act alpha, that is."

Gregg stuck out his skinny chest. "Me, too."

Lucy rolled her eyes. "Unfortunately you two are about as alpha as my little toe."

The awkward, mortifying clips went on like this for painfully long stretches, broken up only by the continual laughter of the audience and a couple of commercials. I closed my eyes at some point, not able to watch any more. I felt angrier by the minute and more sympathetic to the cracker than perhaps I should have been.

It was beyond obvious that Lucy preferred Ray and Max, primarily because they appeared to be rational humans, not spouting *Repercussions* dialogue, pretending to be manly, or having unusual professions like a paranormal investigator or a professional gamer. She showered an inordinate amount of attention on the two normal guys and seemed in near desperation to convince the audience that one of these two guys was her best option. I had to agree that either one of them would have been the best choice of the lot she had left.

The show seemed to stretch on indefinitely until after a commercial, Stone ordered the lights to be dimmed and a weird staccato music blared. Lucy actually appeared nervous as she and the guys were told by Stone O'Hara to stand in a circle for what he called "the results reveal."

"Any last-minute advice for the guys?" Stone shoved the microphone in Lucy's face.

She smiled sweetly, peeking at the television audience over her glasses. "Just be yourself, guys. Be men and be comfortable in your own skin. Don't overthink, just go with your instincts."

Stone nodded thoughtfully, as if she had just said the most intelligent statement in the world. "So, Lucy, do you think the fans will pick the right guy to leave this week?"

"Well, I hope I made it clear which ones I like." She batted her eyes and pressed her hand to her chest. "I have a feeling the audience will agree with me."

I wanted to throw up. Seriously.

Stone smiled back, his teeth overly white in the harsh lighting. "Okay, let's send one of the guys to safety and that is... Ray Lewis."

Lucy seemed relieved and smiled at Ray as he crossed to the stage to stand next to Lucy.

"Next to stay is... Anson Oxlong."

"Anson?" Lucy couldn't hide her disappointment.

One by one the guys were sent to safety until only Max, the British guy Lucy clearly favored, Barnaby Knipple, better known as the *Repercussions* quote guy, and Gregg Magnum, the misguided alpha-wannabe, were left.

Dramatic music sounded. Lucy pressed her hands to her mouth. Suddenly Max disappeared from the stage.

My mouth gaped open. "Huh? Where's Max?"

Kyle misunderstood my astonishment. "Yep. Lucy is going to crap a brick."

I blinked. "No, I mean what happened to him? He vanished into thin air."

"Oh, that. There's a trap door on the stage with a slide and a cushion at the bottom. It's just for dramatic effect."

"They dropped him down a freaking trap door? Words fail me. Really."

Lucy was making noises of her own on the stage. She was furious and didn't make any effort to hide her displeasure.

I glanced at Kyle. "I take it Lucy didn't know in advance."

"No way. Believe me, she's tried more than once to get it out of the staff and me. But Cartwright forbade it. He's afraid of what she'd do."

"I think we're about to find out."

Lucy threw up her arms and stormed off the stage. The camera followed her and then swiveled back to Stone who looked surprised by her departure offstage.

I could hear Cartwright scream through Kyle's headset. "Cut to commercial! Now."

Kyle grabbed my arm. "Let's go."

We ran out of the IT room to the stage. While a commercial played, Cartwright stood at the side of the stage yelling at Lucy.

"Get back on that stage right now."

Lucy got right back in his face. "No! This is intolerable. It's gross. They're gross." She pointed at Barnaby and Gregg. "There is no way I'd ever date those guys, let alone propose to them, and the audience knows it. They *knew* I wanted Max."

"Shut up and do your job." Cartwright's face was beet red.

"I'm an actress, for God's sake."

"Then act the damn part."

"I can't do it anymore. These dorks are driving me crazy. I had no idea it would be this bad when I signed on."

"You are under contract."

Lucy took her glasses off and snapped them in her hands. "Contracts can be broken."

"I'll see you never get work anywhere in this town."

"Don't you dare threaten me. No one will blame me. I am *not* going on one more date or suffer one more disgusting lip lock or clueless groping. I quit."

Cartwright looked ready to have a heart attack. He breathed so hard his face was nearly purple. Still he was smart enough to try another tactic. "C'mon, Lucy. Do it for the show. Turn the other cheek."

"No. Absolutely not."

"Okay, okay. You offer me no choice. I'll give you a raise."

She paused. "How much?"

"A lot. Just get back on that stage."

"Fine. But we negotiate to my satisfaction the second the cameras are off or I'm history." She stalked back on the stage.

Cartwright mopped his brow and turned around. When he saw me, he glared. "You'd better find that hacking idiot and do it soon or I'm going to kill somebody."

Chapter Eight

After the show, the remaining contestants milled about on the side of the stage, looking dejected. Max wasn't in sight. Apparently he hadn't wasted any time between his downward slide, both literally and figuratively, and heading for a bar. I wished I could join him. A lone cameraman stood nearby still filming them.

I walked over to the cameraman. "Seriously? The show is over. Give them a break."

He shrugged, which couldn't have been easy with the heavy camera on his shoulder. "It's the gig. We've got to have them covered 24/7."

"That's asinine."

"I don't make the rules, sweetheart, but if I want a paycheck, I follow them." He took a step back, but kept filming.

Anson spoke first. "Don't worry, Lexi. If we start talking about the hacker, they'll be sure to cut the material. God forbid that they make it public."

Truman snorted. "Like the audience hasn't figured it out yet. Cartwright is fooling himself. The general public isn't that stupid."

"Speak for yourself." Eldrick shoved his fingers in his hair. "I think the people who watch this show are a bunch of morons. But we're the bigger ones for coming on in the first place. Somehow I thought it would be different."

Gregg walked over and tried to throw his arm around my shoulder. I glared at him. "One warning. Keep your hands to yourself. I've got a stun gun and I'm not afraid to use it."

He looked surprised. "You own a stun gun?"

"Of course I own a stun gun. I went to college in the heart of Washington, D.C. Every co-ed has one."

"Baby, you are making me want you so much."

"Ugh."

"Shut up, Gregg." Eldrick moved between us. "We need to focus."

I nodded. "Yes, by all means, focus. Even better, *think*. For God's sake, why in the world are you letting Lucy and the show treat you like this? How can you not stand up for yourselves?"

Eldrick sighed. "Lexi is right. We need to start standing up for ourselves."

"Great idea, wrong plan." Anson frowned. "We signed a contract."

"Yeah, but it doesn't say we can't turn things around and stop acting like idiots." Eldrick leaned against the wall and crossed his arms.

Ray stepped forward. "What Lexi is telling us is that we're not *acting* like idiots, we *are* idiots."

"'Idiots grow like mold on cheese.'" Barnaby shook his finger and then clarified, "Kirk says that to Chardonnay in just about every episode."

I rolled my eyes. "You can quit explaining your quotes, Barnaby. I already told you I'm a fan of *Repercussions*, too."

"Prove it."

I thought for a moment. "'What will happen to Earth if we relinquish the search for knowledge to those with no desire for true understanding?'"

"Ab'Jona to Cypher," Barnaby breathed. "In the episode 'Zone of Proximity.'"

Truman held up a hand. "I hate to interrupt this touching session of *Repercussions* bonding, but can we stick to the problem at hand? I understand what you're saying, Lexi. The problem is that I'm not acting. I really suck at conversation of any kind."

I shrugged. "Hey, I'm not on a high horse. It's not my strength either. Just tell me if there's a point to playing to the stereotype? It's wrong on so many levels. I'm struggling to figure out what prompted you signed up for this insanity. Please don't tell me it's because you're stupid, because I know you're not."

Anson raised his hand.

I sighed. "Jeez, Anson. This isn't school. Just say what you're thinking."

Anson cleared his throat, pushing his glasses up on his nose. "Well, I can't speak for the others, but I know why I'm here. I want to figure out how to communicate properly, with the right amount of emotion and interest, in order to exchange a *girl friend* for a *girlfriend*. It's really not that complex a concept, except for some reason the methodology escapes me."

Barnaby nodded. "'Earthling mating rituals often involve rubber sheaths, liquid that impairs the thinking process, and richly illustrated texts of sexual positions.' Ab'Jona to Kirk in the 'Haunted Vortex.'"

I shot Barnaby an exasperated look. "Look, can't you guys see what's going on here? They're playing you for laughs. Where is your pride? Where's your self-respect? They are exploiting every imaginable stereotype available about geeks and you are playing right into their hands."

Truman shrugged. "Hey, I've got two emails from girls back home who said they saw me on television and are cheering for me. That equals two girls who never noticed me before. Statistically that's a coup for me."

Anson nodded. "He's got a point."

I rolled my eyes. "That is *not* a point. Those girls could be laughing at you."

Truman frowned. "So what? At least they see me."

"No, Truman. They don't see *you*. They see a caricature of you. There's a difference."

"Baby." Gregg strode up to me, hitching his pants. "You've got to relax. We men have got it all under control." Before I could move, his hand shot out, grabbing my shoulder. As I backed up in horror, I almost tripped over Eldrick.

Ray stepped between us. "Gregg, dude. Back off. I mean it. You're like an octopus with eight arms. The fake manly act is *not* working."

"It would work, if she would just relax and go with it."

"She's going to knock you on your ass and the rest of us will cheer."

Barnaby suddenly jumped up. "'A true understanding of women comes from being able to tap the hidden reserve within her soul.'"

We all turned to stare at him.

His cheeks went pink. "Ab'Jona to Cypher in 'Exquisite Disequilibrium.'"

I sighed. "Look, guys, I'm just saying that you should

think about what you are doing and why. You're giving geeks a bad name, okay?"

Eldrick looked at me intently. "So, what do you want us to do, Lexi? Revolt? Shred our contract? Turn the show upside down? Mass exodus?"

I shrugged. "Well, why don't you?"

It was silent for a moment while they all stared at me.

Barnaby leapt up and started pacing. "'I'm scared. It's beginning to look like a three-ring circus out there, and I think I like it.' That was Cypher to Kirk in the episode 'Self-Reflection.'"

We ignored Barnaby, but Eldrick narrowed his eyes as he studied me. "You are almost beginning to sound as if you like this mysterious hacker, Lexi."

"I won't deny that. However, that doesn't mean if I find him, I won't shut him down."

"So, what should we do?" Anson asked, his tone pleading.

I lifted my hands. "Guys, this is *your* show. It's in *your* hands. Put your fine brains together and figure something out. But if I were you, I'd do it sooner rather than later."

Chapter Nine

Despite my intention to stay late after the show and get started on finding the hacker, Kyle and Tony both ganged up on me and told me to get some sleep.

Kyle stood in front of the computer he'd set up for me, blocking it with his body. "The studio closes down in about an hour anyway. Let's start fresh in the morning."

Tony nodded. "Yeah, you need some down time."

I frowned, grumpy. "Okay. We can start fresh tomorrow. But I can walk. It's ten minutes away. I don't need a ride, Tony."

Tony clucked his tongue. "Don't start getting all diva on me. You aren't walking anywhere in L.A., day or night. I'll drive you home and pick you up in the morning at nine sharp. Besides, if anything happens to you, Cartwright will have my ass in a sling."

I didn't argue further because I did feel tired, my stomach was still queasy, and I had a headache from the emotional trauma of having to endure an episode of *Geeks Get Some* up close and personal. My injured hand also ached because I'd forgotten to take some ibuprofen and hadn't done any exercises with the therapy squeeze ball.

As a result, I let Tony guide me to his car. When I got to my hotel room, I changed into my PJs and brushed my teeth. Yet, despite my exhaustion, I was too wound up to sleep.

I surfed the Net, squeezed the therapy ball, paced the room, and jotted down some notes. My mind raced with a number of different scenarios to find the hacker. At twelve fifteen I started to create a spreadsheet to organize my thoughts when my laptop chimed. I clicked on my mail and saw I had received a message from *paranormalexpert@blacknighthome.net*.

You awake, Lexi? Just checking to see if you hold geek hours like we do. If so, want to join us tonight for some gaming?

I tried to remember which one of the contestants was the paranormal investigator. My mind sorted through the guys and landed on the redheaded one named Truman.

Truman, is that you?

Ha! Knew you'd be awake. Just won myself a twenty from Anson.

You serious about the gaming?

I wouldn't joke about gaming. Trust me on that.

Gaming sounds pretty optimum right now. I need to unwind.

We can come get you.

I'm not sure.

Why? Gaming is gaming. Scared we'll trounce you?

I'm hardly scared of a challenge. Just don't want to be part of your filming.

Don't worry. Cameraman is drunk and passed out. We're in the clear.

Still, I'm not sure you guys are at my level. Calculating whether it's worth the effort.

I like a confident woman. We'll be there in ten. You in?

Okay, I'm in.

I emailed the address of the hotel and pulled on some jeans and a sweatshirt. After I wound my hair up in a ponytail, I grabbed my purse and keys and went down to the front of the hotel to wait.

The guy on night duty gallantly asked if could call me a cab, but I told him I was waiting for someone. He didn't even blink an eye that someone was coming to pick me up at nearly one o'clock in the morning, so maybe that's normal in California.

About ten minutes later, a red car pulled up. Truman jumped out of the driver's side and waved me over.

"Ready for some gaming, Lexi?"

I lifted an eyebrow. "Are you?"

"Heck yeah, we are."

He opened the door and I climbed in the front passenger side. There were three other guys crammed in the back and I turned in my seat to see who it was.

I pointed my finger at each of them as I rattled off their names. "Barnaby, Eidrick and Anson. Am I right?"

"Photographic memory?" Eldrick asked.

"Yes, if I'm focused."

"Me, too," Anson said. His hair looked like he'd just had a close encounter with an electric socket. "Great for remembering all the parts of a circuit, but not so great when trying to remember what I'm supposed to say to a girl."

I shrugged. "That's because talking to a girl—or anyone for that matter—isn't a simple list to be memorized. However, I've found that having a small mental reference of small talk topics and phrases to be helpful in certain social situations."

Anson leaned forward in his seat. "Really? You willing to share sometime?"

"Sure. Why not?"

Barnaby gripped Truman's headset and looked at me intently. "'Those who share knowledge, share the path to ultimate understanding.'"

I nodded. "Ab'Jona to Cypher in 'Diffusion Illusion.' I especially liked that episode because Chardonnay outsmarted everyone when she anticipated the Zindi would attack."

I turned around in my seat as Barnaby whistled under his breath.

"She's a true *Repercussions* geek, Barnaby," Anson said. "The real deal. You may have met your match at last."

I glanced at Truman. "So what are we playing tonight?"

Truman shrugged. "Well, we aren't playing any Wicked Fish games—that would be an unfair advantage to Anson, who developed most of them—so we were thinking about 'Zorxx.' You familiar with it?"

"'Zorxx'? Sure, been as far as Level Fourteen."

Eldrick gasped. "I never got past Level Ten. How did you handle the solar niche?"

"Combination blast of synergistic dispersion and thermal focus."

"Whoa. Seriously? I didn't consider the thermal focus."

"It works."

Anson leaned forward. "Hey, I'm on Level Fourteen now. Want to be on my team?"

"No way." Truman took a hard right and we all slid sideways. "We aren't playing 'Zorxx' if you and Lexi are already on Level Fourteen."

I smiled. "Who's scared now?"

The guys started arguing and I felt myself relax. It was nice to be among my peers.

Truman drove up to a gated community. The guard peered in the car. "Hey, you guys aren't supposed to be driving yourselves. Where's your driver?"

Truman leaned out the window. "Come on, Joey. It's one o'clock in the morning. The driver is asleep."

"You know you're not supposed to be driving alone. Legal department makes those rules."

Truman cocked his head toward me. "Give me a break, okay?"

Joey leaned down and peered at me. "Oh, a girl." He looked in the back seat. "With the three other guys in the back?"

"Moral support."

Joey sighed. "That's whack, but I'll let it slide this time. I don't want to see you guys do it again."

"Thanks, dude. You're the greatest."

He lifted the gate and let us in. It was dark, but I could see the hulking shapes of mansions.

I glanced at Truman. "They keep you on a short leash."

"Tell me about it. It's more like prison and less like an exclusive community."

I grimaced. "Why would anyone want to live here?"

Eldrick snorted. "Wait until you see these monstrosities in the daylight."

"I'd rather not."

"'Those with the smallest minds have the largest egos.'" Barnaby patted the seat. "Ab'Jona to Kirk in 'The Triangulated Trio.'"

We pulled into the circular driveway of a mansion that looked like a small museum.

I climbed out of the car and stared at the hulking building. "Really? This is a house? I can't believe people would want to live in a place like this on purpose."

Truman got out as well. "It's our humble abode for as long as we are on the show."

He opened the back door and Barnaby half fell out, pushing the glasses up on his nose. "Exclusivity and taste are not synonymous."

I frowned. "It's pretentious, not to mention hideous."

Truman laughed. "Oh, so true, Lexi. Enter our mansion."

He opened the ginormous front door and we strolled in. The foyer was a cavernous area highlighted by a huge white marble winding staircase and a glittering chandelier. Truman went left, so I followed him with the other guys trailing behind me.

We walked into a huge room with several couches, a

fireplace and a huge plasma screen television mounted on the wall. Pillows were scattered across the floor in front of the television, a half dozen wireless gaming remotes on the floor in front of them and a stack of discs on a nearby table. Three pinball machines lined the right wall and a half dozen laptops were arranged on a long table that had been pushed up against the opposite wall. Three empty pizza boxes and several cans of Mountain Dew littered the nearby coffee tables. Guess the studio executives knew geeks well or had good advisors.

Gregg and Ray were playing something, both of them pounding away on their remotes while swearing like sailors.

I stepped closer, peering at the television. "'Demon Kingdom'?"

The demon on the screen abruptly squashed the knight under a giant clawed foot. Ray swore, tossing his remote to the ground. "She distracted me."

Gregg laughed. "You were finished way before she came." He placed his remote on the coffee table and sauntered toward me, hitching his pants up on his skinny hips. "Ooh, a hot chick in our humble abode after midnight. Want a little loving from a true champion? I'll make it worth your while."

I frowned, taking a step back. "The one certainty of this universe is that I will *never* want that."

The guys all laughed, even Gregg. I took a moment to look around and counted six guys. Barnaby, Ray, Truman, Eldrick, Anson and Gregg.

"Where's Max Sheffield?" I asked.

Ray jerked his head at the front door. "He couldn't wait to hightail it out of here. He left a couple of hours ago."

"Okay, then I guess the gang is all here."

After I grabbed a cold piece of ham, cheese, and pineapple pizza, we sat down to some serious gaming.

The game of choice was ended up being "Quaver" as none of us had played past Level Four. We played in teams, rotated in and out, forty-minute stretches with two of us at a time to be replaced by others on the team. After two hours a couple of the guys disappeared altogether. Some came back and others didn't. By five forty-five only Truman, Anson and I were left. I finished off Truman and then Anson before standing triumphant.

"Good game." I rotated my neck and shoulders. "Now I'm tired."

Anson and Truman both shook my hand. "You were good, Lexi. Better than good. I game for a living, so I am not overstating the fact that you have skills."

"Some skill, but a lot of luck, too. If Barnaby hadn't discovered the Humpbacked Hag in the Ghoulish Garden on Level Seven, she would have finished me off. Luck has to be considered a major factor here."

"Okay, considered. But you're still amazingly good. On that note, I'm going to bed. I should have stayed there when I took a quick nap between Levels Six and Seven." He gave me a salute and disappeared up the marble staircase.

Truman rubbed his eyes. "We're lucky we don't have to film until noon. Six hours will help."

I glanced at my watch. "Crap. I have to be at work at nine."

"I feel your pain."

I wasn't sure he did, especially since jet lag had started to kick in, but I didn't say anything. Truman and I got back into the car and headed back to the hotel.

We passed through the gatehouse and Truman asked, "So, how do you like Hollywood so far, Lexi?"

I shrugged. "It's hard to have a good feeling after one day. But my initial impressions are that it's a bit strange. I'm having a hard time getting past the fact that everyone here seems to have abnormally white teeth."

He laughed. "Agreed."

I blew out a breath. "Hey, Truman, can I ask you something? Why did you do this, really? Put yourself out there, I mean. You dared to come on this show, in front of millions of people, just to figure out how to have a relationship. Is having a relationship really worth all that?"

He stopped at a red light and tapped his fingers on the steering wheel. "I guess I believe there are benefits to being loved by someone else no matter what. So, I put myself out there. No pain, no gain, right?"

I was still thinking about his words when he dropped me off.

I took the elevator to my room and swiped my key card in the door. I dropped my purse on the suitcase stand by the dresser and then stopped cold.

My laptop was open and on. A series of pictures of me walking about the studio, in the studio parking lot, and standing in the hotel lobby, were flashing across the monitor in a screen saver mode.

For a moment I couldn't breathe. Someone had been in my room and messed with my computer.

Someone was stalking me.

Chapter Ten

I whirled around, pressing my back against the wall and scanning the room.

It was empty, but the bathroom door was slightly closed. I inched toward my purse, grabbed my stun gun, and pressed it on. Taking comfort in the quiet hum, I took a silent step toward the bathroom door.

I kicked the door open, but the room was empty. I stepped inside and, with images of *Psycho* playing in my head, ripped back the shower curtain. The tub was empty too. I let out a huge breath, turned off the stun gun and set it on the counter, then perched on the toilet lid trying to catch my breath.

After a moment, I stood and approached my laptop again. I watched as pictures of me entering the hotel, waiting at the elevator in the lobby, lying on my bed in the hotel room, and walking down the corridor at the studio all flashed across the screen.

Anger began to replace the fear.

I reached out to press a key on the keyboard when my phone chirped. I jumped a good half foot in the air and then yanked my phone from my purse.

"Hello?"

"Hey, Lexi."

"Elvis? Is that you?"

"Yeah. You sound funny. Are you okay?"

I pressed a hand to my chest. It was shaking. "I'm not sure."

Silence. "Where are you?"

"Los Angeles. Hollywood to be exact. I'm working a case for X-Corp."

"Hollywood? That's a three-hour difference. I'm sorry I woke you. I assumed you were headed into work."

"It's okay and you didn't wake me. I was already awake."

He paused. "I see. So, what are you doing out there?"

Just hearing his voice had a calming effect on me. I thought about telling him about the photos, but I didn't know what they meant just yet. I needed to check it out before I alarmed anyone.

"X-Corp caught a case. The suits asked for me specifically, I guess."

"I'm not surprised. You working it alone?"

"So far. I just got in yesterday."

"What are you doing?"

"Trying to shut down a cracker who is manipulating votes on a reality television show."

"Sounds prime."

"I don't like Hollywood much."

"Well, I'm not much for television myself. But it sounds like it should be a pretty quick turnaround."

The pictures of me kept flashing across my monitor. I turned away. "I sincerely hope so."

He cleared his voice. "Well, the reason I called is that I noticed some unusual activity on your account last night."

Elvis and Xavier had lent me space on their secure server. It was better than any commercial server on the planet and tighter than Fort Knox, the NSA and the CIA put together. Not surprising, given the twins had created or worked on all of those networks at one time or the other.

I pulled out the desk chair and sat down. I had an upset stomach from all the late-night pizza. "What kind of activity?"

"Sniffing. Someone was probing, checking out the system. They set off the alarms immediately and didn't get anywhere. More interesting, they came back with a different method and a different address, but it was them."

"You trace them?"

"I did. It was a bogus account in Bogota, Colombia." I was silent.

"Lexi? Any reason someone would be checking you out like that?"

I closed my eyes. My head thumped as a headache roared to life. "I'm not sure. It might have to do with the case I just caught. I haven't had a good look at the situation yet. I don't know exactly what I'm up against."

"Well, find out and call me back. I'll keep an eye on things at this end."

"Will do. Thanks for letting me know, Elvis."

"Anytime. Lexi, are you sure you're okay?"

I held out my hand. It no longer shook. "I'm okay."

He hesitated for a moment and then he said, "Take care of yourself. Promise?"

"Promise."

I hung up the phone. I turned the chair to face my

laptop and pressed a key. The pictures of me disappeared.

It took me seven minutes to figure out what had happened. At some point during the day, someone had planted a password-sniffing program on my laptop called Wickercapp. They had used it to perform ARP-poisoning and swipe the security information, including the passwords, right off my laptop. Whoever did that would likely be able to breach the hotel network and steal the key code to my room.

My virtual and physical habitats had both been compromised. I was seriously pissed.

I thought back on my day. I'd left my laptop vulnerable in the IT room. It never occurred to me that it wouldn't be safe there. Unfortunately, it had only routine security software on it since it was a company laptop and not my *personal* one. Still whoever had hacked it was both skilled and resourceful to get past the initial security level. I wouldn't be so sloppy next time.

Who had done this? It had to be someone who had access to the IT room, which meant basically every studio employee and the contestants. But the fact that someone had dared to follow me to my hotel and take photos of me was truly disturbing.

Resolutely, I set aside the creepy stalker photos of myself for inspection at a later point. I then wiped Wickercapp clean, ran several diagnostic programs and installed more stringent security measures. After everything was installed, I initiated several more tests. Finally satisfied all was well and the laptop was virtually impenetrable, I took a breath and opened the folder with the pictures of me.

The first one was of me in the hotel lobby. I looked

at it carefully, noticing the details and trying to determine when it might have been taken.

I assessed and then murmured, "Coming home from the studio tonight after the show."

The next one was one of me sitting in the IT room before the voting started. Another one caught me walking down the studio corridor and could have been at any point during the day. There were two others of me coming out of the restroom and another one of me entering the hotel lobby.

I closed my eyes trying to think, to recall who at the studio might have had pointed a camera at me. It was freaking impossible. The studio was filled with cameras. *Anyone* could have taken these photos from *any* spot in the studio.

The studio photos were bad enough, but the ones in the hotel were worse. Someone had actually followed me to where I was temporarily living, stalked me, and taken pictures without my permission. I hadn't paid attention to who was around me in the hotel, but I would now.

I'd been violated, but I wasn't going to play the victim.

I wasn't sleepy anymore. Using the hotel room coffee pot, I made myself some coffee while I took a shower and changed my clothes. Sipping the coffee, I sat at my laptop and got to work.

Someone didn't like the fact that I'd come and had sent a clear message to let me know that. Was it the hacker who was disrupting the show by manipulating the votes? Or was it someone on the staff who was unhappy that an outsider had been brought in to solve a problem?

Either way, it didn't matter. I had to approach this methodically.

The first order of business was to make a list of everyone I knew so far that was involved with the show. That meant all the contestants, IT staff, stage crew and administrators I'd met so far. I'd get a complete list from Kyle later, but it wouldn't hurt to get a head start on the process. I'd have to ask Tony for a list of any recently fired employees or anyone that may have had a grudge against the studio.

As it stood, all I needed were names to get to work. I started with the IT staff, Kyle in particular. No better place than to start at the top. It took me under fifteen minutes to get a solid dossier of him and his life. One hour later, I had a clear picture of the entire IT staff. All of the tech staff—with the exception of Kyle—were California born and bred. All had gone to college at USC or UCLA. Kyle was an east coast kid, born in Virginia and studied at Virginia Tech. SWM was the first real job for the entire staff. No one had a record or any official blips for cracking or hacking. I didn't see any red flags here.

I moved to the contestants next, reading their bios from the show website and using that as a springboard to search deeper on each of them. Here I found some blips on a few of the contestants' records for hacking and mischief. Nothing too serious, but interesting all the same.

After that, I started going through the considerable studio roster of employees. I began to get into a rhythm with my brain processing and storing information as fast as my fingers could tap the keyboard.

Data in. Data out.

Data filed. Data organized.

A technical waltz I knew well and loved. I was in my element.

Chirp.

Chirp.

Distracted, I tried to bring my focus back to the hotel room. I blinked, glancing over at my phone. It was vibrating on the desk. I picked it up and saw the time. Nine o'clock. Really?

I punched the button. "Hello?"

"Hey, it's me, Tony. I'm downstairs when you are ready."

"Okay. I'm on my way."

I wrapped up my search, shut down my laptop and grabbed my purse. Tony had brought coffee and bagels. I ate one bagel on the way into the studio as I requested the data on former employees.

"Tony, I'm going to need everything you've got, especially on former tech employees, especially if any of them were fired or faced disciplinary action."

He nodded. "Sure. I'll bring it over as soon as it is compiled."

We parted ways at the IT room. Kyle and the rest of the staff were already hard at work.

Kyle came over to greet me as I set up my laptop. "Hey, Lexi. How'd you sleep?"

"Ah, not much. Any news from our cracker after last night's show?"

Kyle shook his head. "He's quiet, but I'm keeping an eye out for any appearance."

He'd already made an appearance to me, but I didn't say anything to Kyle about it yet. Until I felt confident in who I could trust, I would hold my cards close to my chest, which basically meant keeping quiet about the stalker for the time being.

I leaned back in my swivel chair and looked up at him. "Tell me something, Kyle. Why doesn't Cartwright just manipulate the votes how he wants or, by extension, however Lucy wants? What's the big deal? There is no oversight committee and no one has to vouch for the legitimacy of the process. The whole thing is a royal farce anyway."

Kyle shrugged. "That might have worked before the cracker became emotionally involved. Now, if we don't display the votes the way he manipulated them, he's threatened to do something worse. Cartwright has no idea what that means in the scope of things, which is why he hired you."

I blew out a breath. "Okay. Then we're stuck. Now, another question. Who has access to the IT room?"

"Access? Why, any studio employee can come here. We don't lock the door except at night."

"Do the contestants ever come in here?"

"More often than you might think. Several of them are tech heads and just like to hang here and gab."

"Well, until we catch this hacker, I recommend a coded door and no access to anyone who doesn't have a strict reason for being here."

He looked at me for a long moment and then nodded. "Okay, consider it done."

"Good. Now give me some time to get familiar with the setup."

He went back to his office while I surfed around, getting a better view of the system and the security and technical layout. After that, I waded through the mounds of data Kyle had captured from the previous vote manipulations. After the initial review, it confirmed my first conclusion that the hacker was smart and capable. It didn't matter. I'd catch him. He'd slip up at some point and he'd be mine.

While I was attempting to trace the origin of the manifesto emails sent to Lucy and Kyle, Tony stopped by and dropped a file on my desk.

"Here's the list of former employees and contact information." He stared at me. "You've got dark circles under your eyes. Did you sleep at all?"

"Not exactly."

"Why? Isn't the hotel comfortable?"

"It's, ah, fine. Thanks, Tony. I'm good."

"Well, I'll bring you some lunch."

I wasn't really hungry, but I decided not to argue. I stretched and walked over to see what Melinda was up to. I looked over her shoulder. "What are you doing?"

"I've been trying for several days to trace the origins of the manifesto email with no luck. It's led me to a dead end in South Africa."

"He's good, so it's likely to be a dummy account anyway. But shoot what you've found my way and I'll see if I can turn up something."

"Okay, thanks."

I glanced across the room and saw Carlos and Noah arguing about something. I held up my hands in a time-out signal as I strolled over.

"What's the problem, guys?"

Carlos exhaled. "I've spent all morning trying to figure out some pattern for the bad votes, but I'm getting nowhere. The method was random, I'm telling you."

"No way," Noah said. "There has to be a method to

the madness. Otherwise, he couldn't be sure it would work."

"Well, if he had a master plan, I can't find it."

"Because you're not looking hard enough."

"Don't tell me how hard I'm looking."

Time for me to step in. "Okay. Take it easy. I've only been working on the case a few hours, but I can already tell our cracker is skilled. With that in mind, I agree with Noah. There's likely a method. But he's good, so it's not going to be easy to spot. You're going to have to think outside the box, Carlos. I'll help you out and see what I can find. Just keep at it, okay?"

"Like I have a choice." He stomped back to his desk.

Noah rubbed his eyes. "We're all tired."

"I know. Look, I'm going to need your help with a file."

"Sure, girl boss. What do you need?"

I retrieved the file Tony had given me from my desk and passed it off to him. "See if you can link any of these former employees' emails to anything in our system. I'm not leaning toward a former disgruntled employee, but I've got to rule it out."

Noah grimaced. "Oh, man. I get the crap work?"

"Sorry. Someone has to slog through it."

"Well, I sure drew the short straw. And here I was pitying Carlos."

"Suck it up."

"Looks like I don't have a choice either. Okay, I'm on it."

Tony brought me a sandwich while I was doing a careful examination of the studio firewalls. I couldn't find a single bleep, mark or thread where the cracker had left a signature.

"What's happening?" Tony handed me the sandwich and looked over my shoulder.

"I don't like where this is going."

"I'm not sure what that means."

"It means I have no evidence that our hacker cracked into the system from the outside."

"I don't have a clue what that means. Seriously, don't look to me to help you. Tech talk makes me nervous."

After he left, I unwrapped my sandwich and took a bite. After the invasion of my computer, I had already suspected this would be the case, but now I had confirmed it. An absence of threads almost always meant one thing. Insider threat. This would make finding the hacker infinitely harder.

Frowning, I slid my computer glasses off my nose and set them to the side of my monitor. I stood up and lifted my hands above my head in a full body stretch, glancing at Kyle's office. He was typing furiously on the keyboard, a frustrated look on his face. I took another bite of my sandwich, trying to decide the best angle to pursue from this point. I wanted to fill him in, but an inside threat meant I couldn't trust anyone. Unfortunately, keeping him in the dark was going to make things a lot harder for me. So, with no help and no threads to follow, it was going to be like looking for a needle in a haystack.

I knocked on the glass window of Kyle's office. "I'm going out for a bit of fresh air."

He nodded. "Sure."

I grabbed my purse and walked out of the studio. I began to pace up and down the sidewalk. After few minutes, I pulled out my phone. I now had seventeen messages, but I wasn't in the mood to check any of them and then feel guilty about not calling anyone back. Especially since sixteen of said messages were likely from my mother.

Instead I punched in a number I knew by heart.

He answered on the third ring. "Hello?"

"Hey, Elvis. It's Lexi. Are you busy?"

I heard the shuffling of some papers and the tap on a keyboard. "I'm all yours. Sorry again about calling so early this morning."

I sighed. "Not a problem. Actually it was good timing. It was great to hear your voice. What I really need now is a sounding board."

"At your service."

I pressed my hand to my forehead. "It turns out the cracker I'm looking for isn't a cracker."

"Explain."

"I've got no threads, no trails, no nothing."

He was quiet for a moment. "An insider?"

"Yes."

"That's tough. Those are the worst kinds."

"I know. I can't decide how best to take this one down. If he's on the inside, putting up internal barriers may not be enough for the long haul, especially if he's talented."

"True."

"I could probably stay one step ahead of him if I worked here permanently. But I can't stay in Hollywood forever."

"Glad to hear that."

"So, I'm in a bind. I don't want to shut him out completely because then I can't catch him."

"Or her."

"True."

His chair squeaked as he shifted in it. "Unfortunately, Lexi, it's not just a technical problem anymore."

I sighed. "No. It's a people problem."

"Then you're going to have to find a people-centric solution."

"Big problem as I'm not much of a people person. People add too many variables to the equation."

"Then build your defense contextually. Look at how people use the system and create a baseline, searching for the incongruities."

"You mean a behavioral-based approach?"

"Yes. You're probably better at that than you think. As one of the best hackers I've ever met, you can use that to your advantage. Put yourself in his or her shoes and go from there."

I drew in a sharp breath. "Wait. *Wait*. You think... you think *I'm* one of the best hackers you've ever met?"

"You're surprised?"

"Coming from a tech god such as yourself, yes."

He paused. "Wait. You think *I'm* a tech god?"

I laughed. "Of legend status. Oh, jeez. You just made my day, Elvis. Seriously."

"Likewise."

I was glad he couldn't see me grinning like an idiot.

"So, Lexi, this television show you're working on... Should I watch it?"

"Oh, God, no, Elvis. Seriously."

"Okay, if you say so."

"I say so. Trust me."

"I do. I'm still waiting for the gaming and pizza you promised."

"Coming your way when I get back."

"Looking forward to it."

I glanced at my watch. "Well, I'd better get back to work. I really appreciate your insight. Thanks again."

"My pleasure."

"You gave me some good ideas. I'm going to have to think about this."

He chuckled. "In my opinion, that's the best place to start."

Chapter Eleven

I returned to the IT room as soon as I hung up. I needed to start creating a baseline. To do that, I needed to know exactly who had access to the system from the inside, and how many people had accounts within the company. After that I needed to determine if there were any active or inactive accounts not specifically assigned to anyone and whether I should tag them for observation.

I began an immediate series of protocols to match accounts to users and isolate any foreign or sole accounts. When all was said and done I had twenty-seven accounts that weren't openly assigned to anyone. Not that any of them were a red flag, but I'd have them all figured out sooner than later. All of the contestants and Lucy had accounts and all of them were busy. Apparently the emails were publicized so the fans could communicate with the stars. As a studio employee, Stone had an account as well.

I needed to get a better picture of all the people involved.

I knocked on Kyle's door even though it was open. He looked up. "What's up?"

"I need to talk with the contestants again."

"Okay? Why?"

"A couple of them have dings on their records for hacking. Nothing serious enough to warrant jail time, but the skill is there. In fact, a couple of them have tech skills I wish I had. I want to talk to them in more depth, tech to tech, to get a general sense of what they think of our guy."

"What if he's one of them?"

I stopped, stared at Kyle. "You think one of them might be our guy?"

"I haven't ruled out an inside threat, and I bet you haven't either. I figure that's why you're not sharing much. I understand that even though I'm not happy about it. So, why tip by your hand by letting them know they're suspects?"

"If our cracker is one of them, he'll know I'm hunting."

"It will probably piss him off."

"I don't care if he's cocky, anxious, or pissed. If he's among the remaining contestants, I want to rattle him. Rattled crackers are sloppy crackers, and that I like."

Kyle stuck a pencil behind his ear. "Okay. I'm on board if you think it will help. Check with Tony. He'll have the guys' filming schedule."

I managed to track down Tony, who told me the guys would be available after six o'clock at the mansion.

"I'll drive you over then."

"Okay. Thanks, Tony."

I returned to the IT room and decided to work in tandem with Carlos to see if we could find a pattern in the bad votes. It was nearly six o'clock when I spotted it.

"Bingo." I slid the glasses off my nose and leaned back in my chair. "Crapola. It's been staring us in the face this whole time."

"What? Where?" Carlos leaned over, peering at my monitor. "I don't see it."

"Here." I tapped the monitor with my finger. "Look at this string. He swizzled. The bad votes are just copied good votes with the IP addresses and emails rearranged."

"He swizzled? Say what? He left it out in the open? I hate this guy. I really hate him."

"I'm more tired than I thought." I stood up. "I should have seen that about three hours ago. Okay, well, we found out how he's doing it. That's a good thing. I can pull the plug on that technique."

Carlos looked hopeful. "Will it stop him?"

I shook my head. "Doubtful. He'll have a backup plan."

"It's a never-ending nightmare."

I patted his shoulder. "Oh, there's an end, Carlos. We'll get him. Don't worry."

Tony strolled in. "Hey, Lexi. You ready to see the guys?"

"Ready as I'll ever be. Give me a sec to talk to Kyle."

I popped into Kyle's office and brought him up to speed on the swizzle. He pulled up the data and cursed. "Hidden in plain sight." I heard the disgust in his voice. "How did I miss it?"

"We all did. It's a bit unexpected, but clever. We'll learn more about him as we go along. I'm going to see the contestants, then I'll check out for the day."

Kyle turned his chair around. "I'm done as well. See you tomorrow."

Tony and I walked to his car. It was a warm evening, so he left the top down to the convertible as we drove. I dug the small therapy ball out of my purse and squeezed it.

Twenty minutes later we entered the gated community. Since the sun hadn't set yet, I got a better look at the big honking mansions in the guys' neighborhood.

I stared at one of the monstrosities that masqueraded as a house. "That compound is bigger than the National Zoo."

"It's Penny Forester's house. You may know her from the show *Millionaire Model Makeovers*."

"No, I don't know her. I'm sorry to offend her apparent bad taste, but that has to be the ugliest structure I've ever seen. I sincerely hope she doesn't live there alone. There's enough room for the entire population of Estonia."

Tony laughed. "Wait until you see the house next door."

We drove past several more hideous structures before pulling into the circular driveway of the guys' mansion. I followed Tony to the front door and he opened it without knocking and strolled in. "The filming should be over by now. The guys will likely be in the kitchen or the heated pool."

He headed straight for the room where we'd gamed last night. Several of the guys huddled around a table, leaning over something. A lone cameraman was filming them.

I grabbed Tony's arm. "Hey, they're still filming. Wait."

Tony held his ground. "Sometimes they use clips of the guys during their down time as filler."

"They're filming them doing a puzzle."

"The television audience actually finds this interesting? Really?"

"Well, it's a lot more entertaining than what they usually do."

"So, they have absolutely zero privacy?"

"Pretty much for the duration of the show."

Barnaby spotted us first. "Greetings, Lexi and Tony. 'May the fortune of Shangra shine upon you this day and always.'"

The other contestants looked up from the table. They'd been working on a huge puzzle, at least five thousand pieces.

Eldrick waved. "Hey, Lexi. What brings you to our humble abode again?"

"I came to pick your brains."

The rest of the guys wandered over. The cameraman zoomed in on me. I glanced at Tony.

"Can we do something about him? I'm going to need some time here."

Tony considered and then motioned to the cameraman. "Take five. Cartwright would approve."

The guy seemed more than happy to oblige. He shed the heavy camera, then wandered out on the patio near the pool.

Tony patted me on the shoulder. "I'll go keep him company. Come get me when you're ready to split."

"Sure. Thanks."

After he left, I stood alone with the guys and tried to get my thoughts in order. It was awkward until Ray suggested we sit down. I perched in the middle of one of the couches while Barnaby and Anson took a seat on either side of me.

Truman leaned back in a black leather chair and

crossed his arms behind his head. "So, my brain is ready to be picked. What's going on?"

Ray leaned forward. "Yeah, fill us in, Lexi. How's it going finding the nutcase who's manipulating the votes?"

I threaded my fingers together on my lap. "Well, that's why I'm here. I need to partake in the collective wisdom present. So, I'm going to cut to the bottom line. Our cracker is on the inside."

Silence.

Truman finally spoke. "Are you joking? An inside job? Like a studio employee or something?"

"Yes."

Eldrick studied me intently. "No. Not only a studio employee. She thinks it may be one of us. It makes sense. We all have accounts and access."

All eyes turned back to me and I shrugged. "It's a possibility."

Barnaby inhaled sharply. "Fascinating development."

"Dang right, it's fascinating." Gregg chortled. "It's a real mystery. Like the game of Clue or something. Okay, okay. Wait, guys. I think it's Anson Oxlong in the studio with a hypertext transfer protocol."

Anson shot Gregg the finger. "Shut up, Gregg. Lexi, do you really think one of us is the show's cracker?"

"I don't know. Call it a hunch, a gut instinct. I usually trust them."

"So, how can you be sure it's someone on the inside?" Eldrick asked. "Maybe he's just prime. Operates without a trace."

"There's never *not* a trace. If you look hard enough, trace evidence is always there. But I can't find anything."

Ray stared at me. "You're that good?"

"Good enough. Just so you all know, all the pass-words and protocols have been changed and a new ded-icated server has been set up. So, if it *is* one of you, you're going to have to start at square one for your next hack."

Eldrick cracked his knuckles. "Changing proto-cols and passwords won't stop a decent or determined cracker."

"True. I'm just putting it out there as common knowl-edge."

"No, not as a deterrent," Truman said, rubbing his chin. "You don't really think that will stop him. We're all prime suspects. This is pretty cool."

"Cracking isn't cool."

Truman shrugged. "I respectfully disagree. It de-pends on who, when, how, and the all-important why. Besides, you're not one to talk. You've got a blip of your own on record, Lexi."

I turned my gaze on Truman. "You've been check-ing me out?"

"In more ways than one. But yes. I've got a lot of time on my hands. I've pretty much compiled the life story of everyone in this room."

"Same here." Eldrick grinned. "Guilty as charged."

After a moment Barnaby raised his hand. "Guilty as well. 'To admit to an uncomfortable truth is to mas-ter the hidden deception of the heart.' Ab'Jona to Kirk Masters in 'Red Dwarf Revisited.'"

Truman laughed. "Lexi isn't even surprised. She probably expected it of us. Plus, I bet she's already done the same on us. I would venture the assumption that she knows more about me than my mother right now. I bet she also knows Anson still has *Star Wars* sheets on his bed and Gregg likes to play Xbox naked."

Anson reddened. "I do *not* have *Star Wars* sheets on my bed."

"Well, I do like to play Xbox naked, but not with you perverts around," Gregg said laughing. "My door doesn't swing that way."

Truman snorted. "Technically your door should be bolted shut. But, hey, that's why you're here, Lexi, right? To gauge our reactions to your little announcement."

"Partially true. The other part is to elicit your help."

Anson raised his hand and then lowered it when I glared at him. "Right. Sorry. I'm not in a classroom. Anyway, if you think it's an inside job, why are you telling us? If one of us really is the cracker, then you've just given it away."

I scooted back against the cushions and stretched my legs. "I'm being upfront for a number of reasons. One, I really do need your help. I want you to keep an eye on each other. Make it harder for the cracker among us to operate without wondering who is looking over his shoulder."

"You mean, spy on each other?" Eldrick said. "That is very NSA-like, which is, by the way, your former place of employment."

"Sometimes the best approach is an open one."

Gregg cocked his head. "Baby, all this talk of spying is making me hot. But explain to me how spying equals an open approach."

I resisted the urge to smack him. "I've planted the seed. Now all of you are wondering if it's possible that your fellow contestant might be the cracker."

"Sowing the seeds of suspicion," Ray said. "Clever. Bold."

"Subtlety has never been my style. Add in the fact that several of you already have an expertise or experience with hacking. I won't object to anyone who wants to offer any theories on how he's operating or who he is."

"He's got a beef with society." Anson picked up a throw pillow from the couch and squeezed it. "He's been bullied, pushed around."

Eldrick shrugged. "So what? Who in the room hasn't?"

"My take is the guy is on a mission," Ray offered. "He's got a bone to chew."

Truman nodded. "Yeah, he's definitely got a bone, but he's no lunatic. He knows what he is doing and, in a way, he speaks for each of us."

"He makes me feel like I need to grow a pair." Anson pointed at his groin. "That would be balls, Lexi, just in case you hadn't heard that expression."

I grimaced. "Jeez, Anson. Too much information."

Gregg thrust his hips forward. "I've got balls, Lexi. *Big* balls, especially for a guy my size. I can show you if you're interested."

I felt sick at the thought of it. "God, no. We are *not* discussing balls any longer."

"Too bad." Gregg frowned. "It's one of my biggest assets."

"Yeah, *ass* being the key phrase here." Eldrick snorted.

I held up a hand. "Okay, moving on. You've all heard what he had to say in the manifesto. What's your interpretation?"

"Ray is right," Truman said. "The dude has issues so he's on a mission."

Ray sighed, rubbing the back of his neck. "Don't we all?"

"'Each of us, human or not, is the result of a series of unique lifetime experiences.'" Barnaby wagged a finger. "Ab'Jona to Cypher in 'Dispersion Conversion.'"

"Well, we know he likes the movies," Anson pointed out.

"Possibly," I replied. "He references *The Matrix* in the manifesto."

Eldrick frowned. "How can that prove anything? We all like *The Matrix*."

"Well, maybe he's got a background in film." Truman considered a moment. "Or writes movie reviews. Or considered a career in acting but it got derailed because he was too ugly, untalented, or seriously misguided. Probably all three."

Ray pursed his lips. "That just about sums up every person in Hollywood, except for the ugly part."

I felt a headache coming on. I needed to get some sleep and let things percolate a bit more in my head.

"Okay, keep mulling over it and let me know what you come up with." I stood. "I think it's good enough for now. I've got a lot of work ahead of me this week. I want to be ready for our cracker by the next round of voting. Just remember, you see something or hear something that seems off, I want you to tell me. No matter how strange it seems."

Gregg stood as well and sauntered toward me. "Speaking of strange, baby, would this be a good time to tell you I've been told I have the cool sexual prowess of the Zindi?"

Chapter Twelve

The week passed slowly. The IT staff and I spent a significant amount of time strengthening the firewalls, putting protocols in place that would spot and eliminate swizzles, and overhauling the entire system of voting. I checked, double-checked, and triple-checked everything. I had meetings with Cartwright to update him on the progress, called Finn a few times about work-related issues, and went to dinner twice with Tony and his girlfriend.

The contestants had been mum as well, with the exception of Gregg, who sauntered into the IT room one day to invite me over to the mansion to watch an overnight marathon of *Battlestar Galactica*. I respectfully declined after informing him I'd already streamed all the episodes and watched them in order to celebrate my twenty-first birthday.

Our cracker remained silent.

No manifestos. No intrusions. No pictures of me. No nothing.

I wasn't sure whether to be happy or worried.

On the night before the voting, I was reading a book in my hotel room when my phone binged. I'd forgotten all about it and had left it at the bottom of my purse.

It took me a minute to dig it out. It was almost out of charge. Crap.

I checked the text messages.

Cara?

I didn't recognize his number, but that was Slash for you. I typed a response.

Slash?

Si. I've been out of the country. I've missed you. Where are you?

Hollywood on a case for X-Corp. I've been thinking about you, too.

Good to hear. Everything okay?

Sort of.

My phone beeped steadily now. Jeez. It was about to die. I typed quickly before my phone gave out completely.

Just a sec. I need to plug into a cock.

I set it in the dock and then re-read what I'd typed. I gasped in horror. I yanked the phone out of the dock.

No, no. Not cock!

OMG! Cock.

Deck.

Dick.

Dock.

I quilt.

My phone died. I stared at it in mortification.
Holy crap.

I would never *ever* text again. I wasn't sure I'd be
able to look Slash in the eye after talking about dicks
and cocks all in the same freaking text. Just to be on the
safe side, I decided to wait a bit before plugging it in. I
didn't think I wanted to see his response in this lifetime.

Exhaling a deep breath, I stretched out on the bed
to read another chapter. The next thing I knew, I woke
up with the Kindle smashed in my face and slobber all
over the screen.

I'd fallen asleep, fully dressed, and with all the lights
on. I checked the time and saw it was already seven
o'clock in the morning.

Sighing, I plugged in my Kindle and set my phone
in the dock. While it charged, I hopped in the shower,
got dressed, and went downstairs to the hotel lobby for
the continental breakfast.

Despite Tony's warnings about LA, I decided to walk
to the studio. I needed some fresh air to clear my mind. I
retrieved my purse and phone. Now that it was charged,
I saw one text message from Slash had come through.
It simply read, Cara?@$:

My face heated as I stuck the phone in my purse. I'd
have to figure out how to fix the texting disaster later.

The walk and air felt great and I arrived at the studio completely unmolested. Noah came in shortly after, his eyes half-mast.

"Hey, Lexi. Do I look as crappy as you?"

"Well, good morning to you, too."

He tossed his backpack on his desk. "We'd better catch this guy tonight. I don't want another repeat of this week."

"We will."

"You know he's going to be expecting something. A trick or a trap. How can we be sure we're going to get him?"

"We will. We've only got a four-hour window to cover. We're mostly counting on our new firewalls, isolated server, and anti-swizzle traps to keep him out and prevent a repeat of what he's already done. He would really have to think out of the box to get past us this time."

"I hope you're right."

"She is." Melinda came in, followed by Carlos. "We are tight as a drum. We all know what to look for during the voting tonight, not to mention, we know and understand what he's already done. He may not even know we're on to him, so we'll have that advantage."

Noah turned his chair around and sat down. "But is our goal to catch him or stop him?"

I shrugged. "Both preferably, but either option is desirable."

"Okay then. 'May Shangra guide us and lead us into everlasting enlightenment.'"

"Oh, jeez." I rolled my eyes. "Not you, too. You like *Repercussions?*"

"I'm not obsessed like Knipple, but I know of no

better show on television right now, with the exception of *Doctor Who*."

"I'm in full agreement," said Carlos.

Since I couldn't argue with that, I didn't.

The day passed agonizingly slowly because we were ready for the cracker. We'd done everything we could and had only to wait for the voting to begin. Melinda and Noah talked me into taking a stroll with them around the studio at lunchtime. I had frozen yogurt with Kyle in the afternoon. I was literally jittering with impatience when the show finally started to air.

Thank goodness it wasn't a live show. None of the contestants or stage crew were present, and the studio remained fairly quiet. The show was pre-taped, the clips already chosen and the conversations stitched together by frankenbiting, which made them about as fake as you could get. The contestants were at the mansion, presumably watching it. Cartwright was probably in his office, and I had no idea where Lucy or Stone watched, but I was glad it wasn't with me. I could barely stomach the show as it was.

The show started with clips of Lucy and three of the guys at Disneyland. I almost felt sorry for Lucy because the guys were way more into the rides than they were into her. Lucy's boobs—or the promise of seeing them—were no match for Space Mountain. Still the crew had managed to find (or create) plenty of horrible bits of conversation to highlight and exploit.

Next up, Lucy and the remaining three guys went to Venice Beach. They ran around like idiots on the sand and stuck their feet in the water. Lucy laughingly made Gregg, Truman and Anson take off their shirts. Their skin was so blindingly white, I wanted to cover my eyes. More idiocy followed, ending with Gregg and Truman tossing Anson into the ocean.

Every single one of their conversations was beyond painful until finally, thank God above, it was finished.

Kyle let out a deep breath. "Okay, voting starts after the next commercial. Everyone to your stations."

I sat down at my spot in front of the three monitors. I was multi-tasking, but would be keeping an especially close eye on the webserver statistics console. I'd set up an algorithm to map the graph of votes as they were tabulated electronically. If I saw any unusual spikes, it might indicate our cracker at work. The problem would be if our hacker picked the busiest moment to load any fake votes because then they would be harder to detect. But unless he could also monitor the graph, he wouldn't know when that moment would be and would have to rely on common sense and luck. It was possible he could slip them in, but statistically improbable.

Stone came back on the television, urging everyone to vote for the guy who should win Lucy's heart.

"Incoming," Kyle shouted as the voting opened.

The next three hours and fifty-five minutes went fairly smoothly. No spikes, no blips, no evidence of our cracker. I almost felt disappointed.

"Five minutes until closing time," Melinda called out.

Then I saw it. Small consistent spikes on the graph, timed six seconds apart.

"Code Red," I shouted. "All hands on deck. I've got something."

Kyle dashed over, peering over my shoulder at the spikes. "Melinda, you got something on the network?"

"Negative."

"Noah?"

"I've got nothing, boss."

Kyle hurried over to Carlos. "Come on, tell me you've got something."

Carlos shook his head. "I'm looking, but I've got nothing."

Kyle returned to my side. "Where is it coming from, Lexi?"

My fingers flew over the keyboard. "I'm tracing it. Come on, come on." My mind raced as quickly as my fingers.

"Two minutes," Melinda shouted. "Move it."

"Come on, Lexi." Kyle squeezed the back of my chair. "The voting's going to close. Faster."

"I'm right behind him."

Melinda gulped. "Fifty seconds. Hurry."

I kept my gaze steady. "Noah, I need some help here. Where am I?"

I heard him pounding on the keyboard. "Russia. No. India."

"Come on, come on," Kyle urged me.

Carlos leapt from his chair. "Lexi, it's almost time. Hurry up."

My fingers were still typing when Melinda said, "Voting closed. Now."

Kyle leaned forward. "Did you get him?"

I shook my head. "No. He got past me."

The room was silent.

I blew out a breath. "I was really close. He was better than I expected."

Noah swiveled around. "Looks like he used a series of IP addresses in Russia and India."

"I figured he'd be too smart to stay stateside. But he

was fast…almost as if he was anticipating my every move. No blips on the network, Melinda?"

"Not a one. But the good news is that at least we can look through the server logs and wipe the votes that came at the spiked intervals."

I sighed. "Yes, there's that. But this isn't about the legitimacy of the votes anymore. Our cracker is still getting in. He's a serious threat. What if he decides manipulating the votes isn't enough? He could do SWM serious damage, if that's what he wants to do."

Kyle sat down. "So, we're toast. Back to square one."

"Not exactly. Tonight's incident confirmed one important thing."

Noah looked up. "What's that, girl boss?"

"It's definitely an inside job. He came through my door. Now it's just a matter of elimination."

"So what do we do?" Carlos asked.

"First off, we wipe his votes. It will piss him off, but he'll stay invested. I'm not giving him his way this time."

Kyle looked at me in surprise. "But you just said he could do serious damage. Do we really want to tick him off?"

"Actually, I do. I've got a plan."

Chapter Thirteen

I had just walked into the IT room the next morning when Kyle waved me into his office. He looked white as a sheet.

I dropped my purse in his visitor chair. "What's up?"

To my surprise, he walked around me and closed the door. He was visibly agitated.

"Are you okay?" I asked.

"Not really. I'm not sure how to tell you this, Lexi."

"Tell me what?"

"I think we more than pissed off our cracker by wiping the votes."

"What do you mean?" I noticed he was not making eye contact with me. Dread niggled at the back of my throat. "Kyle? What happened?"

Kyle sat behind his desk, resting his elbows on the desk, his hand against his chin. After a moment, he closed his eyes. "There is no easy way to tell you this. You're just going to have to see for yourself."

My legs felt weighted as I stood and walked around his desk. I took one step toward his computer and then stopped, staring in horror at his screen.

He had, on full screen, a picture of me completely naked in my hotel shower. From the angle of the camera, you could mostly see just my boobs, or what little of them there were, but it was no less mortifying.

I blinked. For a moment, I couldn't comprehend how it had happened or if it was even real. I couldn't speak or breathe. Then Kyle pushed a button and I realized it was a video. For the longest twelve seconds of my life, I watched myself take a shower and start to shampoo my hair.

I was going to throw up.

Kyle clicked once and the video vanished. "Lexi, I'm sorry."

I reached out and braced myself against the desk. My legs shook. I'd never felt so violated. I wasn't a prude, but I was an extremely private person. That someone had the audacity to film me at one of my most vulnerable and private moments—and then post it online for everyone to see—was beyond my worst nightmare.

Anger helped me find my voice, but when I spoke, it sounded like I was someone else. "Where'd he post it?"

"Company website and the studio social media. He mailed it to the entire studio staff. I'm not sure where else. I took it down everywhere I could find it. But that didn't stop other people from taking it and posting it elsewhere. I stopped it where I could, I swear. But you know how it goes online, Lexi."

Oh, I knew how it went. And so did whoever posted it.

"He planted a camera in my hotel bathroom," I whispered. "I should have thought of that."

"How could you think of that? How could anyone even fathom something so degenerate?"

"He was in my hotel room the first night I got here. He planted sniffer software on my laptop here in the studio. He took stalker-style pictures of me on my laptop." I swallowed hard. "At least in those pictures, I was dressed."

Kyle looked at me with wide eyes. "Why didn't you tell me?"

I was silent.

He stood and swore. "You didn't trust me."

"I didn't know you, and I'm dealing with an insider threat."

"But you know me now. You *know* I would never do this. You *have* to know that, Lexi."

The look of sheer disgust on his face made me feel better. I inhaled and closed my eyes. "Truthfully, I don't know what I think, Kyle. Not yet. I need time to process."

"Well, Cartwright wants to talk to you right away."

"I'm sure he does."

Kyle blew out a breath. "Lexi, what are we going to do?"

I felt like crying, but instead I straightened. "We hold the course."

"*What*? How can we do that? What if he escalates? What if he does…something worse."

"That's just it. He's trying to scare me and it won't work. But it also tells me something else."

"What?"

"He's scared, too."

I strode out of his office. I saw Melinda, Noah and Carlos huddled together whispering. They stopped and stared at me as I walked through the IT room. No one said anything as I yanked open the door and marched down the hallway. I rounded the corner when Lucy stepped out from her dressing room and nearly collided with me.

"You!" She shook her finger at me. "Why haven't you caught that wacko yet? And why is he sending a naked video of you to everyone?"

"Shut up," I growled. "I'm *not* in a good mood."

She shook her head, her blond hair falling around her shoulders. "What is taking you so long?"

I grit my teeth. "Well, Lucy, maybe you haven't heard that cyberspace is quite vast. Or perhaps you are unaware that plugging a hole from the inside on a compromised vulnerable remote access application is pretty complicated."

She glared at me. "Don't patronize me."

"Then don't bother me."

I tried to walk past her, but she grabbed my arm. "Do you know who's leaving the show tonight?"

"That's your biggest concern?"

"Of course. You think I give a flying crap about seeing your boobs?"

"And if I know who's leaving?"

"Then tell me, for God's sake. I need to prepare myself. It's in the interest of everyone on this show that I handle this properly."

"Why would I want to ruin the drama? It's the best part of your acting."

She narrowed her eyes. "That's a compliment, right?"

I shook off her hand. "Of course. I wouldn't dream of patronizing you…again."

I heard her hiss between her teeth as I turned the corner and headed for Cartwright's office. I had bigger fish to fry at the moment.

Cartwright's secretary waved me in without even

asking who I was. She didn't meet my gaze either, which meant she knew who I was without my clothes on.

I walked past her and into the office. Cartwright sat behind his desk while Tony worked on a laptop at a small conference table.

Cartwright leapt up from behind his desk when he saw me. His caterpillar eyebrows wiggled furiously. "What's the meaning of this? Didn't you catch his ass?"

"Yes and no."

"What is that supposed to mean?"

"He's in a box now. He's mine."

"Can you explain that in plain English? How does a video of you naked in the shower equal having him in a box?"

I flinched and my cheeks heated. "He's mad and he's scared. I almost pegged him and he wanted to strike at me. He's pissed because I know exactly which votes he added and I wiped them."

"How is that having him a box?"

I sighed. "Cybersecurity is essentially a process of elimination. I need to let him do what he does to a certain extent so I can tighten the noose and box him in. I'm close."

Cartwright growled. "He's playing us like a piano. He's got my balls in a damn vise. What do I tell the studio honchos if they ask?"

"Tell them the truth. We figured out what votes he added and we wiped them. The legitimacy of the process is hereby preserved. You can also say we're very close to catching him."

Tony jumped up from his chair. "Do you know who it is?"

I crossed my arms over my chest. "I have my suspicions."

"So, you are going to catch him."

I didn't blink. "Yes."

Cartwright frowned. "You'd better."

"Oh, I will. It's just a matter of time now." I turned to leave when Cartwright spoke.

"Lexi?"

I turned back around. "What?"

"Whoever made that video is a small-minded little jerk. I called the hotel. You're leaving. We're moving you into a nicer, better, and more secure hotel. It's just down the street. We'll absorb any additional cost. I should tell you that hotel security found a small camera planted in the shower curtain. They are beyond apologetic and have no idea how it happened. The police will likely be calling you later to get a statement."

"Okay. Thanks."

"I mean it. What he did sucks. No one should be exposed like that, no pun intended."

"I know. I appreciate your efforts." Still, the thought of more people reviewing the shower video, including the police, made me sick. "I'll be okay."

"Good, because we need you."

Chapter Fourteen

I needed to focus and push the humiliation of the video of me naked from my mind. The studio was abuzz with activity ready for the results show. The stage crew ran around the set adjusting the lighting and the making sure the trap door worked properly. A couple of sound guys were testing the wireless microphones that Stone, Lucy and the contestants wore. The contestants themselves were dressed, combed and waiting none-to-happily in the staged Red Room. Lucy stalked about the stage in a little black dress with mile-high heels and a new pair of fake black glasses. Kyle waved me over. He stood by the side of the stage with a headset that had a small microphone. "Front seat view just for you."

"Do we have to? I'd rather watch from inside the IT room."

Maybe it was reality or maybe I was paranoid, but I felt like everyone's eyes were on me, imagining me naked in the shower. I wondered if I'd ever feel secure in the shower again.

"Cartwright wants us here for moral support."

I frowned. "How in the world am I supposed to offer moral support? Do I look like a people person?"

Kyle shrugged. "He's the boss, so we're standing

here. Besides, I've got Noah, Carlos and Melinda on duty watching in case anything comes up."

I sighed and leaned against the wall. Stone strolled onto the stage, the lights dimmed, and someone yelled, "Two minutes."

Kyle put on his headset and leaned back against the wall next to me. "Get ready. The crap is about to hit the fan."

"It could get interesting." I noticed his hands were trembling slightly. "You really are nervous, Kyle."

"It's Lucy. She's in rare form tonight."

"Doesn't that make for good reality television?"

Kyle lifted his shoulders. "We'll see."

The On-Air studio light began flashing red. We all fell quiet as a crewmember starting counting down with his fingers. When he got to zero, the music cued and Stone started talking.

"The beauty and the geek. Who have you chosen for Lucy? She doesn't know yet, but you have spoken and tonight we will find out who is going home on *Geeks Get Some*."

The stupid music played and the lights flashed. I stuck my finger in my mouth as if I was gagging. Kyle caught the gesture and smiled as the show went to commercial. When the show came back, Stone introduced Lucy and they started rolling clips from the previous week's filming.

It was ten wasted minutes of mindless, forced social interaction. Ten minutes of my life that I would never get back. Lucy made fun in not-so subtle ways of the guys with the exception of Ray, who seemed to be the only one clued into her fakeness. Although he was clearly the favorite at this point, he didn't seem comfortable with her in the slightest, despite her near desperate fawning over him. Two more commercials with interspersed clips and, thankfully, we were nearing the end of the show.

"Hold on," Kyle mouthed to me.

Stone's voice boomed. "Now it's time for one of our contestants to go. Did you choose the right guy to leave the show? We're about to find out. Dim the lights."

Someone cranked the dramatic music. It all seemed unbelievably stupid and cheesy to me, yet I could feel the tension in the air.

"Wait. Not yet!"

I blinked as Anson stepped forward holding out his cell phone. The music stopped and the lights flickered and then brightened. I saw Cartwright stand up from his director's chair, a horrified look on his face. It didn't take a high IQ to realize this part of the show was not going as planned.

Stone darted a worried glance offstage at Cartwright and then smiled brightly at Anson. "Ah, yes, my man. What's up?"

Anson planted his legs apart and I had a weird flashback of a cowboy getting ready for a shoot-out. "There is only one person who should be going home tonight." He waved his cell phone above his head. "And that person is you... Lucy."

He pointed at her in a dramatic fashion and the entire stage hushed.

Lucy looked at him like he was an alien from another planet before stalking across the stage.

"Don't you *dare* tell me what to do, you dork." She looked over her shoulder at Cartwright. "What is this?

Some kind of script deviation? No one told me about this."

Anson cleared his throat and wagged his finger at her. "Don't call me a dork. I'm not going to take it anymore. None of us are. We know the truth about you." The other guys shuffled forward and crowded behind him in support.

Lucy narrowed her eyes and I exchanged a worried glance with Kyle. He shook his head and lifted his hands as if to say he had no clue where this was headed.

Stone stood looking completely dumbfounded as if he, too, could not deal with a script change. He glanced over at Cartwright, who started making a slicing motion under his throat.

"Uh—" Stone started when Anson cut him off.

"*Get Lucky with Lucy.*" He shouted at the top of his lungs, waving his phone like a maniac. "You aren't a geek at all. You are a soft porn star wearing fake glasses. I found a video of you on YouTube. You're so dense that light bends around you."

Barnaby shook his fist. "Yes, woman, you are a fatuous example of the human species."

She stared at Barnaby. "Did you just call me fat?"

Anson laughed. "You're *so* not a geek."

"Cut!" Cartwright's voice boomed so loudly through Kyle's headset, he ripped it off his head, wincing. "Cut to commercial. Cut, cut, cut."

Lucy paled, glaring at Anson. "You dim-witted loser. How dare you insult me!"

She launched herself at him, clawing at his face. Ray managed to grab her around the waist just as she collided into Anson, who fell backward into a few of the other guys, knocking them over like bowling pins.

Lucy screamed, her arms flailing about, shouting about killing all of them. Stone leaned over to help and the back of her fist hit Stone square in the eye. He howled, dropping his mike and covering his face.

The cameramen, not sure what to do, zoomed in and then out. I stood frozen in shock. Kyle's headset was on the floor, and I could hear Cartwright screaming. "Go to commercial! Right now!"

The television monitor blacked and a tampon commercial came on. Stone lurched toward Cartwright, who had ripped off his headset and was yelling something unintelligible, his face purple.

Tony ran over to Cartwright. "Boss. Boss! What do we do now? We've only got thirty seconds to decide."

Cartwright started barking orders. "Get Lucy off the stage and into a soundproofed room. Knock her out if you have to. Nerds, pull yourselves together and stand up. You—" He pointed at Anson. "I'm talking to *you* later."

Tony ran to the stage and together he and Ray managed to pull Lucy still screaming and clawing into the arms of a very large security guard.

Cartwright kept shouting. "Stone, play the shocked card. We didn't know. We're flabbergasted and will look into any and all of the sordid details. You've got five minutes of show to fill. Be shocked, be sorry, and do it right or we're all dead."

"But my eye." Stone moaned and lifted his hand where his eyes had turned red and starting to swell shut. "Oh, my God, she hit me in the face."

"Suck it up. You're a professional. Take one for the show." Cartwright ran from the stage as the crewmember began to count backwards from ten.

To his credit, Stone straightened and began to talk, despite the fact his eye had almost swollen shut. "Ah, welcome back to *Geeks Get Some*. We had, um, a bit of a surprise as you may have seen before that last commercial. It was revealed, rather shockingly I might add, that our very own Lucy Shoemaker might have had a previously unknown job before coming onto the show. It would also imply that she is *not* a geophysicist."

Anson glared at him, his right cheek scratched and bleeding. "No kidding, Sherlock."

"Lucy was a bit dismayed by the revelation and accidentally caused injury to a few of us while, ah, displaying her dissatisfaction."

Ray climbed back onto the stage, panting. His shirt was ripped at the shoulder. Apparently Lucy had torn it in her attempt to maim and disembowel Anson.

Stone looked between the guys, his eye looking more hideous by the moment. I could almost hear the wheels turning in his head, trying to figure out what to say and do next. Cartwright tersely ordered for cameraman number one to zoom in on Stone's eye. He would milk this for whatever he could.

Stone swallowed. "Ah, yes. Well, anyway, I can't tell you how *shocked* we here at SWM Productions are at this unexpected complication. To think Lucy had fooled all of us is a stunning development."

Truman snorted. "Save it, Stone. Look, one thing we are not is stupid. Yeah, we knew Lucy wasn't a geek a long time ago, but we went with it in order to hopefully get some guidance on how to interact with girls. Instead, you created a travesty. You didn't help us, you created a show that magnified the bullying that most of us already have endured and then put it on display to entertain millions of others."

Gregg put a hand on Truman's shoulder. "Yeah. We aren't going to take it anymore. We've got a list of demands if you want us to continue."

To my surprise, Anson glanced over at me and gave me a thumbs-up. When I had suggested a revolt, this wasn't exactly what I had in mind, but I wasn't going to stop it while they were on a roll.

Stone looked nervously over at Cartwright, who had started to pace, his hand on his head. He couldn't stop the live show, and they still had several minutes to fill.

Anson pulled out a piece of paper from his pocket and began to read. "No one is proposing an end of the show. Not at this point anyway. But we are done with the fake part. No more frankenbiting our conversations or piecing together unrelated phrases just for drama's sake. No bogus girl. We want to keep this show transparent. Additionally, we want the girl herself to vote on which one of us she likes best. Fans can still voice their opinion and guide her, but ultimately, the choice must be hers alone. She is not an idiot. It's a disservice to all woman to think she can't make up her own mind about one of us."

Stone swayed on his feet, his eye now completely swollen shut. "Uh, well, okay, I guess. Transparency is good. Right?" He looked in desperation at Cartwright, who stood stage left. His ears were turning a weird shade of purple.

Ray stepped forward. "Now, the most important demand of all is the girl."

Stone shook his head, confused. "Ah, given the

shocking revelation about Lucy's past profession, I believe she will no longer be continuing on the show——"

"Good." Ray smiled. "Because we've already got a candidate of our own. A true-blue geek girl. The real thing."

To my horror, he pointed offstage, in my direction. I looked over my shoulder in desperation as all the cameras suddenly swiveled toward me. A spotlight shined directly in my face. A guy with a boom mike started running in my direction.

I took a step back into Kyle, squinting as the relevance of what was happening hit me.

Ray laughed. "*Geeks Get Some* audience, meet Lexi Carmichael. She's one of the computer whizzes behind the show and our new genuine geek girl."

Chapter Fifteen

I sat next to Kyle in Cartwright's office, adrenaline racing through my veins. My foot kept jiggling as if it were ready to leap up and race a marathon all on its own.

Cartwright paced around the office like a caged lion. He looked horrible, his face like a neon light changing from red, to violet, to deep purple. Tony hovered over him like a nursemaid, waving a bottle of pills he kept trying to shove into Cartwright's hand.

"Boss, you've got to take your meds."

Cartwright glared at Tony, who backed up two steps

Cartwright cleared his throat and then looked at me. "Is this part of your brilliant plan to catch the hacker?"

I shook my head. "No. Absolutely not. This in no way has anything to do with catching him."

"Well, now it looks like *you* have my balls in a vise. So, let's just cut to the chase. Lexi Carmichael, SWM is officially inviting you to be the next girl on *Geeks Get Some*. Looks like whether we like it or not, you've been chosen by popular demand."

I clasped my hands together on my lap, my stomach churning. "Gee, thanks for the offer, not to mention the stunning vote of confidence, but no."

Cartwright blinked in surprise. "No? Did you say no?"

"I said no."

"Are you nuts? This is prime time television we're talking about."

"Apparently I'm not being very clear. As a result, I'll give you three options. No, no way, and *hell* no. Clear enough now?"

Cartwright threw up his hands. "You can't say no."

"Then why did you ask?"

"It's a formality, for Christ's sake. You have to agree. I hired you. I'm paying you."

"To catch a hacker. *Not* to star in a television show."

"You'll still be hunting the hacker. Just in front of a camera instead of behind a computer screen."

"Don't be ridiculous."

Cartwright's eyebrows wiggled furiously. "Look, this idiot may still be after us. How can we know for sure? Who knows what that sicko will do next if you refuse to go on."

I lifted a hand. "Slow down. First, I'm *not* going to have any say because I'm *not* going to be in front of the camera." The thought of the video of me in the shower made my stomach lurch. "I don't even like to have my picture taken."

"That's perfect! You won't have to worry about watching yourself. I'll have it put in your contract."

I narrowed my eyes. "Second, it can't be that hard to find another girl to stand in for Lucy. This is Hollywood. Doesn't everyone want to be a star?"

Cartwright growled. "Everyone but you, apparently."

"Well, then there you have it."

Cartwright shook his head. "The guys don't want *another* girl. They want *you*."

"I'm sure you can convince them to accept someone else. Get your lawyers on it."

Cartwright started pacing again. "Okay, I'm going to be straight with you Lexi. We had the highest ratings in the history of the show tonight. It's going to be the buzz at every water cooler in the country tomorrow. The suits are beyond delirious. We've already had three requests from talk show hosts to have you on. At this moment, you are the best thing that has ever happened to this show. I've got the name of a good agent who can review your contract and guide your career."

"I've already *got* a career."

"But this is *the* career. You'll go places. Besides, you're perfect for us. The sky is the limit."

"I've already arrived at the place in life I want to be."

"I'll pay you more. A lot more. More than double what I paid Lucy."

I crossed my arms. "This is not about money."

"Fine. We'll throw in a vacation or two. All expenses paid. A car or three."

"Are you even listening to me?"

"Of course, I'm listening. But let's get one thing straight. You *will* be on this show because your ultimate job is to bring down this hacker. It's in your contract."

"That's exactly why I'm *not* going to be on this show. My contract is for working with computers, not cameras."

"Technically, it doesn't say that. If the best way to catch the hacker is in front of the camera, then you are bound to agree, in principle, of course."

"I'm not bound by any such thing. Stop trying to intimidate me. I'm not Lucy. You do know my boss, Finn

Shaughnessy, is also a lawyer, right? He's not going to let this just slide by."

"Honey, I have a boatload of shark lawyers of my own—the best Hollywood can buy. I'm sure Finn is a bang-up lawyer. But do you really want to spend all your company's money in court? Look, I don't want to argue semantics, laws or loopholes with you. I just want to catch this lunatic, once and for all, so I can continue producing the best reality shows on television without the shadow of him hanging over me. If that means putting you in front of the camera, I'm on board."

"Stop calling me honey. I assure you that this show hardly qualifies to be in the same sentence as the word 'best.' If you want my honest opinion—which you probably don't but I'm giving it to you anyway—this show sucks. It would be a blessing for the entire human race if this travesty of a show disappeared."

He beamed. "You are *so* going to be the perfect girl for this show."

"No!" I shouted.

Cartwright took a deep breath. "Let's talk bottom line. I want you to catch this guy. You want to catch him. We have a mutual goal. SWM absolutely cannot have him ruining whatever show I might produce now or in the future. It's your responsibility to catch him. I'm paying you good money to shut him down. If you have to do that in front of the camera, then so be it. Personally, I don't give a crap. If it adds to the ambiance of the show, then I get an added benefit. But above all, I need *you*."

"Nice speech, but those are all moot points. If the show doesn't have voting that matters, I can't catch him anyway."

"We *are* going to continue the voting in one capacity or the other, if for no other reason than to help us catch him. The problem is, if we don't have a show at all, we can't get him."

"Fine, then we're back to the easiest solution. Find another girl to be your champion and continue with the show. I'm willing to stay on *behind* the show to catch him. He's mine. But I'm *not* going to be your star and that's final."

Kyle cleared his voice and we all looked over at him. "Um, Lexi. You might want to see this. It's an email that came to Cartwright just after the show ended."

He unfolded a piece of paper he held clutched in his hand and passed it over to me. He didn't meet my eyes as I took it.

My stomach did a funny flip as I looked down and read.

For once in the existence of this miserable show, things are getting interesting. The guys finally got some balls and have banded together to protest their unflattering portrayals. This is a fascinating development, one I like. The power is now theirs. Until this moment, my goal was to end this travesty of a show. Now, I'm intrigued. The show may continue...for now. I would suggest you accept all their demands and keep Lexi Carmichael on the show. Put her in front of the camera instead of having her play housekeeping with the keyboard. She cannot beat me there. If you don't keep her on the show, more than just this show will go down. The future of SMW now hangs in the balance. I have the power. I've been accommodating so far. You must choose, but choose wisely."

I looked up from the note. "*Indiana Jones.*"

"Huh?" Cartwright frowned at me.

"*Indiana Jones and the Last Crusade.* It almost sounds like he's referencing that movie at the end of the note."

Cartwright snatched the paper from my hand. "What? The choose-wisely thing? Why did he say that?"

"I don't know, but he's referenced two movies in the two notes we've received from him. First *The Matrix* and now *Indiana Jones.*"

Kyle rubbed his chin. "It might be prudent to remember that Walter Donovan, the character who desires the Holy Grail and betrays Indiana Jones, did not choose wisely."

Cartwright stared at me, his eyebrows wiggling. "Didn't that guy drink from the wrong grail and then die a horrible death? Is this guy threatening me with death?"

I considered. "More like he's insinuating the death of the show, and possibly other SMW productions. However, he's definitely blackmailing you."

"Exactly. You can see why we need you, Lexi. Please. You have to help us."

"We can't give in to blackmail."

"We can't afford to ignore it. Just be on the show, even if it's just temporarily. I give you my word that as soon as we have him, you can be off the show. Whatever you need, you'll get. Just don't abandon SMW."

"There has to be another way."

"Believe me, I'd take it if I could find it. But look at the facts. He wants you. The guys on the show want you. The audience wants you. I want you. No, let me rephrase that. I *need* you. Come on, help us out here."

Kyle nodded. "Look, Lexi, as much as it pains me to say it, Cartwright may have a point. It sounds like this guy will stay invested as long as you participate. That's a good thing if we still want to catch him. If the show goes away, he goes away, or worse, he intensifies his attacks against the studio."

I stood. "I'm sorry. I really am, but I just can't do this. I truly can't. I am not the type to be on television. You need someone who's pretty, has blinding white teeth, and can make interesting small talk. I can't do any of these things."

Cartwright put his hand on my shoulder, which surprised me since he had an aversion to touching others. "Look, all of that is why you're perfect for this role. Lexi, you've already met the guys. You know them. They know you. They actually *like* you. That's half the battle right there. We'll make the rest easy, I promise. We'll cater to you like we've never catered to another star. We'll work to make this the most comfortable experience you can possibly have. There's much more at stake than just one television show. We're talking the future of this company."

I pinched the bridge of my nose, hoping it would help ease the throbbing headache that had started behind my forehead. "I'm sorry, but my answer still has to be no. Being in front of a camera is something I just can't handle."

Cartwright waved his hand. "Okay. Everyone get out. Everyone except Lexi. Now."

I looked up in surprise. Tony scurried out first and

Kyle exchanged a puzzled glance with me before rising from his chair and exiting.

I crossed my arms and looked up at Cartwright. "Look, no matter what you say, I'm not going to change my mind."

"Maybe. Maybe not. However, just so you know, I'm going to fire them. All of them. Kyle, Tony, and their entire staffs, too, if you don't work with me."

"*What?*"

"They are canned. Gone. All of them. They are useless to me...unless you help them find that jerk."

"You wouldn't."

"I would."

"That's blackmail!"

He shrugged. "I'm desperate."

"They're just kids."

"We're talking about a lot of money and the future of this company. You find that hacker and there might just be a raise in store for them."

"You are contemptible."

"Which is why they pay me the big money."

"It's disreputable. Despicable."

"It's Hollywood, honey."

"Don't call me honey!"

"Fine. I'm only asking you to reconsider."

"You're not asking me to reconsider. You're trying to blackmail me into a decision."

"I won't deny it. I already told you I need you and I'm desperate."

My brain searched for an alternative, but I couldn't find one. "Don't you dare fire anyone. I'm going to think about it. I need to talk it over with my boss and then with the guys on the show. At some point, I'll make my decision. However, let's be clear. Don't rush me, and I'm not in *any* way saying yes."

Cartwright released my shoulder. "Works for me as long as you aren't saying no. Do what you need to do. I'll be here waiting."

Chapter Sixteen

Kyle was waiting outside the door, leaning against the wall. "Everything okay?"

I plastered a fake smile on my face. "Sure. Just dandy. I need to make a phone call, but I want you to assemble the team and get them working their angles on finding who sent that latest email. Maybe he made a mistake—got cocky or careless. Let's see if we can nail him."

I sincerely doubted they would find anything. But right now, I had to give them something to do other than worry about the thin thread that was holding them to their jobs.

Kyle nodded. "Okay. What was that all about with Cartwright? Why did he want to see you alone?"

"He tried to use his forceful powers of persuasion."

"Did it work?"

"That's yet to be determined."

I walked past him and out of the studio, needing some fresh air and a chance to calm down before I called Finn.

I walked around the parking lot for about ten minutes before I could bring myself to call Finn. In short, clipped sentences, I brought him up to date on all the developments. He didn't interrupt, but I heard him swearing under his breath on several occasions. When I finished, his voice exploded through the phone.

"No. Hell, no. I hope you said that."

"Using those exact words. But the hacker is invested now. He wants me on the show."

"This is the same guy who planted a camera in your bathroom. He posted a video of you on the internet. You *cannot* give him what he wants."

I closed my eyes, wondering if Finn would look for and find the shower video. I felt like throwing up just thinking about it, but pushed the feeling to the side.

"I have no intention of giving him what he wants, Finn. I just want him to think I am. The truth is if I leave, he wins."

"So, don't leave. Work behind the scenes."

"That's what I want to do, but it's not so easy."

"Of course it's easy. The show, if we can call it that, will go on. They'll get another so-called star. You continue your work behind the scenes as we planned. Or the show folds and that's that. I think we're in full agreement, it won't be a loss to the world of entertainment either way."

"Look, I'm in full agreement that this show bites, but he's threatened to do serious damage if I don't go on."

"All the more reason to get you out of there. Let Cartwright hire someone else to worry about it. Who cares?"

I sighed. "I do. I accepted this job and honestly, I'm not comfortable leaving it unfinished. I'm close to catching him, Finn. That hacker is mine now. Besides, I've already made progress. It's an inside job and I'm dramatically narrowing my lists of suspects."

"I don't care how close you are to catching him, Lexi.

I don't like this situation. I'm not going to make you go on television to catch a hacker. I'm not comfortable with someone targeting you like that."

"It won't be good publicity for X-Corp if we leave the job unfinished."

"I don't give a crap about publicity. I care about you. Everyone else can bloody well sod off."

I took a moment to compose myself, feeling better for Finn's support. "I appreciate you saying that, Finn. More than you know. Look, here's the bottom line. Cartwright is going to fire the entire IT team and his assistant if I don't stay."

"That guy is a bloody wanker. It's rank, but it's not our problem." His voice was hard.

"Unfortunately, it *is* my problem. Cartwright made sure of that. I like them, Finn. They're kids. It's their livelihood on the line. It's not going to look good for them if they get canned on their first job."

"Those *kids* are probably just as old as you are."

"Maybe, but they're green. If they get tossed, it's on me."

"That is absolutely, one-hundred percent, not true."

"Yes, it is. Indirectly, but still as a direct result of my actions."

"Listen to me, Lexi. Don't you see what is happening? Cartwright is blackmailing you."

"I know. Unfortunately, so is the hacker. I'm getting squeezed from both sides. The IT team doesn't deserve this, and neither does Tony. They are doing their best. Not to mention, the poor contestants on the show are vulnerable right now. They're good guys. I wouldn't treat them the way Lucy did."

"Mary, Mother of God. You're actually considering this."

"I can't believe that just came out my mouth, but it did. Finn, I can catch this hacker. I know I can."

He was silent and I could hear the sound of his shoes slapping against the floor. He was pacing his office and hard. "Lexi, think about it. Do you really want to do this? Go on television in front of millions of people on a show that's a farce?"

"I don't *want* to do it. I'd rather hang upside down by my toenails while being waterboarded by a hundred secret agents. But I *need* to do it. That hacker issued a challenge. He violated my privacy. That's what I can't walk away from. Him and those IT kids. But I'm not going to do it if it's not right for X-Corp."

"Wait. You're putting this on me?"

"Seems like the right thing to do, seeing as how you're my boss."

"That's a bloody difficult spot you're jamming me in."

"Agreed. Guess being the boss isn't all fame, glory and a great salary."

He sighed in exasperation. "Okay, let me put it this way. Yes, I'm your boss, but I also care a lot about you in ways I'm not even sure what do about yet. Look, I'm not going to make this decision for you, Lexi. In terms of X-Corp, I support you in whatever you decide. The call is up to you."

I'd barely hung up the phone when a call came through from my assistant at X-Corp, Ken Kurisu.

"Hey, Lexi. How's it going in Hollywood?"

"Don't ask."

He chuckled. "That good?"

"Worse."

"Well, I don't want to alarm you, but X-Corp got hacked last night."

My breath caught in my throat. "*What?*"

"Whoever it was didn't do any damage. First, he didn't get far. He ran into trouble at the second firewall. As soon as I got the alert, I followed all the security protocols and closed everything up. He won't come back in—at least not that way again. Plus, Jay and I are on the lookout for him."

I made a mental note to review and overhaul our security at X-Corp. "I just talked to Finn and he didn't say anything about it."

"I haven't told him yet. I wanted to talk to you first because, well, I don't know how to put this. The hacker, he left a message behind."

My heart leapt to my throat. "What…kind of message?"

"A coded one, but I unraveled it pretty quickly. It's for you."

I closed my eyes. "What did it say?"

"It said, *Lexi Carmichael, the showdown is coming. Stay or else.* I don't know what it means. Does it make sense to you?"

This whole situation was getting uglier by the minute. My phone beeped and I looked at the number. It was my dad.

"I'll take care of it, Ken. I'll call you later. Go ahead and tell Finn. Right now I've got an incoming call I've got to take."

"Sure. No problem."

I hung up with Ken and pressed the button to bring my dad on the line. "Dad? Is that you?"

"It sure is. How are you, sweetie?"

"Oh, I'm just great." I probably said it with too much fake enthusiasm because my dad was silent for a moment.

"Are you sure everything is fine?"

My breath lodged in my throat. I hadn't thought about my dad, about my mom. What if they had seen the video? I closed my eyes, swallowed hard.

"I'm okay. Work is just a bit stressful. Why do you ask?"

"Well, our law firm was hacked today. I guess some jokester sent out an email to the entire staff."

"That stinks. Is your IT staff handling it?"

"Yes, yes, of course. But there was this one odd thing."

My heart sunk. "What odd thing?"

"Well, the email mentioned you."

"*Me*? What did it say?"

"It said, *Tell Lexi Carmichael to stay or else.* Do you know what that means?"

I exhaled. "Yeah, I understand. Don't worry, Dad. I'll fix everything."

"What does it mean?"

"I'm working a difficult case in Hollywood and it's probably connected. It's complicated. I'll explain it all later."

"You're in Hollywood? Look, I don't care about computers or fake emails. I care about you. You're still recovering from your injuries. Are you sure it was wise to rush out on a new job so quickly?"

"I'm sure, Dad. Really, I'm fine. Don't worry. How's Mom?"

"Since you left without saying goodbye? Since you

won't pick up your phone and call her back? Madder than you can imagine. You're going to have to make it up to her big time."

I cringed. "Tell her I'm sorry, i really am. This trip was unexpected. I'll make it up to her. I promise."

"Good luck with that. She was convinced you were on your deathbed and then suddenly you're in Holly-wood."

"I'm perfectly fine, just a little sore in spots. My hand feels much better. It's just this case is complicated, Dad. But I've got it under control. Sort of."

I talked with him for a few more minutes and then hung up, pressing the phone to my forehead. Things were going from bad to horrific. I needed to talk tech speak with someone, and I knew exactly whom I needed. I punched in the numbers.

"Lexi?"

"Hey, Elvis. You got a moment?"

"For you, always. How are things?"

"Not so good. Can I ask you a question? Have you had any intrusion attempts tonight on your home servers? Anything out of the ordinary?"

"Funny you ask. Just had an attempt an hour ago, but no dice."

I wasn't surprised. Not even an exceedingly excellent hacker would ever breech the genius that was the Zimmermans' network.

I leaned against a car. "Someone's on my tail."

Silence. "Okay, spill."

I told him the whole story, ending with the Cart-wright's insistence I go on the show and the cyberat-tacks on X-Corp and my dad's law firm.

There was a long silence. "He planted a camera in your hotel bathroom and posted video online?"

I felt tears spring to my eyes. "Yes."

"Bastard."

I wasn't sure I'd ever heard Elvis say that word. Somehow, it made me feel better. "Now he's targeting my work and family."

"Lexi, I'm not clear on why he wants you to go on this show. I thought you said he wanted it shut down."

"He did. But he's suddenly changed course. I'm not sure if he's trying to distract me and keep me too busy to find him or whether he has an ulterior motive. Truthfully, I have no freaking idea why it's suddenly so important to him."

"Humiliation?"

"Possibly. He scored big on that when he posted that video of me. But it didn't stop me. I may have failed to catch him up to this point. But I'm close. I think he may be running scared."

"He wants to be in control. This is his way of regaining the upper ground."

I considered. "Yes."

Silence again. I could almost hear him thinking. "Who would profit the most if the show continued?"

"Everyone has an agenda, but I think SWM has the most to gain. But they also have the most to lose." A headache throbbed behind my eyes. "Our cracker has a new plan and somehow I've become part of it. It may throw a wrench in my plan."

I began walking around the parking lot again. "I think the revolt was an unexpected crimp in his plan. It was spontaneous. Organic, if you will. However, I think rather than being annoyed by the revolt, he's pleased, perhaps even amused, and is embracing it. The problem is me. I *have* to cooperate in order for things to progress in a way he now finds interesting. If I don't participate, he's sending me a not-so-subtle message that he intends to make my life, and the cyber lives of my friends and family, a living hell. I can't be everywhere at once, Elvis, protecting everyone I know."

"Personal cracking is the worst kind."

"I can't see a way out. Do I have a choice?"

"You always have a choice, Lexi. What does your gut tell you to do?"

"It tells me I can't let him get away with this. He's not going to control me. He's not going to own me. I know he's on the inside, and I may even know who he is. But this changes the game, and I wasn't ready for it."

"You may be on even footing then. He likely wasn't ready for it either."

"But he's called me out. I'm not walking away from that."

"So?"

I exhaled. "So, game on."

A long pause ensued. "Are you sure about this, Lexi?"

I closed my eyes and tried to steel my resolve. "Yeah, I'm sure. Thanks for helping me think this through, Elvis. I needed that. You've helped me more than you know. Guess it's official. I'm the new girl on the show."

Chapter Seventeen

Cartwright had moved my things to the new hotel and I spent a lot of time looking through the room and bathroom before feeling comfortable enough to settle down. It was a nicer room, a suite, but I found it hard to appreciate it given what had happened.

The next morning at the studio, before I made any official announcement, I found Tony and asked him to drive me out to the guys' mansion.

A cameraman met me at the door, his camera rolling.

I glared at him. "Get lost. I mean it."

Tony nodded at the guy. "Do it. Her word is gold now. Orders come from Cartwright himself."

The guy lowered his camera and headed out to the pool. Eldrick walked down the stairs in a gray T-shirt and pair of soft shorts, blinking sleepily. "Hey, Lexi. Tony. What are you guys doing here?"

It was time for me to get my head in the game. "Get the other guys and assemble them here."

The sleepiness vanished. "What happened?"

"I'll explain it, but I only want to do it once. Get everyone down here."

"Okay. We were up late with a marathon gaming

session of 'Vector Fission IV.' Barnaby slaughtered us, but it was a good time."

I perked up. "Really? I like that series. I haven't played version IV yet. Is it as good as the others?"

"Better. The effects are prime."

"As expected. Thanks for the update."

"Sure anytime." He paused, shifted uncomfortably on his feet. "Look, Lexi, I want you to know I think it's awful what the cracker did with that video of you. He's a coward of the worst kind. We all deleted it without watching it. Well, except maybe Gregg. But at least he was mad about it on your behalf."

I wasn't sure what I could say to that. "Uh, thanks, I appreciate it."

He turned and jogged up the stairs.

I looked at Tony. "No offense, but I need to talk to the guys alone."

He shrugged. "Sure, I don't even understand what you guys say to each other half the time. I'll join the cameraman poolside. No skin off my nose."

"Appreciate it."

I wandered into the living/gaming room, but was too nervous to sit. I examined the fireplace and then turned around as Gregg strolled in. He smoothed his hair with his hands and adjusted his sweats on his bony hips, swaggering toward me. I was surprised his pants didn't just slide off as he moved.

He eyed me appreciatively. "Holy Batman. Girl in the geek cave. How are you, babylicious?"

"I feel like hurling when you talk like that, actually."

"I bet you've come for a little Gregg-lovin' in the wee early morning hours."

"Unequivocally, no."

"So, what did you think of our show last night? We showed Lucy who we really are. We had balls in abundance, didn't we?"

I grimaced. "I'd rather not discuss balls in any shape or form."

"I'd show you mine in a parsec if you just gave the word."

"*Gregg!*"

Ray walked in, plopped sideways into a plush armchair. "Stop making a royal ass of yourself, dude."

"Hey, some girls dig the dirty talk. I happen to be an expert at the sex talk. Just ask me, Mr. Fifty Shades of Gregg."

I was saved from answering when Anson walked in blinking and rubbing his eyes. "Hi, Lexi. What's up? Are they shutting down the show after our revolt last night? I kept expecting Cartwright to call me in and haul me out, but he didn't." He looked around the room. "Hey, where are the cameramen?"

"Gone temporarily."

Eldrick walked in with Truman and Barnaby. I waited until everyone was seated and made sure all the guys were present and accounted for. I remained standing.

"So fill us in, Lexi," Eldrick said. "How did the suits take our mini-revolution last night? Is the show done? Who got voted off? Even more importantly, did Lucy get canned?"

I felt significantly better that everyone was way more interested in the fate of the show than in a video of me naked in the shower. I appreciated it more than I could verbalize.

I pondered the best way to present the issue and then

decided I just needed to go with it. "The show is not cancelled and no one got voted off. Apparently the episode last night got the highest ratings in the series history."

"I figured," Eldrick said. "They were talking about it on all the late night talk shows last night."

"However, as far as I know, Lucy is history."

Truman punched a fist in the air. "Yes! We got rid of her."

Ray laughed. "Dude, you couldn't wait to get a piece of her a week ago."

Truman sniffed. "That was before my standards were raised...by Lexi. You are going to be our new girl, right?"

"About that..."

Anson leapt to his feet. "You can't say no. You just can't."

I held up a hand. "Technically, I can do whatever I want. I didn't sign a contract to star on a television show and I do have standards. Somewhat."

Barnaby frowned at me. "'But our neural conduits have melded into an acute awareness that has become both mutually beneficial and satisfying. We are one in many ways. You cannot leave me behind.' Ab'Jona to Chardonnay in 'Diffusion Disaster.'"

I smiled. "I didn't say I *wouldn't* do it. I'm considering it but only because I have a plan to catch this hacker and being on the show might actually help me."

Eldrick leaned forward, placing his hands on the coffee table. "Interesting. What kind of plan do you have in mind?"

"Sorry, the plan is mine alone. However, I need you to back me up on my requirements for being on the show."

Ray crossed his ankles. "What kind of requirements did you have in mind, Lexi?"

"Well, I'm in full agreement with you guys about no frankenbiting and no cruel or stupid jokes or situations. I also want to have a say in who stays and who goes on the show. But I need you guys to be open to the idea of audience voting as well."

Eldrick studied me. "Why?"

"Why do you think?"

Truman laughed. "She's keeping the cracker engaged. Good thinking."

"But doesn't it make you nervous to know that this may be the hacker's plan all along?" Anson asked.

"*You* guys worry about the show and leave the cracker to me."

Ray lifted his hands. "Okay. I'm on board."

"Don't agree just yet. We need to make a few things clear." I took a deep breath. Even among my peers, this was going to be a hard speech to make and I had to be perfectly clear.

"There is not going to be any kind of proposal— marriage, sex, or otherwise—during or at the end of show. Plus, there will be no sexual hanky-panky of any variation. I'll be upfront and say I have no intention of sleeping with any of you now or in the near future. We will simply use this show as an opportunity to practice our social skills and maybe show off the smarter side of our personalities. *Capisce?*"

Truman looked at Gregg. "Did she just say hanky-panky? I might be in love."

Gregg laughed. "She had me at *capisce*."

I smiled, relief sweeping through me at their apparent support. "Plus, I'm going to insist on no bathing suits, no hot tubs, and no hotel rooms. Everyone on this show will be required to keep shirts and pants on at all times."

Anson whistled. "Okay, now I think *I* may be in love."

I walked over and sat on the couch next to Truman, then pulled out a small notebook from my purse. "Now let's put our collective heads together. If anyone has any other requirements to add to the list before I take it to Cartwright, now would be the time to do it. For once, I think we have him right where we want him."

Chapter Eighteen

I had Cartwright over a proverbial barrel and he knew it. He accepted all my demands, including the one that I was history as soon as I caught the hacker. He wasn't thrilled about accepting that one, but he did. Whether it was because it was nearly the end of the show's season or he didn't think I'd catch the hacker before that, I couldn't be sure. He also reluctantly agreed that I wouldn't have television cameras on me 24/7, just when we were filming. Unfortunately, as the guys hadn't negotiated that in their contracts, they were stuck with round the clock coverage.

In any event, I teleconferenced Finn in on my discussions with Cartwright and the studio lawyer. There was a point during the negotiations where I thought Cartwright might cry with relief at my so-called capitulation. Several hours later, all was agreed to and the studio lawyer said he would write up the contracts and send them to Finn for signing.

Cartwright stood up. "We have to stick to our filming schedule. That means you need to be in front of the camera in about three hours. Got it?"

I swallowed my anxiety and reminded myself that this was all part of my plan and I could manage it.

He insisted Tony take me to my dressing room. On the way there, I heard my phone ring. I grabbed it out of my purse and checked the number. I didn't recognize it, but I knew who it was. I looked over at Tony.

"Can I have a minute?"

"Sure. I'll meet you in the dressing room."

I stepped to a quiet corner of the corridor and punched on the phone. "Hello?"

"*Cara?*"

"Slash?" I felt a lump in my throat. It was good to hear his voice.

"How are you?"

I swallowed. "I'm hanging in there. I'm having a bad day."

There was silence and then he said, "I talked to Elvis. I heard what happened. Come home."

I closed my eyes. "I can't, Slash. I'm not going to let him get away with this."

He swore under his breath. "You don't need to play the hero."

"I'm not playing the hero. I'm doing my job."

"I will hunt him down for you. I will find him. You know I will."

I opened my eyes. "I know. But this is *my* hunt, *my* solution."

"He hurt you."

"Emotionally, yes."

"He's dead."

"It's okay, Slash. I've got it under control."

"I don't doubt that. But you don't have to do it when you have me."

"But I do. I need to do it my way. This is about him

and me. He didn't post a video of *you* naked on the internet."

He growled. "No, I'm not going to just hunt. I'm going to find him, string him up, and torture him before I kill him."

I appreciated his fierce support. "Thanks, Slash, but I can handle it. It's just…completely humiliating."

"You shouldn't be humiliated. You have lovely breasts."

For a second I couldn't speak. "What? You…you *saw* the video?"

Dead silence. "Ah, well, I…ah…"

"Slash? You *watched* it?"

"No, no, *cara*. Of course not. I turned it off immediately."

"Don't lie to me."

He sighed, paused. "*Si*, I watched it."

"How many times? The truth, please."

"Once." Silence. "Twice. That's all."

Disbelief swept through me. "How *could* you?"

"*Cara*, I know you are upset, but in Europe things are different. A woman often goes without a top at the beach and no one thinks twice of it. It's natural."

"I'm *not* European." My eyes filled with tears. "I *wasn't* on a beach."

"I know. You are absolutely right. I'm not handling this correctly. That isn't what I meant at all. I didn't watch it to see your breasts…although they were perfectly fine." He swore under his breath. "Now *that* came out completely wrong."

I heard a noise behind me and turned to see Tony waving at me and pointing to his watch.

I took a breath. "Look, Slash, I have to go. I'll talk to you later."

"Wait, *cara*..."

"I really have to go. I'll talk to you soon."

I punched the button on my phone and stuck it in my purse. I was upset at him and needed to think about what Slash had said, but I didn't have time right now. I was about to go in front of a television camera and right now *that* required all my concentration and emotional energy.

Summoning an inner courage I wasn't sure I possessed, I walked into Lucy's dressing room.

No it was my dressing room now. I had to be confident in my ability to pull this off or the hacker would get away. I looked around. Under my instructions, Kyle had moved my computer setup to the dressing room and it had been nicely placed in one corner of the room. One side of the room was floor-to-ceiling mirror and a peek into an open door to the right revealed a large bathroom.

The black make-up chair intimidated me, so I went to sit on the leather couch instead next to Tony. Just as I got comfortable, a guy dressed in ripped jeans, a Dodgers T-shirt and a head full of dark dreadlocks strolled in.

Tony rose from the couch. "Hey, Lexi, this is Ace Keener. He's going to be your dialogue coach."

I felt a grip of panic around my throat. "Dialogue? What dialogue? I thought the show is unscripted."

Ace gave me an easy smile. "Relax. There is no scripted dialogue. I'm here to help only. For example, I can make suggestions on topics to talk about or ways you might want the conversations to go, if needed. I'll be here to throw you a bone, so to say."

"A bone." I considered the offer and calmed down. "Okay, good. I'll probably need you."

"Glad to know I might be useful."

Tony slapped Ace on the shoulder and gave me a thumbs-up. "Okay, Lexi, Ace will get you acquainted for what happens on the show. Go get 'em, guys. Have fun."

I returned the thumbs-up with only half-hearted enthusiasm and then let out a breath as he left and Ace sat down on the couch next to me. "So I understand today will be your first time being in front of the camera on the show."

"On *any* show." I put my hands on my lap, feeling sick. "God, I think I made a mistake."

He patted me on the shoulder. "Hey, don't talk like that. You'll do great. Let me see what's up on the shooting agenda." He fumbled with something in his pocket and pulled out his smartphone, then slid his finger across the phone a few times and read something while stroking his chin.

"Hmm..."

I looked up quickly. "What does that mean?"

"It means I need to talk to Mandy and Rena about make-up and costume. We've got to get you ready for the L.A. Comic Book Convention tomorrow."

I perked up. "A comic book convention? I get to go to a comic book convention?"

"You sure do."

Relief swept over me. "Well, that's...fantastic. I wasn't expecting that. I love comic book conventions. In fact, I haven't been to one in years. Hey, maybe this won't be so bad after all."

Ace stood, pocketing his phone. "Of course, it won't be bad. I'll be back in a jiffy with the girls. Don't go anywhere. After that we'll discuss today's programming."

I stood up, stretching. Thank God. I could manage a comic book convention. I would totally be in my element and, in fact, I might even enjoy myself. Things really were starting to look up.

I walked over to my computer terminal and did a quick review of the server weblogs. I checked my email and reminded Kyle to keep me apprised of any developments.

Ace returned several minutes later with Mandy and another woman I assumed to be the costume expert, Rena. Mandy carried what looked like an artist's palette and Rena had a length of black leather draped over her arm.

"What's that?" I pointed at the leather.

Rena smiled. "Your costume. Well, actually it was Lucy's, but it's going to be yours now. We don't have time to make a new one." She stuck out a hand. "Nice to officially meet you. I'm Rena."

I shook her hand. "I don't normally wear costumes to comic book conventions."

"This isn't time to be normal. You're going to be a star."

"I don't want to be a star."

"How wonderfully refreshing. I'll take care of you, I promise."

I gulped. "Do I at least get to guess who I'm going to dress up as?"

"Sure. Guess away."

I studied the leather. "Batman?"

"No."

"Darth Vader?"

"No."

"Zorro?"

Rena laughed. "God, no."

"Wait, I know. Neo from *The Matrix*."

Rena shook out the leather, which was when I realized it wasn't a cape. "Yes, *Matrix*, no Neo. You are a woman. You are going as Trinity."

"Trinity?" Trinity was the kick-ass heroine of *The Matrix*, and Neo's sexy love interest. She was beyond cool, but, she wore a skintight black leather jumpsuit for most of the movie.

I took a step back. "Uh, I'd rather be Neo."

Ace came up behind me propelling me toward the makeup chair. "You go as Trinity. You're a girl."

"A girl who doesn't wear clothes that fit like a second skin. Especially leather ones."

Rena clucked her tongue. "It's not clothes. It's a costume. It's a fantasy."

Ace put his hands on my shoulders, pushing me toward the dressing room. "It's all in fun. Just go with it."

"Can't I go with it as Neo?"

"No."

"Zorro? Did I mention I like Antonio Banderas?"

Rena pressed the leather suit into my arms. "Change. Now. I'm going to have to make some alterations."

They shut the door in my face and I locked the door and turned around to look at myself in the mirror. There were dark circles under my eyes, my hair hung limp, and my skin was a pasty white. Why in the world had I agreed to go on television?

I stripped down to my undies and bra and wiggled into the jumpsuit. Wiggled is the code word here. It was tight in every imaginable place, except for the boobs.

There, it sagged like a jawless fish as I examined my reflection from side to side.

"My bra is showing." I spoke loudly so it would carry through the door.

"Take the bra off."

"My boobs will show."

Rena tapped the door. "No worries. I'll fix it. Come out."

"I repeat, either my bra or boobs will show."

Rena wiggled the doorknob. "Open the door. We're all girls here."

"Hey," said Ace. "I take offense to that."

Rena rattled the doorknob harder. "Come on out, Lexi. I can't fix it if I can't see it."

"No."

"No, what?"

"I'm not going out there. There's a guy out there."

Ace laughed. "Trust me. I've seen boobs before." There was a sudden pause and then he spoke. "Not that I've seen *your* boobs before. I didn't look at the video. I swear, Lexi."

I pushed the sick feeling down. "I believe you, but I'm not coming out with you there."

There was silence. After a moment, I heard the murmur of voices and Mandy called out. "Ace left, Lexi. It's okay. Come on out."

I unlocked the door and peeked out. Ace was gone. I stepped out, clutching the suit to my chest. "This is ridiculous. I am so not Trinity."

Rena gently took my hands away from my chest, a bunch of straight pins in her mouth. "This is Hollywood. You are who we make you. If we want you to be Trinity, you will. Hold still."

She started bunching the material and sticking pins in it.

"Hey, be careful." I tried to step away, but Mandy put her hands on my shoulders, holding me in place.

"Hold still." Mandy angled me toward Rena. "Look, let's just clear the air. We all got the email of you in the shower and we're all royally pissed on your behalf. It's just some prick getting his jollies. Whoever he is, he's a big-time loser. I think it's refreshing that you care about modesty and decency. Those are rare commodities these days in Hollywood. Take my advice. Don't let one loser get you down. That's what he wants."

"I know. Thanks."

Rena nodded. "We women have to stick together. I don't know if it will make you feel any better, but we are beyond overjoyed to have you on the show."

I winced as Rena squeezed tighter and pinned the material under my arm. "You mean you're glad Lucy is gone."

Mandy laughed. "That, too, but we like you, Lexi."

Rena yanked, pulled, pressed and pinned until she was satisfied. "Okay, you can strip now."

"How? I'm pinned in."

She loosened some pins and helped me remove my arms from the sleeves. I appreciated the piece material she draped over my naked chest without saying a word.

Rena pushed the leather down over my hips and legs, being careful not to stick me. "Okay, it should take me no time to fix this up."

She headed out of the room, and I darted back in the bathroom and pulled on my slacks, bra and shirt.

Ace was waiting for me on the leather couch when I came out. My cheeks heated as I sat next to him.

He patted my shoulder. "There, that wasn't so hard, was it?"

"Honestly? I'd rather have thirty-six root canals than do that again."

He chuckled. "You're going to be fine. Luckily, you don't need a costume for tonight. You get to dress casual for today's show."

I closed my eyes. This was going to be a lot harder than I thought. "Define casual."

"Jeans and a blouse. The girls have your measurements, so they'll pick out something for you."

"I have my own jeans."

"Wrong. These will be designer jeans. They will fit you nicely. Trust the girls. They're professional stylists. They will make you look fantastic."

"I don't want to look fantastic. I just want to look like me."

"You'll be the same Lexi, just better. You don't have to worry about a thing."

I sighed. "Somehow, I don't think it will be that easy."

"It will. I promise you. Now let's talk about today's programming. We start filming in a couple of hours right here in the studio."

"I'm not sure I'm ready—intellectually or emotionally."

"You don't have to be ready or prepare for anything. You get dressed, go to the stage, and ask the guys some questions that have already been prepared. That's it. No prepping, no practice, and most importantly, no scripted dialogue."

My heart started pounding. "What if I mess up?"

"You'll read questions off a card. Pretty hard for a smart girl like you to mess that up."

I nodded. "Okay. Reading questions off a card. I can do that."

"Good. Besides, even if you messed up, it's not live. We can do re-takes as necessary."

"That's good. Then what?"

Ace tapped his pen against the clipboard. "Then the guys answer your questions. You can either respond to them or just read the next question. Your choice."

"How will I know where to stand, where to go and when it's my time to ask questions?"

"There will be a chair for you on the stage." He checked his clipboard and flipped up some papers. "Of the seven remaining contestants, you will question five of them today. You'll go on dates with the other two tomorrow."

I started to breathe faster. "Define dates?"

"Let's take one thing at a time. Trust me. Today's filming and the dates tomorrow will be painless. Easy peasy. Cartwright insisted."

"I'm *already* in pain and filming hasn't started yet. I think this may have been a really bad idea."

"It's a really great idea. You're going to be wonderful."

"I'm going to be sick."

He stood up. "Here come Rena and Mandy. Let's get you dressed and camera ready."

"Do I have to?"

"Yes."

"Fine. Anything to get this over with as quickly as possible."

He smiled. "Now that's the spirit."

Chapter Nineteen

It took a lot longer to get dressed than I expected. Ace wisely disappeared as soon as Rena carried in six pairs of jeans. I wasn't happy to discover I had to try them *all* on even after the first pair fit. I then had to try on two final choices while Mandy and Rena poked, prodded and adjusted me before concurring on the winning pair. The pair they chose didn't even come up to my belly button.

"You do realize these jeans are sitting on my hips, right?" I said.

Rena fussed with the waist. "Of course. They're low-rise jeans."

"Low being the operative word here."

"They look great. You have nice legs."

"Long, you mean."

"In Hollywood, long legs are an asset. We're going to play them up."

I frowned. "I like jeans that go to my waist."

"These look better on you."

After that we went through at least thirty pairs of shoes before they settled on a medium-high white-heeled shoe.

"I'm already taller than most of the guys on the show. Can't I wear sneakers?"

Rena crossed her arms. "No."

I sighed and went with it. Nonetheless, I was seriously cranky by the time Mandy carried out the blouses.

I crossed my arms against my chest. "I'm not wearing pink, anything with flowers, or anything that shows cleavage. Not that I have any cleavage to speak of, but in principle."

Rena sighed and then set aside three blouses. "Doesn't matter, I think I already know which one will look best on you."

She handed me a white tank top and a gauzy blouse that went over it. It was kind of pretty and more importantly, simple, so I decided to go with it.

As soon as they decided on the clothes, I had to take everything off and get into a white robe. Mandy washed, dried and combed out my hair.

I wanted her to pull it into a ponytail, but she pulled back a few strands on each side, clipping it in the back, and left the rest long.

After that, Mandy made me sit in the chair and glooped all kinds of creams and lotions on my face. She patted, smoothed and brushed on endless types of foundation and blush. They didn't let me look in the mirror and I had visions of my face being buried under pounds of pancaked makeup. She swiped mascara on my lips and different powders on my brows. I was so fidgety that Mandy snapped at me twice. I couldn't imagine how actors enjoyed doing this for a living.

Just when I was certain I couldn't wait another moment to get out of the chair, Mandy announced she was done.

Rena made me get dressed again in the jeans and blouse and I was done. A quick glance at the clock on the wall indicated I had about twenty minutes until filming. My stomach turned over and I pressed my lips together.

Mandy spun the chair around so it faced the mirror. "So what do you think?"

I climbed out of the chair and examined my reflection. The jeans fit snugly and the blouse and tank top were casual enough that I didn't mind them. What was really surprising was my face and hair. They looked very natural, with the exception of the lipstick, which was too girly for my taste. My hair looked nice, all straight and shiny and just pulled back slightly. No weird curls or anything.

"So?" Mandy asked.

I nodded. "You did pretty good. I'm just not sure about the shoes." I looked down at the delicate white heels. "Are you certain I can't wear sneakers?"

"I'm certain."

Ace walked over. "You are perfection. Are you ready?"

"Do I have a choice?"

He took my hand. "Nope. Come on. Let's go to the stage."

We walked out to the stage and I saw the crew had completely changed things around. There was a fancy yellow armchair next to a small round end table with a fancy lamp on it. Beneath the armchair was a big brown rug. Across from the armchair were three bar stools. Two guys were arguing over the angle of the barstools to the cameras.

I looked at Ace and frowned. "What's this?"

"The stage."

"I mean, why are the guys sitting on barstools and I'm in some fancy armchair?"

"That's just the layout for the program."

"Why can't they sit in normal chairs next to me?"

Ace steered me toward the chair. "Don't worry about how the stage is set up. Just go with it. It's simple. Sit down and ask the questions, okay? That's it."

I tried to control the clawing nervousness. I turned and saw Cartwright sitting in his director's chair. Tony was reading him something off a tablet. Kyle was standing off to the side, leaning against the wall and watching me. He saw me looking at him and gave me a thumbs-up.

I turned back to Ace. "The show's not live, right? If I mess up, we can cut it, right?"

"Right. But don't mess up too often or the crew will get cranky. People have lives and families and like to go home on time. Okay?"

"Okay." I took the index cards that Ace pressed into my hands.

"Now remember, just smile once in a while, okay? Don't look so terrified."

"Easy for you to say."

I almost resisted when he turned me and gave me a little push toward the stage. "Go sit, Lexi. The camera guys want to check out the angles and lighting."

I blew out a breath and carefully climbed the few stairs to the stage.

I gingerly sat in the chair. The low-rise jeans gapped in the back, and I fidgeted until the cameraman yelled at me to hold still.

Stone strolled on to the stage and walked over to me.

His eye was still swollen, but the makeup team had tried to camouflage it. He still managed to pull of the tanned, plastic-style handsome look despite it.

"So, you're the new girl?" He raised an eyebrow. "Hope Cartwright knows what he's doing."

He said it with such distaste that I almost stood up and decked him. But before I could move, the intro music started playing.

"Show time," Stone said to me and flashed his pearly whites.

I grit my teeth and tried not to squint as the lights seemed to get even brighter. Then someone cued the horrid staccato music and we were on. I started breathing faster and my palms got sweaty. I swallowed hard, hoping I wouldn't hurl on myself.

"Welcome to *Geeks Get Some*." Stone's voice carried throughout the studio. "Tonight we are introducing you to our new girl. The guys found her in our computer room and decided she was the girl they wanted to get to know."

I heard the cheering and clapping of a non-existent audience. They must be using a canned audience soundtrack.

Jeez.

Stone strutted around the stage as if he owned it. "She's twenty-five and never been kissed. She likes circuits, guys with pocket protectors, and reciting the square root of Pi. A graduate of Georgetown University with a degree in mathematics and computer science, meet Lexi Carmichael."

The audience soundtrack was turned up so loudly I winced. Stone walked over behind me and put his hands on the chair.

"Welcome to *Geeks Get Some*, Lexi. Are you excited to be on the show?"

It was awkward talking to Stone when he was behind me. "Well, Stone. I'm not sure excited would be the exact modifier I'd use."

He laughed a bit too heartily. "Well, I'm looking forward to getting to know you as much as the guys are. How about you, audience?"

The soundtrack roared and I tried not to roll my eyes.

"But first, we need you to meet our guys. Lexi, are you ready?"

"As ready as I'll ever be."

He laughed again as if I had said the most hilarious thing in the world. I really, really wanted to smack him.

He walked out from behind the chair, clutching the wireless microphone. "Okay, Contestant Number One is a professional gamer who likes pinball festivals and multiple-choice questions, and believes combing his hair should be optional. Meet Anson Oxlong."

There was noisy clapping and Stone smiled broadly as Anson walked onto the stage and climbed on the first barstool. He gave me a nervous smile. I wanted to smile back except I was so nervous my mouth was frozen in a grimace.

"Contestant Number Two is a software engineer for a large firm. He enjoys playing the guitar, brushing his teeth with baking soda, and has a strong aversion to pixie fairies. Let's give it up for Ray Ferris."

Ray strolled onto the stage as I looked at Stone with a mixture of disgust and disbelief, wondering who in the depths of hell wrote this crap. I didn't believe for one second it was the guys. I glanced over at Cartwright and he was positively beaming.

"Contestant Number Three is a paranormal investigator. Yes, he chases ghosts, demons and the boogeyman. He likes stargazing, poltergeist movies, and Michael Jackson. Hello, Truman Clark."

I closed my eyes. This was cringe-worthy stuff.

Stone waved out a hand. "Our final contestant for the evening is a cybersecurity expert for a Los Angeles company. He is looking for a girl to join him on a mission to explore new biospheres, unravel complex computational codes, and boldly go where no fanboy has ever been before. Put your hands together for Eldrick Faston."

Once the guys were all on the stools, there was more clapping, and then someone called out, "Cut!"

Stone dropped the smile and lowered the mic. "How did that go?"

"Great." Cartwright hopped out of his chair. "Excellent start."

I frowned. "Wait. Who made up that crap? I've been kissed before. And no one wears pocket protectors these days."

Stone shrugged. "Stop complaining and just go with it. Who cares?"

"I care. There should be at least a modicum of effort to make this show accurate."

"It's entertainment. Accuracy is not important."

"It is to me."

A crew member walked up to the bottom of the stairs. "Okay, let's keep going, gang." He held up his hand and silently counted down backwards from five.

Stone picked up the cue effortlessly. "Welcome back to *Geeks Get Some*. We just met our new girl, Lexi Carmichael, and four of the guys she will be getting to know better over the next few weeks. Lexi, we are breathless to see what kinds of things you want to learn about the guys."

I looked down at the index cards I held in a death grip in my hand. I wondered what I wanted to know, too.

"We're going to start by having you ask the guys some questions. Go to it, and good luck."

I loosened my grip on the cards and picked up the first one.

"Contestant Number One, Anson, if I were a cupcake, what would you fill me with?"

I leapt to my feet, holding up the card. "Wait. Cartwright, what kind of question is this?"

"Cut!"

Cartwright stormed over. "What are you doing?"

"This question is absurd. I'm supposed to be getting to know these guys not talk about stupid things like cupcakes. None of us are so dense that we don't see how you are masquerading cupcakes as a euphemism for sex. Seriously?"

Cartwright looked about ready to say something and then he took a deep breath. "Yes, I know it all seems ridiculous, but there is a method to the madness. Trust me. We want to *entertain* people. I know what I'm doing. Just ask the questions on the cards. Seriously, it's not that hard. Start over. Okay? Think you can handle that?"

I frowned. "Okay. But I'm on the record for saying this is idiocy."

"Fine. So noted." Cartwright stomped back to his chair. I exhaled and read the question again.

Anson took a moment and then answered, "Well, Lexi, I think if you were a cupcake, I'd fill you with...

jelly. Lots of jelly. Or a hot dog. Yeah, I'd fill you with a great big hot dog. Ha, ha. Get it?"

The guys all started laughing.

I rolled my eyes. "That was seriously mature, Anson. Not."

The guys all dissolved into laughter again.

I slid that card to the bottom of the pile and picked up the next card. "Contestant Number Two, Ray. Tell me why dating an engineer would be exciting."

"Hmm... Well, engineers know heat transfer, can act with great precision, and can strip more than just wires. That good enough for you?"

I laughed. "Yeah, that's pretty good."

I shifted in the chair. "Okay, Contestant Number Three, ah, Truman. What was the last fun thing you did at home before joining the show?"

"Let me think about that. Oh. Yes. I perfected my zombie escape plan because, hey, you never know when the Zombie Apocalypse will hit."

I gave him a thumbs-up. "Good answer. May we all be so prepared." I relaxed a smidgen. Maybe things weren't going as badly as I expected.

"Contestant Number Four, Eldrick. What's your best pick-up line?"

"Me? Um, let me see if I can remember. Well, technically it didn't work, so I'm not sure it's my best line."

"Spill anyway."

"Well, in my defense, I was participating in a sci-fi session of speed dating at the time. She smiled nicely at me, so I said, 'Your mouth says shields up, but your eyes say a hull breach is imminent.' Unfortunately, she moved on."

I winced. "Hard break."

"You're telling me."

"Same question, Ray."

"Oh, it's my turn?" He paused for a moment. "Best pick-up line. Okay, here's my favorite. 'You know, girl, it's not the length of the vector that counts, it's how you apply the force.'"

I groaned. "Jeez."

"Awesome, dude." Truman gave Ray a high five.

"Hey, Lexi," said Anson. "I've got a good line for you."

"Okay, Anson. Give it your best shot."

He cleared his throat. "Hey, baby, looking good. Someone must have shot you with a phaser set on 'stunning.'"

The guys burst out laughing and I shook my head. "Okay, no more pick-up lines, guys. I beg you."

There was some more hooting and laughing from the canned audience feed. I tried to ignore it.

I started to read from the next card and then jumped from my chair. "Wait! Cartwright, I'm *not* asking this question. I've barely met these guys. I'm certainly not going to ask one of them something so personal right out of the gate. Not to mention, I don't even *want* to know the answer to this question."

"Cut!" Cartwright stalked back over. "I'm fully aware of the fact that it's a highly personal question, but that's what makes it fun. If you want to blush or giggle behind your hand while you ask it, be my guest. It would add to the flavor."

"What? I am *not* blushing or giggling behind my hand. Seriously?"

Cartwright sighed. "Just ask the stupid questions. Yes, some of them are strange, some are obvious sexual euphemisms, and some are just plain idiotic. It's like that on purpose. We can always cut the ones we don't like, if need be. We made up a few extra questions and we'll whittle it down take the best of the lot for the final show. Okay? Just sit down and ask the questions. Let us do the rest."

I blew out a breath. "Fine."

I sat down as Cartwright stomped back to his chair. The crew member counted down again. As soon as Cartwright indicated we were rolling, I picked up the index card.

"Contestant Number Four, Eldrick. Where is the most unusual place you've ever…ah…imagined making love?"

The guys looked at each other and murmured among themselves. Finally Eldrick asked, "The *most* unusual place?"

I looked down at the card for a double check. "Yes. The *most* unusual."

"Um, let me think about that one. Okay… I'm going to go with the ear."

I froze in disbelief.

Cameraman Three was the first to go down. He snorted and then erupted into a howl of laughter, abandoning the camera and falling to his knees gripping his stomach.

The guy holding the boom mic went next, laughing until tears streamed down his cheeks. As if on cue, the entire studio exploded into howls of screaming laughter.

I was paralyzed by incredulity.

"What?" said Eldrick. "What's so funny? She said *unusual*."

I saw Cartwright laughing so hard I thought he'd

have a heart attack. Tony was wiping his eyes and Stone was smacking his head.

I tried desperately to think of a way to extract poor Eldrick.

I had to practically yell to hear myself. "Ah, Eldrick, I believe the question referred to *place* meaning locations. Unusual locations. Not places as in *bodily orifices*."

Eldrick's face turned beet red. "Oh. You didn't specify. Well in that case, I'll go with the kitchen table."

The studio dissolved into manic howling again. I pressed my hand to my forehead and then stood up. "Cartwright, we can cut that part out, right? *Right?*"

No one even looked my way. Eldrick hid his face in his hands. Even the other contestants were laughing.

"Cartwright? Ace?"

I don't think anyone heard me. Everyone was shaking with laughter. The guy with the boom mic had managed to retrieve his equipment, but was still sniggering. Cameraman Three remained incapacitated and writhing on the floor. I wasn't sure the show could go on.

I reviewed the chaos around me and crossed my arms over my chest.

I seriously needed to catch that hacker.

Chapter Twenty

A new dawn, a new day. Well, at least that's what I tried to tell myself.

Mandy was waiting for me at the makeup chair when I arrived at the dressing room. She patted the chair. "Good morning, Trinity. Are you ready to face the Matrix?"

I stopped in my tracks and crossed my arms over my chest. "Ah, I wanted to talk to you about that. You're not going to go all crazy on me with the Trinity makeup? I'm just not into that level of costuming."

Mandy wiggled a finger at me. "Trust me. Okay?"

"Only if you promise me no weird lipstick."

"Weird, no."

"No blue or green eye shadow?"

"Not as Trinity."

"Not as me or as anyone. Ever. That's an ultimatum." She sighed. "You drive a hard bargain, but deal."

I loosened my hands and walked to the chair. "Just in case you couldn't tell, I rarely wear makeup."

"Really? Don't worry. I'll make it as painless as possible."

As I sat in the chair, she fluffed my hair. "Trinity

had short black hair, so we're going to cap your hair and put a wig on."

"What? A wig?"

She patted my scalp. "Relax. We'll put your hair up in something like a shower cap and put a short dark wig over it. You'll be a dead ringer for Trinity. You have her tall, thin shape."

"Bony, you mean."

Mandy smiled. "Kick ass is what I mean. Remember, this is just a costume. Relax and have fun with it."

A knock sounded on the door. "I assume everyone is decent, correct?"

"Come in, Ace. She's decent."

Mandy smeared something cold on my cheeks. I resisted the urge to swipe at it. "I'm not sure how decent I am with this gunk on my face."

Mandy snorted. "Don't be such a baby. It's a moisturizer base. I haven't even got to the good stuff yet."

I kept my eyes closed. I considered it a denial of sorts.

Ace's voice moved closer until I could tell he stood next to the chair. "Glad you're up and ready to go. Okay, Lexi, today we're filming you and two of the guys at the L.A. Comic Book Convention."

"Okay. I can manage that. We just walk around, look at the displays and have a good time, right?"

"Right. But there needs to be some interaction between you and the guys. You can't just focus on the goods."

"By interaction, you mean talking, right?"

"At the very least. The rest is up to you."

"What do you mean by 'the rest'?"

"I mean you're a grown woman. You can decide to do whatever you want with those men."

"Trust me, talking will be it."

"Okay, whatever works. Do you know what you're going to talk about?"

I felt a niggling of panic. "I have to plan it in advance? How can I do that if I don't know how they'll answer?"

"Of course, you don't have to plan the conversation in detail, but it doesn't hurt to have something in mind in case the conversation runs dry. With this group, it's a distinct possibility."

I thought for a moment. "Oh. Who are the two guys?"

"Barnaby and Gregg."

"They were the two missing from the show yesterday. Why do they get one-on-one time when I didn't even get to see the other contestants?"

"Cartwright calls the shots. I don't write the script. Just babysit the star."

"Very amusing. Not."

He chuckled. "You'll be fine."

"Why do I have to go with them separately? Can't we just go altogether as a group?"

"No. We go with Cartwright's plan."

I sighed. "How am I supposed to carry on a conversation with Barnaby when he only talks in *Repercussions* quotes?"

"You'll think of something. You're familiar with *Repercussions*?"

"Intimately. But I don't see how quoting lines from the shows equals conversation."

"Go with your gut. The audience will love it."

"If you say so. Gregg, however, is another problem.

He's like a freaking octopus with his hands everywhere at once."

Ace laughed. "That guy is totally unreal. He's genuine, however, which makes it interesting. He has no clue he's making an idiot of himself."

"I'm going to deck him if he tries anything. No kidding."

"Jesus. This episode is going to be spectacular. I don't know why you need me."

"I'm afraid you're overestimating my ability."

"I doubt it. You'll handle him just fine."

I sighed. "We'll see. I just hope I'm not making a colossal mistake."

An hour later my hair was beneath a tight cap and a short dark wig sat on my head. Mandy had smeared stuff on my cheeks, eyes and lips. True to her word, it wasn't as bad as I'd expected, except for the blood red lipstick.

"Can't you tone the lipstick down?" I complained. "It's really red."

"It's part of the costume. It's supposed to be dramatic, over the top. It's perfect."

I didn't argue because I figured I'd just wipe it off the first chance I had. "Okay, whatever."

Rena returned with the leather jumpsuit and a pair of short boots. "Go put them on."

I wiggled into the costume and examined my reflection in the mirror. She'd fixed the costume and I actually did look a little bit like Trinity.

I sat on the toilet and put on the boots. They had a heel, but I was thankful it wasn't too high. Still, I wobbled slightly when I stood up. Taking a deep breath for courage, I opened the door and walked out.

There was silence and then Rena finally said, "We need to pad her."

I put my hands on my hips. "What do you mean pad me?"

"The boots look good," Ace offered.

Rena pursed her lips. "We're going to have to add some padding to the front of your costume, Lexi."

All three of them stared at my chest.

I stepped back and crossed my arms. "No padding."

Mandy cocked her head from side to side. "You're right. I can't see how to fix it short of padding."

"Did you hear me? No padding."

"I know you are sensitive about this subject in light of what just happened, but trust me, it will give you shape. I'll be right back."

She darted out of the room.

I shook my head. "I am *not* wearing a padded bra. That's weird, not to mention false advertising."

Mandy clucked her tongue. "It's just some padding. Don't worry. Rena will fix you up. You look pretty remarkable right now as it is."

"You're just saying that so I'll be compliant and wear it."

She laughed. "Maybe. But it will fill out the costume. Seriously. You make a great Trinity. Just walk with a bit more confidence. Remember Trinity was all about being kick ass."

"*You* try to be kick ass in heels, tight leather and neon red lipstick. It's not exactly a walk in the park."

Mandy chuckled. "I'm sure it's not."

Rena rushed back in the room with what looked like two small pieces of nude-colored foam.

I eyed them. "What is that stuff?"

"Padding. It's hypoallergenic, easily removable, and sits just below the curve of your breasts to offer a bit of a push upwards. If arranged properly, it can even give you cleavage."

Mandy shook her head. "How will they stay in place if she doesn't wear a bra?"

"The jumpsuit is snug enough to hold it in place."

Without a word, she reached down the front of my jumpsuit.

"Hey!" I leapt backward.

"Hold still. I need to arrange the padding."

"I don't want to wear padding. It's worse than a padded bra, not to mention…cheating."

Rena stopped, waved the foam at me. "For heaven's sake, it's a costume. You need this."

I glanced at my profile in the mirror. There was nothing to indicate I had a chest at all. No curves, no bumps, no nothing. Rena was right.

"Okay." I held out my hands. "But I stuff it in myself."

"Have you ever used foam padding before?"

"God, no."

"Then better leave this to the hands of a professional."

"Fine. But it should go on the record that I'm not happy about this."

Rena walked over and shoved her hand down the front of my jumpsuit. I tried not to flinch at her cold hand. She groped around for my breast and then shoved the foam beneath it. It actually pushed what little boob I had up and out, so I guess that was a good thing.

She stuck the padding beneath the other boob. Once the pads were both in, she and Mandy began pressing and arranging until everything was symmetrical. I couldn't decide if I were embarrassed, mortified, exasperated, or all three.

Finally they were finished. Ace showed me something small and black in the palm of his hand.

"What's that?" I examined it. "Wait, a wireless microphone. Excellent."

He snapped it on the front of my jumpsuit. "All of the contestants wear one of these. You can turn it on and off as needed. For example, when you go to the bathroom." He indicated a miniscule button on the side of the microphone. "But if you turn it off, you'd better turn it back on. Otherwise you'll have to do your date all over again."

I shuddered. "I'll remember."

"A few additional caveats. Don't get it wet. Speak in a normal voice and don't lose it. They're expensive."

"Got it."

"You're going to be a star."

"I sincerely doubt that."

I grabbed my purse and Ace took my arm. Together we walked into the hall where Tony was waiting.

"Holy crap." Tony's mouth fell open. "You look… amazing."

"I'm supposed to be Trinity from *The Matrix*."

"I know. Rena and Mandy worked magic. You really do look like her." He extended his arm. "Let's go. The limo is waiting."

He led me out of a studio side door where a crisply dressed driver stood next to a black limo. "Good morning, miss." He didn't even blink at the fact that I wore a low-cut leather jumpsuit, dark sunglasses and boots. Guess that's Hollywood for you.

"Good morning to you, too." I tried to sound upbeat instead of hot and anxious. The limo door was already open, so I climbed in.

Tony and Ace climbed in after me. The driver closed the door as I leaned against the seat. My heart was beating way too fast and I felt nauseated.

"Ace, I'm not sure I can do this after all. No, it's worse than that. I don't know *how* to do this. It's like living my worst nightmare. I'll be forced into meaningless conversation, only now I'll have to do it in front of millions of people."

Ace patted my knee. "You'll be fine. Ignore the cameramen and be yourself. You already know these guys, no surprises there. Plus, a comic book convention is cool."

"But I'm with Gregg and Barnaby. What in the world are we going to talk about?"

"The show truly is unscripted, Lexi. Say whatever comes to mind."

"But there's not going to be any frankenbiting. No cutting pieces of our conversation and pasting them together. What the audience sees will be the real deal. It will likely the most boring show in the history of television."

"It will be genuine and it will be far better that way. Look, my advice is this. Just hang with them. Get to know them better. Ask them to tell you something about themselves, something personal you couldn't find on a resume, for example. Then tell them something interesting about yourself. The audience wants to get to know you, too."

I opened my eyes. "There is nothing interesting

about me. Oh, God. It's all too much to remember. Can you write that down and send it to my phone?"

Tony sighed. "Man up, Lexi. You can do this. Remember, it's all about the hacker."

"Right." I tried not to hyperventilate. "The hacker. This is all about him."

"Yes. You've got to keep the show going and lure him into getting cocky. He's bound to slip up and then you'll nab him."

"I will. I'd better. But Cartwright is right. The sooner the better."

Chapter Twenty-One

We arrived at L.A. Comic Book Convention where a mob of people still stood in line to get into the conference center. The second I climbed out of the limo, two cameras were on me from different angles. Tony and Ace faded into the background, although I they were both within shouting distance. People were beginning to look at me and a bunch of guys began screeching catcalls.

"Hey, Trinity, walk my way."

"Trinity, I'll be the One for you."

I ignored them and tried not to throw up. I could do this. I really could. I didn't have to remember any lines or do anything I didn't want to do. It was in my contract. I just had to attend a comic book convention and socialize a bit with two fellow geeks who were probably as nervous as I was. How hard could that be?

At least I resembled Trinity. I took a deep breath, clutched my purse to my chest and began to walk toward the entrance where Tony and Ace stood wildly gesturing at me to follow. I wouldn't have to wait in line. Guess this job did have some perks after all.

The security guard at the entrance let us through. One of the cameramen nearly brained me as he rushed past and then whirled around to film me. I tried not to be distracted by him and looked around the conference center.

The center was enormous, and there were already hundreds of people inside. Exhibition booths were lined up along the walls and a raised stage sat in the middle of the room. Someone stood up there now, trying to direct the crowd to various deals and events. A dark-haired young woman with a tongue ring, ten holes up the entire length of her earlobes, and a tattoo of the Star Trek Enterprise on the back of her hand pressed a brochure into my hands.

"Looking good, Trinity. Here's a map of all the exhibition booths and the location of the Dealer's Room."

"Thanks." I perked up. The Dealer's Room typically held a wide selection of collectibles for sale, including comic books, action figures, movie memorabilia and costumes. I usually came without my credit card to events like this, but today I'd forgotten to take it out and I had it with me in my purse. Maybe I'd buy just a little something to mark the occasion. Knowing the pricing on most of the collectibles, it would have to be *really* little.

"Now what?" I said to Tony.

"Go ahead. Look around. Do what you would normally do at one of these events. You're in control."

I shrugged. "Okay."

I ignored the cameramen and stopped at a booth. It held science-fiction novels from Baen Books. I browsed through several of them, wishing I had more time to read. I was headed for the next booth when I saw a gaggle of people and two more cameramen headed my way.

I stopped. "Uh-oh."

Barnaby Knipple headed toward me. He wore a nice suit, but he'd already rumpled it. His glasses were askew, and his curly blond hair had somehow resisted all of Mandy's efforts to tame it. Some people, possibly show groupies, were talking to him and trying to get his autograph. He stopped and signed a few. But he had eyes only for me...well, Trinity.

He walked up to me and gave the *Repercussions* greeting salute, which was the thumb and middle finger pressed together and the other three fingers straight. He tapped his nose first, then the lips, and last, the forehead. "Greetings, Trinity, it is an honor. You look stunning and those shades are truly spectacular."

I lifted the sunglasses. "It's not Trinity. It's just me, Lexi."

He smiled. "It's all spectacular." That's when I noticed he had something on his other hand.

"Barnaby, is that a sock...puppet?"

He lifted it up and a closer examination indicated that Barnaby did indeed have a sock puppet on his left hand.

"You made that?" I was both impressed because he had done an excellent job creating it and appalled that a grown man was carrying around a sock puppet. I examined the elongated head, oddly shaped ears and almond-shaped eyes.

"Is that Ab'Jona from *Repercussions?*"

Ab'Jona opened his sock mouth and spoke. "It is I. You are quite observant for a human. It's an admirable quality."

Unbelievable. I couldn't see Barnaby's mouth moving. "Do you always bring a sock puppet on a date?"

"You are actually quite fortunate, my lady. I assure you that Barnaby does not show me to just anyone."

"Well, that's a relief. I think. Jeez, I'm talking to a puppet."

For a minute, we just stood looking at each other until I decided that I couldn't think of a single intelligent thing to say to a sock. I took Barnaby by the arm. "Come on, Ab'Jona, let's look around."

Barnaby, the puppet, the cameramen, and a small but growing crowd, followed me. I was stopped for several photo ops with Spiderman, the Green Lantern, a guy who was a dead ringer for Fox Mulder on *The X-Files*, and Catwoman. Finally, I wanted to browse the booths in peace, so I told the crowd that some guy from *The Twilight Zone* was signing autographs a couple of booths over. Everyone stampeded away, leaving us, along with the cameramen, at a booth with some bored-looking guy sitting next to a stack of photos.

Barnaby held up Ab'Jona. "What is your commerce, sir?"

The guy stared at the puppet. "Hey, is that Ab'Jona from *Repercussions?*"

"Yes. I am Ab'Jona. Have you a question for the mightiest mind in the universe?"

"Yeah, like when are you going to make your move on Chardonnay? Even an alien should be able to see she is hot."

"Ah, but women are like a fine wine. Chardonnay, pun intended, needs to come to the realization that Ab'Jona has the answers she seeks. Then she will come to him."

The guy thought about it and nodded. "Yeah, I see what you mean. She's not ready for him yet. But you'd better watch out. She may end up with Cypher if you don't make your move."

I couldn't decide which was more bizarre, that someone was having an actual conversation with a puppet or that Barnaby was providing witty conversation via a sock.

The guy held up a shot of him in costume on the set of what I presumed was the *Stargate* set and smiled. "So, are you guys interested in an autographed photo? I starred in a few episodes of *Stargate SG-1* many moons ago. It's only twenty bucks."

Barnaby thrust the puppet in my face. "My lady? Have you a wish for this man's portrait? I shall purchase it for you if you so desire it."

I stepped back. "Ah, thanks, but I think I'll pass."

Ab'Jona turned to the guy. "I regret to inform you that the lady declines."

"Yeah, I got that much." He looked at the cameramen crowding into the booth, filming us. "I think the more fitting question is who are you two?"

I sighed. "Just a couple of ordinary geeks. Come on, Barnaby, let's go."

We left without a photo and the guy looked kind of dejected.

After a minute, Barnaby made the puppet talk to me again. "My lady, I have a scientific inquiry for you."

"What is it, Ab'Jona?"

"Are those breasts real? As one of the brightest scientific minds in the universe, I feel it is my duty to touch them to make certain of their validity."

I rolled my eyes. "That's lame, especially for Ab'Jona. Please tell me you didn't memorize that from pickuplinesforgeeks.com."

"Actually, pickuplinesthatwork.com."

"Note this in your scientific journal—epic failure."

"So noted."

We wandered around the exhibit floor for a bit, looking in the booths, chatting with the exhibitors and examining the science fiction books, comics, gaming software and upcoming films. Despite the cameraman trailing us, the crowd was so large we were able to remain mostly anonymous. Ace and Tony were nowhere to be seen. There were so many people we kind of blended in. No one seemed to notice that we were the ones being filmed, which made me really happy. Half of the attendees were in pretty wild costumes, so my Trinity costume and Barnaby and his Ab'Jona puppet almost seemed normal. I began to enjoy myself a little.

After a while my feet began to hurt in Trinity's boots. I hobbled over to a bench.

"Let's sit down for a bit."

Barnaby wiggled the puppet at me. "As you wish."

We sat there for a few minutes in silence. "Why do you do it?" I finally asked.

"Do what?"

"Hide behind television quotes, puppets and God knows what else you have in your arsenal? You're a pretty talented guy. Anyone who studies theoretical astrophysics at MIT has got to have an interesting mind. Why hide it?"

He was silent for so long I thought he wouldn't answer. Then Barnaby lifted the puppet and spoke. "'I am the sum parts of my existence thus far. Shaped, melded and now forced to live in a world not of my choosing. We all have our burdens, and I must carry mine alone.'"

I smiled. "Ah, yes. Ab'Jona to Chardonnay in the episode 'The Synergistic Effect.' That's one of my favorite *Repercussions* episodes ever."

"I am pleased you are so familiar with my world."

"It's not *your* world, Barnaby. It's Ab'Jona's. And while I'm a bit of a *Repercussions* geek myself, I think I'd like Barnaby a lot better, if I had the chance to get to know him. No offense, Ab'Jona."

"That's illogical."

"Not in the slightest. You know, you're good with the ventriloquist act. I can't see your mouth moving and you've got Ab'Jona's voice nailed. If the astrophysics thing doesn't work out, you've always got that voice talent to fall back on."

I glanced sideways and saw him smile. I stood and stretched. "Come on, let's go see what they have in the way of food and drink. I'm thirsty."

We wandered over to a side room that had a small cafeteria and some vending machines. Barnaby had forgotten his wallet, so I sprang for two sodas and a bag of chips to share. I felt sorry for the cameramen. They looked tired and thirsty, too, but I had run out of change. Big signs indicated that we wouldn't be allowed to take food or drink out of the room, so I looked for an empty place to sit. The room was packed and no seats were available, so I motioned to Barnaby to follow me over toward a raised counter where people were standing and talking. I had almost reached it when I heard an *oomph.* I whirled around just in time to see Barnaby and his puppet falling. I dropped the sodas and reached toward him, but I was too late.

One of the sodas exploded. It hit the floor just as Barnaby plowed, face-first, into a table. He bounced off, then crashed to the ground. The people at the table jumped up, shouting.

I dropped to my knees next to him. "Oh, my God. Barnaby!"

I rolled him over. His nose gushed blood and his glasses were askew and possibly broken, but he was conscious.

"Hey, bud, are you okay?"

"I took a spill."

"I know. You're okay, just be still." I tried to stay calm even as his nose spewed blood like a geyser. "Someone get me some napkins. Quick."

A guy shoved a bunch of napkins into my hand. I gently removed Barnaby's glasses and pressed the napkins to his nose. Barnaby moaned, his eyes rolling around in his head.

I looked over at a guy who had knelt beside me. "See if you can find a doctor."

He took off. The blood from Barnaby's nose had already soaked through the cheap napkins. I needed something more absorbent. Without thinking, I reached down the front of my jumpsuit and yanked out one of foam breast pads and pressed it to his nose. The bleeding slowed.

Another minute later a young woman pushed her way through the crowd and knelt beside Barnaby.

"I'm a doctor. Is he your friend?"

"Yes. Well, no. I'm not sure. In the technical sense, that is."

She gave me a strange look. "Do you at least know his name?"

"Barnaby. Barnaby Knipple."

The doctor leaned down closer to him. "Barnaby. Can you hear me?"

He lifted an arm. "Yes, of course, I can hear you.

My ears are fine. It's just a nosebleed. I get them all the time. I'm a klutz."

Relieved he was coherent, I looked up and saw Tony and Ace making their way through the crowd. I waved at them and they pushed their way to me.

Tony seemed out of breath. "What happened?"

"He tripped, I think. His face got up close and personal with that table."

"Are you okay?"

"I'm not the one with the bloody nose."

Barnaby was sitting up now, holding the pad to his nose. "Please, everyone, go away. I'm fine." His voice was muffled.

The doctor put a hand on his chest. "Stay down. You took a hard fall. Did you lose consciousness?"

"No, but I wish I had."

"Can you track my finger?"

Barnaby dutifully followed her finger with his eyes.

"Okay, that's good. Let me see that nose now."

She lifted the padding and examined his nose, pressing on one spot. Barnaby winced.

She frowned. "Your nose may be broken. You should get checked out at a hospital."

Tony knelt beside him. "She's right. Come on, dude. We're going to the hospital right now. I've got the limo standing by. I'm not taking any chances." He put a hand under Barnaby's elbow and he and the doctor lifted him into a stand.

Barnaby swayed on his feet, holding the pad to his nose. "I don't want to go to the hospital."

Tony put his arm around Barnaby's waist. "Too bad. It's not an option. Say goodbye to Lexi."

Barnaby, apparently resigned to his fate, held up the

Ab'Jona puppet, still safely ensconced on his hand, although spotted with blood. "'Farewell for now. May Shangra guide you and lead you into everlasting enlightenment.'"

I stood and hesitantly gave him the *Repercussions* salute.

His eyes widened and then he smiled from behind the padding. "Hey, Lexi."

"What?"

"I'm touching your breast after all." He wiggled the pad.

"Enjoy it. It's the closest you'll ever get."

"Ouch."

I smiled at my witty comeback. That kind of banter didn't come easy to me, even geek to geek.

Barnaby winced as he and Tony made their way out of the room. The two cameramen trailed after them.

I let out a breath and turned to Ace. "I can't believe that just happened. I hope he's okay. There was so much blood."

"It's a face wound. There's always a lot of blood when the nose gets hit. He seemed okay. Don't worry. Tony will take care of him."

"I hope so. Let's get out of here."

"Um, you can't. You have another date."

I stared at Ace. "What? You can't be serious. After this?"

"Yes, after this. I'm completely serious. We're on a strict filming schedule. We have to squeeze all your dates in on the times we've already arranged or we won't make the live show on Wednesday. Gregg is already here waiting for you."

"I can't possibly go another date. My first date just

left with a bloody nose. I'm a mental wreck. I've got Diet Coke and blood on my hands and probably on my costume. Plus my feet hurt in these boots."

"So, you'll wash your hands and take your boots off for a few minutes. I'll spot-check your costume for blood. Come on, Lexi, you can do this."

"No, I *can't* do this. I'm in no condition to go on a date, especially with Octopus Man."

"Gregg is harmless. You can handle him."

"In this condition? I can't even handle him and his eight arms when I'm at my best."

Ace steered me toward the restrooms. To my surprise, he went to the Family Restroom and opened the door. He gave me a push in and then followed me inside, locking the door.

"Hey, what are you doing?"

"Getting you back in shape. You want to catch this hacker, right? So, suck it up. Go on these dates and get it over with. But first, wash your hands. I'll spot clean your costume. You can hardly see it anyway. Blood doesn't show up well on black material." He grabbed a paper towel, wetted it, and began dabbing it on my leg.

"Jeez. No hacker is worth this." I turned off my microphone, then washed my hands with Ace trailing behind me, blotting at my knee. Once my hands were clean and dry, I removed my boots and wiggled my toes on the cool tile of the floor. "I couldn't imagine doing this kind of gig for a living."

Ace laughed. "I feel the same way about computers."

"Computers are so much easier to understand than people. Computers are logical and purposeful. They aren't emotional and unpredictable."

"Now *you* sound like Ab'Jona."

He was right, so I shut up and let him finish searching my costume for blood.

When he got to my chest area, he regarded me with a cocked head. "Why are you lopsided?"

I looked down at my chest. "Oh, I used one of the pads for his nose."

He closed his eyes. "Please tell me you didn't."

"It was a medical emergency."

Ace sighed and held out a hand. "Now I get the breast crack Barnaby made. Give me the other one."

I pulled out the foam and handed it over. "They weren't very comfortable anyway."

He dropped it in the trash, adjusted the wig on my head and told me to put my boots back on. I obliged and we exited the bathroom past a young mother and two kids who stared at us with wide eyes.

"Now what?" I asked, scanning the crowd. The two cameramen straightened from leaning against the wall and began filming us again.

"Turn on your microphone and let's get this show on the road."

Chapter Twenty-Two

I spotted Gregg and his two cameramen almost immediately. Who knew Batman was so skinny?

Ace pushed me toward him and stepped out of the view of the cameras. "Go on. Get his attention, Lexi."

I half-heartedly waved a hand. Gregg rushed over, the black cape flying out behind him.

"Holy Matrix." He gave me a thorough once-over. "Trinity, you are rocking the outfit."

"It's Lexi."

"Of course it is. Today, however, you are Trinity and I'm Batman. However, I'd be happy to be your Neo, if you'd like. It's all fantasy anyway. You can take the red pill and I'll show you just how far the rabbit hole goes."

I stared at him. "You didn't just say that."

"That one didn't work for you? I could have said I am a sorcerer and when I look at you, baby, I detect magic all over."

"Ugh."

He reached out to put an arm around me, but I stepped back and held up my hands. "No touching either. I'm not kidding."

"Hey, baby, I got it. No messing up the costume. It's all clear."

"It better be."

Ace tossed us a couple of Cokes and we drank them without another word. Fueled by a sugar-and-caffeine rush, as well as a genuine interest in the contents of the exhibition booths, I motioned for Gregg to follow me.

We walked through the convention hall, passing other people in costumes. A man dressed as Han Solo walked by. Gregg shouted at him, "Han shot first."

The guy gave him a thumbs-up.

We stopped to browse at a booth. I glanced through a couple of super-cool, antique, exhibition-only, Avenger comic books that were protected with plastic sleeves. I wished they were for sale but probably couldn't have afforded them, even if they were.

Gregg was making noises over a comic book at the end of the table, so I went to see what had excited him.

"Look, Trinity, a Green Hornet comic book. Man, this is beyond prime."

I peered over his shoulder. "It's not just any issue. It's the *first* issue, dated December 1940. This was the first of a six-series run of the Green Hornet comics, based on the radio show of the same name. These are very rare."

"Excellent." Reverently he set it down. "Baby, I love me a woman who knows her comic books. Seriously, Trinity, you are turning me on."

He scooted closer so I took a step back, wagging a finger at him. "Admire from a distance."

He smiled, his eyes gleaming from behind the Batman mask. "You should know I get all fired up over a woman who plays hard to get."

I rolled my eyes and we left the booth. We perused several more exhibitions, and even more stacks of comics, before heading for the Dealer's Room.

Greg touched me on the shoulder as we walked. I jumped, whirling into a karate stance. "What part of no touching you didn't understand?"

He held up a hand. "Easy, baby. I just wanted to know whether or not you're going to buy anything."

I narrowed my eyes. "Can't you ask that without touching me?"

He sighed. "Working with you, it's not easy, you know. You're making me train you like a skittish colt. We both know it's only a matter of time before you're begging for my mojo."

"Wow. Just wow. That's beyond gross, not to mention seriously disturbing."

"Just give me a try, baby. I'm virus free."

"Arrgh. Come on, let's go and don't even think about invading my personal space again."

The Dealer's Room was chock full of tables with individuals selling collectibles. There was everything from action figures to DVDs to movie-set pieces. It was truly geek heaven. My pulse quickened despite the fact that I was stuck with the Batman from hell.

"Will you look at this?" I picked up a set of three Iron Man helmets. The helmets were metal and wired. When I pressed a button, the helmet lit up with blinking lights, followed by Jarvis, Iron Man's computer, telling me to sit down and relax a while.

"Sweet." I pressed the helmet again and Jarvis asked if I needed to hear the status of the weather. "I seriously wouldn't mind having this, but it's too expensive." I set it down.

"Well, it's not sweeter than this." Gregg pointed to a toaster that would imprint Captain America's shield on the center of your toast.

I examined it and nodded. "Not bad. But I wouldn't pay four hundred and two dollars for it. I mean, really?"

We wandered around some more and then I stopped at a stack of books and picked one up. "OMG! It's an original, signed edition of Kevin Mitnick's *Ghost in the Wires*. This is excellent."

I checked the price and it was in my budget. "It's mine now." I clutched it to my chest and headed for the cashier.

"Shall I buy it for you?" Gregg followed behind. "I can be gallant in that way."

"No, thanks. I'm perfectly capable of buying my own collectibles."

"But it would be the manly thing to do, right? Plus, I'm loaded, and I mean that in more ways than one."

"Stop. Just stop. Please. I beg you."

"Stop wanting you? It's not going to happen. You have the hottest multi-touch interface I've ever come across. How 'bout I run a sniffer to see if your ports are open."

I covered my ears. "I am now scarred for life. Seriously, Gregg, give it up already."

"I never give up. I know that's what you like best about me."

I blew out a breath and got in line. Gregg slipped in behind me.

I turned around and glared at him. "You can't be in this line unless you are buying something."

"Says who?"

"Says me. Other people are waiting."

"Don't be such a line Nazi. You just don't want me to be in such close proximity."

"Guilty as charged."

"Too bad. I am buying something." He held up the Iron Man helmets.

I raised an eyebrow. "You're buying that?"

He nodded. "As a gift for someone special."

"I hope it's not me. As much as I like that, I am *not* susceptible to bribes."

"Baby, I'm not telling you who it's for. I'm keeping it a secret. Besides, women like a man of mystery."

I sighed and turned around. When there was just one person in front of me, I fumbled in my purse to get my wallet out. I swore under my breath as I struggled to get the credit card out of the wallet sleeve with just one hand.

"Need help?" Gregg held out a hand.

"No."

I muscled with it some more to no avail and then finally handed him my purse and the book. "Just hold these for a minute, okay? My credit card is stuck."

"Of course. Batman is always at your service."

"Right. Thanks."

Using two hands, I yanked the card out of the sleeve. I snapped my wallet shut and turned to get my purse.

"Hey, is this your stun gun?" Gregg held it up and brought it close to his face. Unfortunately, he held it backwards, with the gun pointed directly at himself.

"Did you just snoop around into my purse?"

"Hey, I swear I just took a little peek and this just fell into my hand."

"A stun gun doesn't *fall* into anyone's hand."

"Hey, I didn't mean to. Seriously. I was shifting the book and the purse and it just fell out. I thought you were joking about it."

"I don't joke about stun guns. Now give it to me."
I reached to swipe it, but he lifted it out of my reach.

"Chillax, baby. I must admit I'm fascinated. I've never met a woman who carried a stun gun before. Have you used it before?"

"I haven't used it yet, but I may before this day is over."

"I love it when you talk alpha to me. It's so hot. Come and take it from me, baby."

He laughed and I lunged for him. Unfortunately, I wobbled on the Trinity boots and fell into him. He staggered backward and tripped, landing directly on the hand holding the stun gun. I heard the horrifying hissing sound of an electrical discharge as it went off.

"Oooooooorgh."

Gregg's eyes rolled back in his head and his body convulsed several times before going still.

I stood there, shell-shocked, trying to get my head around what had just happened. "Gregg? Tell me you didn't actually turn it on."

People stepped out of line and fell silent. I dropped to the floor and lifted Gregg's head onto my knees, pressing my hand against his cheek. "Gregg, talk to me. Are you okay?"

He blinked. Tried to move his mouth. Blinked again. *"Thaaaaarrrrr."*

Some guy shouted, "Red alert! Batman's down."

People started to crowd around Gregg.

I began to hyperventilate. "I told you to give it back to me. By the way, you don't have a heart condition I should know about, do you?"

"Agguuuulaaaaa."

I patted his cheek, tried to act natural, calm. "It's

okay. You're okay. According to the operating manual, you should be back to normal within a minute or so. The effects pass quickly. Not that I know that from personal experience, but that's what the manual says. Fortunately, I have it set it at a low stun as a precaution."

Ace came out of nowhere, sliding in beside me on his knees. "I go to the bathroom and all hell breaks loose." He looked down at Gregg, who was still twitching. "For the love of God, Lexi. What did you do to him?"

"I didn't do anything. He stunned himself."

"No one stuns themselves."

"He did. I swear. He took it out of my purse. I was trying to get it back from him when he fell and stunned himself. He was holding the darn thing backwards."

Ace looked first at me and then at Gregg lying on the floor. "You may be a danger to all men, not to mention society. This makes two for two and it's only your first two dates."

"I repeat. This is not my fault."

Gregg opened his mouth and moved his jaw around as if trying to stretch it. "*Keeeeeeeew.*"

I looked at Ace. "What did he say?

"I think he said 'cool.'"

"He thinks it's cool that he stunned himself?"

Ace frowned. "How would I know? You're the geek."

I put my head down closer to Gregg's face. "What did you say, Gregg? Is something cool?"

"I kneeew…"

I glanced at Ace. "Not cool. Knew. I think he's trying to tell us that he knew something." I leaned down closer. "You knew what, Gregg?"

He smiled, but it was a lopsided one. I studied his face. His skin was stark white beneath the Batman mask and his pupils were small pinpricks. But his eyes focused on me and at least he'd stopped twitching.

"Closer." He barely whispered the word.

I bent even lower. "Gregg, what is it? You knew what?"

"I knew...you wanted me."

Then he kissed me.

Chapter Twenty-Three

"You stunned one of your dates?"

I held the phone away from my ear as Basia shrieked with laughter. "Oh, my God. That's the funniest thing I've ever heard."

"There is nothing amusing about getting stunned. And I didn't do it. Why does everyone keep saying that? He did it to himself."

"He'd rather stun himself than go on a date with you?" She exploded in laughter. Again. "Oh, God." She gasped for breath. "When is this show airing? I absolutely cannot miss it."

"*Basia!*"

"Okay, okay." I heard her take a deep breath. "I'm gaining control."

"Well, do it quick, because I'm scheduled to go on four more dates tomorrow. It's obvious I made a colossal mistake agreeing to star in this show. I need some help here. I can't focus on what's important—like finding the freaking hacker—because I'm all tied up with this television crap."

"You're not *really* getting tied up. Right?"

"*Basia!*"

"Okay, okay." She laughed again. "Oh, how I adore

you. Finn okayed everything. I'm already at the airport. I'll be there late tonight. My plane leaves in forty
minutes."

"Thank goodness. Did Glinda get you a room at my
hotel?"

"She did. I'll take a cab there. Don't wait up for me."

"You'll help me out on the set tomorrow?"

"Of course. I wouldn't miss it for the world."

I hung up the phone, relieved she was on her way.
Basia was my social compass, my guide in sticky situations. If anyone could get me through this disaster,
she was the one. I could leave the social maneuvering
to her, and I could concentrate on what I did best—
hunting hackers.

I took a shower while wrapped in a wet towel, which
wasn't easy, but I wasn't taking any chances. At last,
I went to bed exhausted. When the alarm woke me at
nine o'clock the next morning, I rolled over in bed and
called the hotel concierge.

"Did Basia Kowalski check in last night?"

"One moment, ma'am. Yes, she did."

"What's her room number?"

"I'm sorry I can't give you her room number, but I
can connect you to her room."

"Okay, please do that."

The phone rang six times before I heard Basia pick
up. "Hello?"

"Basia, you're here."

"Lexi?" Her voice was thick with sleep. "Really? It
can't possibly be morning. I just went to sleep."

"It's nine o'clock. What room are you in?"

"Um…602. Look, I'm still jet lagged. I got to the
hotel after one o'clock. Can you go to the studio by

yourself and I'll catch up with you later? I need at least another hour of sleep, some coffee and a long, hot shower."

"You can sleep even longer. I'll have Tony pick you up in front of the hotel around one o'clock. I have to be at the studio around ten for a wardrobe fitting and makeup."

"It all sounds very exciting."

"Actually it's been one of the worst experiences of my life. I don't think Hollywood agrees with me."

She laughed. "We'll change that. I'll see you in a bit."

"Good. I really need you."

"Yes, you do. See you soon."

I hung up and rolled out of bed. I had told Tony yesterday I would walk this morning because the fresh air would make me feel better and I felt more comfortable about the trek. I would have rather swung from a trapeze over a tank of hungry sharks than suffer through a wardrobe fitting and makeup, but I'd made my bed and had to lie in it. So, I sucked it up and got myself ready for the day. I strolled to the studio, got waved in by Manny, the gate guard, and arrived at the studio promptly at ten.

I swung by the IT room to check in with Kyle. He wasn't in his office, so I stopped to chat with Noah. "Where's Kyle?"

"He's in a meeting with Cartwright. We miss you in here. What's it like in front of the camera?"

"Truthfully? It sucks. I don't get why so many people want this job."

He laughed. "What? You don't like being a star?"

"Not in the slightest. So, any news?"

"Nope. Our cracker is silent."

I nodded. "Okay. Silent is good. He's watching and waiting. So am I."

I left the IT room and headed for the dressing room. Ace, Rena and Mandy were sitting around talking. They stopped the second I walked in.

I dropped my purse on the table next to my computer. "How are Gregg and Barnaby?"

Rena approached me with a tape measure and started measuring my waist. "Both are alive and kicking. Gregg is back to his annoying self and Barnaby is spouting *Repercussions* quotes minus the sock puppet, but sporting two black eyes. He fractured his nose, so he's also got a bandage across the bridge."

"Jeez. Who knew dating could be so dangerous? Well, what's on the agenda for today?"

Rena measured the circumference of my neck. "We have to decide what you are going to wear this evening, hence the tape measure."

Rena turned me around and measured the length from my hip to my foot.

I dutifully turned to the right and then the left when Rena snapped her fingers. "Ace, who am I so-called dating today?"

"Well, there's been a bit of a change of plan seeing as how things went down yesterday. Cartwright decided to have a group date, figuring there was safety in numbers."

"I knew this whole dating thing was a bad idea from the start."

Ace stepped up beside me. "No one is blaming you. It's just a precaution. Call it a friendly recommendation from the studio lawyers."

"Jeez."

"Anyway, this group date will be a cocktail party. Then, at some point during the evening, you'll have one-on-one time with each of the remaining four contestants. The good news is no hot tubs are involved."

"That *is* good news. Especially as I had it written into my contract."

He smiled. "You drive a hard bargain."

I sat down in the makeup chair, my cranky side rearing its ugly head. "So, what dumb thing do I have to wear to this shindig tonight?"

Rena held several swaths of material against my skin. "The 'shindig' is a classy cocktail party. The 'dumb thing' you are required wear would be a dress. Something simple, yet elegant."

"I don't want low cut, slits or anything that might result in a wardrobe malfunction. The heels in the shoes have to be low. I can't manage all that fashion stress, plus think of something to say at the same time."

Rena slid the tape measure under my armpits and across my chest. "Okay. I'll try my very best to figure something out within the parameters of your concerns."

I pressed my hand to my forehead. "Crap. I know I sound like a jerk, Rena. I'm sorry. I'm nervous and cranky."

She patted my cheek. "I know and I understand. It's okay."

I sighed. "Thanks. I appreciate it, even if I still feel like a jerk."

Rena left and Ace consulted his clipboard. "You are scheduled to arrive at the guy's mansion via limo. There you will meet with Truman, Eldrick, Ray and Anson. You'll all be in a group in the beginning and then you'll split off for some private one on one."

"Why does it have to be private?"

"Well, it won't be that private. We'll all be there watching, okay? I'll have a whiteboard and I'll provide some cues if you need them."

That made me feel better. "Okay."

"What's with the limo thing? Can't we just take Tony's car?"

"The limo adds dramatic appeal, so, no, we can't use Tony's car."

"Seems ostentatious to me."

"Let the pros handle how you get to the cocktail party. You just worry about the guys."

"I *am* worried about the guys. Look what happened to the last two."

"Point taken, believe me. However, I'm sure you'll manage. You'll mingle for forty minutes to an hour with the guys as a group."

"An hour?" I pursed my lips. "Define mingle."

"Small talk. Chit chat. Bull. Whatever you want to call it."

I started to hyperventilate. "I hate that."

"You did just fine yesterday."

"In what universe would that be considered fine? One ended up with a broken nose, and the other was stunned and twitching on the floor."

"Yes, and as a result, new precautions are in place for tonight. There will be additional security staff on hand, as well as a doctor and a nurse. What could possibly happen?"

"I'm not usually superstitious, but in this case, I wish you wouldn't jinx things by saying that."

Ace grinned and put his hand on my shoulder.

"Relax, Lexi. Just be yourself. Things will work themselves out."

"Promises, promises."

"I do promise. Look, just ask the guys questions about themselves. Try to get to know them more than just superficially. Dig a little and try to get a feel for what makes them tick. If you feel safer, steer the conversation to topics with which you are familiar."

I brightened. "You mean we can talk computers and technology?"

"To a certain extent. Just remember the purpose of all of this is to get the guys comfortable with an average girl. If they yammer on for ten minutes about a microchip, they're going to start losing her, not to mention the audience. So, ask them a little about themselves and their work to loosen them up. Touch briefly on their passions and even their fears. You'll find most people don't mind talking about themselves."

"This group is not most people."

"That's okay. They're still men. Just go with it."

"I guess I can do that."

"That's the spirit."

Ace's phone rang and he left the room to take a call. I told Mandy I was heading over to the IT room for a while.

She looked up from whatever she was mixing in a small white bottle. "Be back in an hour and a half tops. Your dress should be ready by then and I'll be finished mixing the makeup."

I eyed the bottle with mistrust. "Why the heck do you have to mix makeup?"

"Why does one computer chip work better than the other?"

"Are you telling me to mind my own business?"

"You *are* smart."

"Very funny. Alright, I won't ask again."

"Good plan."

I strolled into the IT room and my blood pressure immediately dropped. This was where I belonged—among computers, cables and the anonymity of cyberspace. I closed my eyes for a moment and took a deep breath of the overly cool air. This was my home, my Zen.

Noah slapped me on the back. "She's back, the star of the decade."

I rolled my eyes. "Not amused."

He laughed. "I just heard you took out two of the contestants. That's one way of eliminating them."

"Very funny. They're both alive and kicking."

Carlos came over, then perched on a corner of one of the desks. "The gossip mill is going wild."

Melinda giggled. "Did you really stun one of the contestants?"

"I didn't stun or knock out anyone. Forget about the gossip mill. What's happening on the IT front?"

Noah shrugged. "Still nothing."

Carlos nodded. "Yeah, it's dead. It's almost a letdown."

Melinda nodded. "I bet he's waiting to see what happens."

I pursed my lips. "Quiet is good. Once I get the filming over tonight, I can be back in the IT room for the next few days while they cut and edit the clips together. It can't come a moment too soon."

"Don't worry, we've got it covered on this end. I bet you'll knock them out tonight. Literally and physically." Carlos bent over and howled with laughter. "I'm good."

Noah gave Carlos a high five. "Funny, dude. I can't believe I know a movie star. Can I have your autograph, Lexi?"

"Get real." I looked around the room. "Where's Kyle?"

"Dentist, I think. He's out until three o'clock or so."

"Okay. Well, I'm just going to take a quick look around the network and then I have to return to my dressing room to get ready for tonight."

Melinda's eyes shined. "Tonight? What's on the agenda?"

I sighed. "A fancy shindig. Wish me luck. I'm going to need it."

Chapter Twenty-Four

It literally took hours to get the makeup on, my hair styled and the dress fitted just right. Thank goodness Basia arrived just as I reached my exasperation point or I might have lost it completely. She interceded on my behalf several times, including defending my reluctance to wear a lot of jewelry and dangly earrings. I truly might have lost it at the dangly earrings if not for Basia.

She also hit it off immediately with Ace and was able to talk to Mandy and Rena in a language involving fashion terms and makeup that was beyond my comprehension. It was more than a relief to have her handle that part of the work. It gave me much needed time and peace to sit back and let my mind drift to places it needed to be in terms of catching the hacker.

When I was dressed and gussied to everyone's satisfaction, the gang stood in a circle to take a critical look at me. I'd never felt so self-conscious.

After a minute when no one said anything, I spread my hands in exasperation. "What? Is it that bad?"

Basia shook her head, her hand covering her mouth. "No. Not at all. Lexi, you are lovely. Rena and Mandy have created a goddess. You look stunning."

Ace nodded. "Basia is right. They nailed it. Each

one of your assets is on full display in that dress. Long legs, small waist, pretty hair and eyes. Girl, you are one sexy lady."

I looked down at the tight-fitting blue sparkly dress. I didn't feel sexy. I felt like Lexi. The shoes were a bit too high for my taste and the front cut was a little daring, but it would have been worse with the extra jewelry and dangly earrings. I could live with it.

Mandy had fixed my hair. She'd smoothed it out and sprayed something on it that made it feel super soft and smell good. Every time I moved, it swung around with me. I'd revolted against curlers, but Basia had convinced me to permit her to use something called a flat iron to smooth it out. Once they assured me I wasn't going to have Shirley Temple hair, I'd agreed to it.

Ace informed me that I'd have to ride to the guys' mansion alone in the limo.

"Why can't you ride with me?"

Ace spread his hands. "The cameramen will be waiting for you to arrive. It's a big part of the show. Stone will greet you and help you out of the car."

"Ugh. Why him?"

"Because he's the host of the show." Ace clipped my microphone discreetly to the corner of my dress, turned it on, and gave me a kiss on the check. "Play nice and knock 'em dead." He stopped and gave me a serious look. "You know I didn't mean that literally, right?"

I smiled. "Ha ha."

When it was time to go, everyone walked me to the limo. I felt abandoned going it alone, but Basia reminded me that they'd all be there waiting for me as soon as I arrived. Seeing as how I didn't have another choice, I settled in for the ride.

The limo pulled up into the circular driveway. To-night the place was ablaze with lights. Stone was wait-ing for me and opened the door to the limo. He made a big deal of helping me out of the car and then tucked my arm in his. I didn't feel comfortable with him. He seemed more plastic than real with his perfect tan, per-fect hair and perfect white teeth. Tony kind of looked like him with his surfer boy good looks, but Tony had a personality. Stone seemed made of plastic. He was stiff and almost creepy with all his perfection.

"You look absolutely gorgeous," he said loudly, even though he'd hardly given me a cursory glance.

It was definite bull, but I wasn't always the best judge of people, so I tried to be friendly. "Your eye looks bet-ter."

"It's the makeup. Smile." He grinned and turned his head, probably to give the cameras his best side, as we walked past.

I tried to smile, too, but it wasn't genuine. I was sure everyone could tell I just wanted to throw up. How long could I hide in the bathroom and get away with it?

Stone walked me into the mansion where the guys were herded into the dining room and the adjacent liv-ing room. The dining room table was loaded with fancy hors d'oeuvres and desserts. A chandelier dripping with crystals that sparkled and dazzled in the dual lights of the mansion and the cameras hung over the table. A fire roared in the fireplace and the mantle was ablaze with a dozen or more candles and vases of fresh flow-ers. To the right, behind an open bar, a bartender stood at attention in a crisp white suit and red tie. The living room had a couple of couches and chairs. But the main feature was the elaborate French doors that led out to the patio. Tonight they were open, and I could see a swimming pool filled with floating candles.

Eldrick and Anson stood together in the dining room, while Ray and Truman sat on the couches in the living room. Everyone, with the exception of Ray, looked miserable in the stiff tuxedos.

Eldrick waved. "Hey, Lexi. Looking good tonight."

I disengaged from Stone and walked over to them.

"Hi, Eldrick. Hey, Anson." I gave them both a fist bump.

Eldrick leaned forward, lowered his voice. "So is it true you punched Barnaby and stunned Gregg?"

"What?"

"It's okay if you did. Was it a tough love kind of thing? You know, manning them up and all."

"Wow. No. Just stop here." I made a time-out motion. "Let me be clear that I did not, in any way, punch or stun anyone. Barnaby tripped and fell into a table, and Gregg stunned himself with a stun gun he swiped from my purse."

Anson fidgeted. "Well, you're not going to *accidentally* brain me or something tonight, are you? After all, the odds of physically disabling both of your dates within a few hours are statistically significant. So you can understand why I might be just a tad bit nervous."

"I'm not going to brain you, Anson. You either, Eldrick."

"That's good to know." He sighed in relief. "I thought it was a bit harsh even for you."

"You can't possibly think I'd do something like that on purpose."

"Well, Lucy dumped Gregg's drink down the front of his pants on the second week of the show when he tried to get to first base with her. I've heard of weirder things happening on these reality shows."

I couldn't argue with that since I'd never even *seen* a reality show before this one. However, the conversation was raising my nervousness quotient.

I examined Anson's glass and sniffed. "What is that?"

"Whiskey on the rocks. I don't usually drink alcohol at all, so I may be visiting the bathroom soon."

I was seriously considering imbibing, as well. "I don't drink much either, but I may need one soon. I hope there's more than one bathroom in this place."

Eldrick stared at Anson's drink. "I'd rather have a beer, but the producers said this was a more *sophisticated* gathering."

I considered that. "I didn't realize beer was viewed as unsophisticated."

Anson looked around nervously. "I just hope this night is over and fast. I am not enjoying this at all."

"Me neither." I cocked my head. "However, you guys actually look pretty good in those tuxes."

Eldrick snorted. "These penguin suits? Constricting and itchy." He tugged at the bow tie.

"Consider yourselves fortunate. At least you don't have to wear panty hose and breast padding." I paused. "Well, I'm not wearing any padding tonight."

That comment was a mistake because both guys started staring at my chest. I blushed and snapped my fingers. "Hey, up here."

Anson's eyes shot up. "Ah, that's true about the breast padding and panty hose. Sounds pretty hideous. But at least you don't have to wear jock straps. Not that I would wear one with a tuxedo. Actually, not that I've *ever* worn one. Just saying." He paused. "That was too much information for a casual conversation, right?"

"Beats me. I'm probably not the best person to ask about that seeing as how I was just talking about breast padding."

Anson took a nervous gulp of whiskey and then coughed. "What do they put in whiskey?"

"Fermented grain mash. Some more potent than others." I patted him on the back. "But I'm guessing you meant that as a rhetorical question rather than an actual query."

"Yes. I do that all the time. It bugs the heck out of my mother."

"Hey, I'll get you a drink, Lexi," Eldrick gallantly offered. "What's your poison?"

My stomach rolled. "Better not yet. My stomach is a bit shaky at the moment. Nerves and all."

"Right. Okay."

For a minute the three of us just stood staring at each other. Not one of us could think of anything conversation worthy. Eldrick developed a weird eye tic and Anson gulped the rest of his whiskey before erupting into another coughing fit. The silence stretched into unbearable territory.

Then I saw Ace over Eldrick's shoulder waving a dry-erase board with something written on it.

I squinted. *Technology.*

Relief flooded through me. I'd forgotten. As long as I didn't drone on forever, I could tech talk. I took a deep breath. "So, guys, what do think of Juniper's new SDN controller?"

The guys let out an audible breath of relief.

Anson's face lit up. "You heard about Juniper? It's

good stuff. Did you hear they made it available as open source code?"

We were off and running for the next several minutes until I saw Ace giving me a chopping signal on his neck. He then pointed to the other group of guys. I looked over my shoulder at Ray and Truman who were sitting on the couch, talking.

I had been enjoying the conversation, so I rather reluctantly told the guys I was going over to talk to Ray and Truman. Still happily talking about Juniper's controller, they headed for the food table. I wished I could follow them and the interesting conversation.

Instead I headed for the living room. Ray whistled as I approached. I rolled my eyes and sat on the couch next to him. At the last second, I remembered to cross my legs. My mother would never forgive me if I showed up on television with my legs wide open. It's just I wasn't used to walking around in a dress and heels. It felt unnatural.

"Hey, you look great, Lexi." Ray leaned back against the cushion and studied me. "You've even got makeup on."

"They told me I had to wear it."

Truman nodded. "The warm peach-colored hue of your lipstick serves to offset the pale pigmentation of your skin and creates an inherent balance of color and harmony when one looks at your face." His cheeks turned pink. "That was a compliment, by the way."

"I figured. Thanks, but it's all Mandy's doing. I just sat there and let her smear it on. I couldn't do this myself."

Ray touched a strand of my hair. "They did something nice to your hair, too. It's kind of wavy and smooth."

"I usually wear it in a ponytail."

"It looks good loose. It makes you look…approachable."

"I don't normally look approachable?"

"I meant this is just a softer look for you. Also, you aren't much for direct eye contact, so if a guy was trying to connect with you from across the room, it would be hard for him."

"Why does a guy have to connect with me from across the room? Why not just come over and say hello?"

"Guys want to make sure the girl is interested."

"How can you tell from across the room if she's interested?"

Ray shrugged. "You just can."

"I can't," Truman offered.

I frowned. "That seems counterintuitive. I sincerely doubt you can tell much about a person from nothing more than an exchange of glances across a room."

Ray laughed. "You'd be wrong about that, Lexi."

"Apparently I seem to be wrong about a great deal of that stuff. Which is exactly why I avoid it."

Truman nodded. "Me, too."

We fell silent again and I started to dread these pregnant pauses in the conversation. Why people went to parties to do this very thing for fun completely mystified me. I saw Basia waving at me, opening and closing her fingers in the universal signal to talk. But what the heck was I supposed to talk about?

"Uh, guys, how about that weather?" I cringed, but at least I had said something.

Surprisingly, Truman perked up. "Actually, today

the atmospheric thickness and wind conditions were quite favorable for Los Angeles at this time of year."

Ray grinned. "Agreed. The weather has been fabulous. It's one of the best things about living in the City of Angels."

"Right."

We fell silent again. I was just about to bring up a tech subject when Ray spoke first.

"So, what did you do today, Lexi?"

I looked at him in surprise. "Me? You want to know what I did?"

"Sure. Tell me about your day."

I thought a moment. "Um, nope I've got nothing. Nothing interesting happened."

Truman leaned forward. "I can tell you what I did."

Thankful to be off the hook, I nodded eagerly. "Great. Tell us."

He thought for a moment. "Okay, well, I got up before the alarm went off. I sat up in bed and stretched. My neck muscles were sore. That is probably because it's a different pillow than the one I have at home, plus I've had a couple of stressful days in a row. Then I got up, checked my teeth and tongue in the mirror, and went to the bathroom."

Ray held up a hand. "Whoa, dude. You don't have to give us the details of every second. Just the highlights."

"Those *were* the highlights."

Ray and I fell silent.

I looked over at Ace hopefully. He was furiously writing something on the board and then held it up.

Food.

I jumped up from the couch, surprising both guys. "Let's eat. Thank goodness."

"Excellent idea." Truman followed on my heels, seemingly as relieved as I to have a reprieve from conversation.

Ray trailed behind Truman and me as we made our way to the table. We passed the other two guys, who were already cramming food in their mouths, dropping crumbs down the front of their tuxedo jacket. I looked down at my sparkly blue dress and wondered if I'd make it through the night without spilling anything on it. The odds were not in my favor.

I went to the table and began to calculate how much I needed to load on my plate and the time it would take me to chew it in order to minimize the minutes I'd have to spend talking.

I filled my plate based on my rough calculations and then got a club soda with a lot of ice before heading into the living room. Everyone already sat around the coffee table. I'd just sat down on the couch next to Eldrick when Stone strolled over.

"So how goes it, guys?" He smiled his million-watt smile. "Feeling like you know our girl any better?"

"She doesn't drink much," Eldrick offered.

"And dislikes wearing padded bras," Anson added. "Although I forgot to ask if she's ever seen a jock strap before."

I closed my eyes. I sincerely hoped my mother did not watch this show. She was either going to kill or disown me. Probably both.

Stone beamed. "Excellent." He turned to me. "Lexi, we have arranged an intimate table on the patio for you to meet and chat with each of the remaining guys alone. This will give you time to privately get to know each other in a safe environment."

"Define safe environment."

Stone laughed. "An intimate, romantic, cozy, candlelit table for two. The perfect setting to kiss and fall in love."

I choked on the egg roll thingamabob I was eating. Anson pounded me hard on the back just as I grabbed my club soda. The half eaten eggroll popped out of my mouth at the same time the glass flew out of my hand. The eggroll mash plopped on the coffee table, while the ice-cold liquid splashed directly onto Stone's crotch.

"*Aaaaaaaah!*" Stone leapt backward and did an Irish jig kind of dance.

I grabbed a napkin and tried to press it to the wet area on Stone's pants. "Jeez. I'm sorry, Stone. Anson hit me a little hard on the back and—"

Stone screamed like a girl. "No. God. Don't touch me there." He jigged backward behind the cameras, clutching his crotch. "What is it with the girls on this show trying to cause me bodily harm? Cartwright, we are so cutting that section. It's cold. Wardrobe! Get me some new pants."

Sighing, I picked up the mashed egg roll from the table with my wet napkin and then retrieved the glass, which had tumbled unbroken onto the carpet.

Anson's face was beet red. "I'm so sorry, Lexi. I should have done the Heimlich maneuver instead of a thump on the back. It was just an instinctive kind of thing."

"It's okay. Actually, I wasn't really choking. It was just a temporary catch of food in my throat. But it's the thought that counts."

Eldrick burst out laughing. "I'm sorry, but that was the funniest thing ever. Did you see Stone's face? His pecker probably shriveled to the size of a pecan given all the ice in that glass…unless it's already that size."

The other guys burst out laughing as well.

I spread my hands. "Hey, just so we're all clear here… I did *not* do that on purpose."

I heard more giggles and saw several of the stage crew and both cameramen were laughing. Guess Stone wasn't as well liked as I'd thought. I blew out a breath and stood.

"Okay, let's just get this next part over with. I think we're all clear that there will be nothing intimate about our conversation. Especially since there will be me, one of you, the cameramen, the stage crew, and everyone out in television land listening in. It's all a bit ridiculous, if you ask me. But since no one asked me, I guess we forge onward."

Ray patted my arm. "We'll survive. Get to work."

Reluctantly I picked up my plate wandered out to the patio. Just as Stone had said, there was a candlelit table under the stars and moon next to the shimmering pool filled with candles. The two cameramen had recovered and stood quietly in different locations, adjusting their lenses. It was kind of dark on the patio, and I wondered I how they were able to film without adding extra lighting. My mind wanted to explore the potential technical issues associated with that. Unfortunately, I had to focus on what was more important for the moment—talking to a bunch of guys about personal issues. Crapola. I'd rather endure getting fake nails while being forced to listen to Cher, but it wasn't like I had a choice at this point.

The table had a white tablecloth, a vase with a single red rose bud, and a champagne bucket and two flutes.

I set my plate and drink down and sat nervously in my chair. The house was ablaze with light and I could hear laughter coming from the living room. It felt weird to be isolated out here in the dark with two silent cameramen.

After a minute I saw Truman walking out with his plate and drink. He sat opposite me and put his napkin in his lap. I'd forgotten about that, so I did it, too, and then we sat looking at each other.

He finally exhaled a deep breath. "Okay. Here we are."

"Yes, here we are."

"They sent me out first."

"Lucky you."

"Not really." He looked up quickly. "I mean I'm lucky I'm with you, it's just not lucky that I'm first."

"I understand. I think."

We fell silent. My appetite fled and, apparently, so did Truman's. I tried desperately to remember Basia's and Ace's instructions. Try to get to know the person beyond the superficial level. Ask them questions about themselves. If all else fails, talk technology, at least for a while.

"Ah, okay. So, Truman, tell me something about yourself that I may not know."

"Like what?"

"I don't know. Something you want to tell me."

"I really don't *want* to tell you anything. I don't like talking about myself, but if I have to…"

"Yes, you *have* to." I said that a little too desperately, but we are who we are.

"Okay. Well you know I'm a paranormal investigator."

"Yes, I knew that. How did you get into that field?"

"It's something I always wanted to explore. I graduated from high school at twelve, got a degree from UCLA in computer science at fifteen, and finished my PhD in Cognitive and Computer Science at the same university by nineteen. I started my own company, Intelligence Services LLC, offering hypothesis testing, intelligence enhancement, and artificial intelligence engineering services the same year. I got a loan from my grandparents and hired three of my friends. I hired fourteen more employees as the year went on and we cleared six million in the first year. After six years, I sold the company for seven hundred and ninety-nine million dollars. I retired and decided to pursue a leisurely career in a field less explored by science."

I stared at him. "That's impressive. Retired at twenty-five. I actually considered a career in cognitive computer science as well."

"You actually know what it is?"

"Sure."

"Most people don't have a clue."

"They should. It's a great field."

"It truly is."

I saw Ace waving the board and glanced over.

No more technology talk.

Get MORE personal.

Truman saw the sign, too, but neither one of us knew how to take the conversation to a more personal level. It was already *way* more personal than I liked. Giving myself time to think, I shoveled food in my mouth. Truman did the same and after we finished, we took a drink, and then stared at each other some more.

Ace was not happy with our silence and had started dancing around and waving the dry-erase board, looking like he was having apoplexy. Why was it so important for people to get personal?

Then I thought of the hacker who would be watching and took a deep breath to calm down. I was just about to ask something, *anything*, when Truman abruptly spoke.

"Okay, Lexi. I think it's your turn to tell me something personal."

My heart skipped a beat. I felt truly uncomfortable talking about myself, especially knowing a million plus people were listening in. But I guess it was fair play since I was asking him to talk about himself.

"Uh, Truman, my life is pretty routine…most of the time. I go to work. I come home. I eat, game, and sleep. That's about it." I took a sip of my champagne.

He leaned forward. "Do you masturbate?"

I spewed the champagne all over the table and all over Truman. "*What?*"

Truman began dabbing his cheeks with his napkin.

"Well, I just wondered, you know, if girls like to do that."

I fumbled for my own napkin and pressed it to my mouth. I wanted to cover my face with it and crawl under the table, but he was looking at me so earnestly, I just couldn't do it.

"Jeez, Truman. I'm not an expert on dating, but I think that may be too personal a question for a first date."

"I thought we were supposed to get personal."

"Not *that* personal."

He frowned. "Well, it's not like they spelled out the difference."

I sighed. "I know."

Truman looked dejected, and I felt like an idiot.

"Look, Truman, why don't you tell me more about...
your new business instead."

I saw Ace writing something on the board. He held
it up. *No!*

Not his job.

GO BACK TO PERSONAL.

I pretended I didn't see it, and so did Truman.

"I'm glad you asked. My company is called Black
of Night. I've got all the top-notch equipment to search
out and find traces of paranormal or otherworldly be-
ings such as ghosts, demons, poltergeists, vampires,
and cryptic animals like werewolves or Big Foot. My
business also handles possessions, voodoo, witchcraft
and psychic activity."

"You do aliens, too?"

"No, that's an entirely different angle."

"Found anything yet on the paranormal front?"

He stabbed a meatball with his fork. "Not yet, but
part of the fun is debunking everything with science."

"Actually, that does sound like fun."

"I assure you, it is."

"Don't your clients mind if you can't find a ghost or
vampire hidden in their basement? It seems rather an-
ticlimactic to explain it all away by science."

"Actually, most people are relieved when I am able
to find a science-based reason for their fears."

"Cool."

"You'll have to come by the office sometime. I'll
give you a tour."

"Hey, I'd like that."

Again the conversation stalled. I gulped my soda
water and started to get a raging headache from all the
work of conversing. I wanted desperately to be alone

and out of my tight, sparkly dress. But I still had three more guys to go. Then I steeled my resolve and decided honesty would be the best approach.

"Look, Truman, it's abundantly clear you and I totally suck at this conversation stuff, so I'm just going to cut to the chase. Can you please tell me something personal about yourself so we can move on? Don't tell me something overly personal—especially if it involves bodily functions or orifices—and don't talk about your education or employment history. No technology. Just tell me something that I couldn't read on your resume. Is that a clear enough guideline?"

He crinkled his brow. "Something that wouldn't be on my resume?"

"Yeah. You know, something most people wouldn't know about you, I guess."

"Okay, let me think." He paused, considered. "Well, I don't think most people know I eat Count Chocula for breakfast every morning. It's been my favorite cereal since I was seven." He paused and then brightened. "Oh, I also made out with a topless inflatable doll once."

I stood up so quickly; I hit the corner of the table with my leg. The champagne flutes toppled sideways and rolled off the table, smashing onto the flagstone. Truman caught the champagne and its bucket, but the remains of our dinner was splattered on top of the shattered glasses.

Truman glanced at me alarmed. "Lexi, are you okay?"

Other than the fact that I would never *ever* be able to get the image of him making out with a topless inflatable doll out of my mind, I was fine.

"I, ah, have to go to the bathroom. I'm sorry, Truman."

Stone came running out to the patio in dry, freshly pressed slacks. Ace and Basia followed on his heels.

"What happened?" Stone stayed two steps away from me. "Does anyone need a doctor?"

I shook my head. "No one needs a doctor. I just need to visit the ladies' room. I knocked into the table when I stood up, and a couple of things rolled off and the hit the ground. No biggie."

I think Stone was disappointed I hadn't speared Truman or knocked him over the head with the champagne bottle. He waved his hand at the cameramen. "Take ten while we clean up this mess. What a klutz."

I glared at Stone as I ran past him and headed for the bathroom. Basia chased after me. She caught up and linked arms with me. "Lexi, are you okay?"

I stopped and fumed. "No, Basia, I am *not* okay. This is a nightmare. A nightmare of my own making. All I want to do is catch a hacker. Instead, I'm roped into conversation with people whose communication skills are on par or worse than mine. Even worse, I have to do it front of millions of people who are going to be laughing their heads off at our idiocy. It's a nightmare compounded by a nightmare. I better catch this hacker and soon."

"You will."

"I have to because I don't know how much more of this I can take."

"It's okay. Inhale a deep breath. Settle down. Take your time in the bathroom. I'm going to talk to Ace about a better way to approach this situation."

"Fine." I slammed the door shut, turned off my mic, and sat on top of the closed toilet. Putting my head between my knees, I took deep breaths. When I finally was able to collect myself, I used the facilities and washed my hands. I hadn't taken two steps out of the bathroom when someone grabbed my arm and pulled me down a hallway.

"Ray?"

"Is your mic off?"

I looked down at the mic clipped to my dress. "Yes. I turned it off in the bathroom and haven't flipped it back on yet. What's wrong?"

His normally coffee-colored skin looked unusually pale. "I need to tell you something." He exhaled. "Look, I'm not who you think I am."

"Okay, who are you?"

"I'm a fraud."

"A fraud?"

"Yes. I'm not really here to win the heart of a girl, geek or otherwise. I'm also not here to figure out how to get it on with a girl."

"Can I admit that this doesn't surprise me? You seemed light years ahead of us in intuition."

He smiled. "I figured you'd be on to me."

"So, go ahead and tell me. Why are you here in a fraudulent manner?"

He pressed his hand to his forehead. "I'm a software engineer. That's true. But I already have a girlfriend and we want to get married someday. My thing is...well, I have this dream. Tanya, that's my girl, she told me to chase it while I'm still young."

"What dream?"

"I play the guitar and sing. I may be good at math, but I want to be a songwriter and singer. I thought if I came on this show, I'd have a chance to play for Lucy. I hoped I'd get noticed and maybe even get offered a recording contract or something. In hindsight, it was a really stupid idea. What was I thinking? To make matters worse, Lucy was a royal pain, and wasn't remotely interested in my singing abilities. She ridiculed me while at the same time trying to stick her tongue down my throat. It was pretty awful. Add to that, the producers cut both times I sang for her. It's all been quite the epic failure."

"I'm sorry to hear that."

"Anyway, I like you, Lexi. I don't want to deceive you. Plus, I miss Tanya. This was sheer lunacy. I'm really sorry. I'm telling you this because I'd appreciate it if you'd choose me to leave. I could act like a prick to make you and the audience hate me so it is easy for you to get rid of me, but that's not my style. If you could just pick me to go home instead of one of the other guys, I'd appreciate it. I've gotten to know them, and they're good kids. They are the real deal and came on this show to get some solid advice and some interaction practice. It took a lot of courage for them to do it, and it sucks the way they've been manipulated. The way we've all been handled."

"Agreed." I considered for a moment. "Although I really do like you...in a friendly way, I mean. Anyway, I'll do what I can."

"I appreciate it, Lexi. I have no doubt you'll make some guy very happy someday."

"That's highly doubtful, but trust me, it's the least of my problems right now."

To my surprise, he laughed and gave me a peck on the cheek before disappearing down the stairs. I leaned back against the wall and tried to get my thoughts in order.

Before I could make any headway, I saw Basia coming up the stairs. "Lexi, are you okay? Why are you standing in the hallway?"

"I'm hiding."

She pulled on my arm. "Look, don't worry about it. I've talked to Ace and he's promised to calm down. You can talk about whatever you want, however you want, and the producers will have to figure out what to do with it."

"They can't frankenbite anything. I had it put in the contract."

"Good. They're professionals. They'll figure it out. Talk about what you want. I promise. Just be who you are."

"The person I am wants to go home and crawl under the covers. But I'm going to catch that hacker. In order to do that, I have to survive talking with three more guys on national television."

"You can do it. Remember the end game. We're all rooting for you."

I closed my eyes. "Okay, I can do this. Do you know who is up next?"

"Eldrick, I believe. You asked me to come here to help you, so I will. Ask him to tell you why he thinks he has trouble communicating with girls. Ask him what's his favorite movie and why. Those two questions should be enough for him and then move on to the next guy. If it's not enough, talk geek to your heart's content and screw the producers."

I hugged her. "Now I remember why you're my best friend."

She gave me a squeeze. "And don't you forget it."

Chapter Twenty-Five

We headed downstairs and back out to the patio. The glass had been swept away and the tablecloth refreshed. The champagne bucket and bottle remained in the middle of the table, as did the candle and two new flutes. I felt like popping the cork and guzzling the champagne for the buzz, but I already had a headache and I supposed I had to maintain some measure of decorum.

I turned my microphone back on as the cameramen hefted their cameras. Stone, with his annoyingly fake smile, led Eldrick to the table.

Stone patted Eldrick on the shoulder. "Good luck, and have fun, kids." His laughter trailed after him.

Eldrick waited until he was out of earshot. "Condescending jerk."

I chuckled. "He's going to hear that. National television and all, remember?"

"They won't play it. He's a favorite son. Trust me, it will be the first thing Cartwright cuts."

"You're probably right."

Eldrick picked up the champagne bottle. "It's full. Didn't you drink it with Truman?"

"No. We got to talking and never got around to it."

"Truman actually talked?"

"Well, sort of."

"Good for him, but bad for me. That's a lot of pressure for me to follow up."

"Don't worry. You'll do fine. Trust me on that."

He sighed. "If you say so. Do you want some champagne?"

"Actually, yes. I could really use a drink."

He grabbed the bottle. "Got a corkscrew?"

The bartender magically appeared. "Let me assist you with that, sir."

Eldrick looked at little startled at his sudden appearance, but handed over the bottle. "Thanks."

The waiter uncorked the bottle, poured the champagne in our glasses and then disappeared.

Eldrick picked up his glass. "Is it just me or was that a bit creepy the way he just materialized."

"Kind of reminds me of Alfred Pennyworth."

"Ah, Batman's butler. He seemed show up whenever Batman needed him, whether he was summoned or not."

He lifted his glass. "Well, how about we have a toast?"

"To Batman?"

He smiled. "No. How about a genuine conversation regardless of who is listening?"

"If you believe that is a feasible goal then I'm in."

I lifted my glass and we clinked them together. I took a sip and the bubbles tickled my nose.

"You know, Eldrick, the idea of a genuine conversation begs the question, why exactly did you come on this show? Was it really to get some?"

He set his glass down. "Technically, yes. I didn't mind sex being the end prize, or even a side prize, if it were to happen."

"Really? I mean it all seems rather ridiculous. You didn't even know Lucy and you thought you might actually sleep with her?"

"Why not? It happens all the times on these reality shows."

I took another sip of my champagne. "Another reason why I am *so* glad I don't watch much television."

"I'm with you on that. Look, the truth is I make enough money that hiring hookers on a regular basis wouldn't be a problem if it were just for sex." He sighed. "Although I am a bit of a germaphobe. Still, I thought Lucy was really going to be a real girl. You know, genuine. It seemed like a good idea at the time, which sounds really stupid right now."

I nodded with sympathy. "Some things are better visualized than actually put into practice."

"True, but I really wanted to figure out how to meet and talk to a woman in a way she'd appreciate. My problem is finding a woman that I can like and respect. For me women are like internet domains. The ones I want are already taken."

I had no idea of the appropriate response to that, so I took a large gulp of champagne and started to feel a bit light-headed. Thankfully, Eldrick didn't take offense to my silence and instead continued talking.

"You know, I can understand how a woman might not want to get sucked into the nerd-o-sphere which dominates my life. But I can be interesting on occasion. I hope. What do you think?"

He looked at me. I wasn't sure how to answer that, so I glanced over at Basia and Ace. Basia had grabbed the dry-erase board and had written *Ask him what he wants in a girl.*

"Uh, I think... I think... I want to know what exactly you are looking for in a girl."

He blinked in surprise. "You mean other than sex and relatively intelligent conversation?"

Unsure, I glanced over at Basia, who was nodding furiously. "Um. Yes. Yes, that's what I want to know."

He rolled the cloth napkin into something resembling a light saber. He held it up and looked through it at me like a telescope. "You know, that's actually a good question."

I threw Basia an appreciative glance. "Ah, thanks."

"So, what do I want in a woman? Well, I want a lady who can appreciate me for who I am. I don't want her to try to change me or fix me. She should love me as I am for all my quirks and oddities."

"That seems fair."

"Of course, it's fair. I mean she shouldn't care if I alphabetize my pantry, have a foot fetish, or wear my underwear in the shower. It's all about who we are on the inside."

I stared at him. "Ah..."

He narrowed his eyes. "Right?"

I stood up. "I have to go to the bathroom again."

Cartwright stormed onto the set, pulling off his headset. "Oh, for Christ's sake. The conversation was just getting interesting. Do you have the smallest bladder on the planet?"

I brushed past him. "I'm *not* discussing my bladder with you."

The cameramen, laughing, dropped into patio chairs. Basia once again linked arms with me on the way to the bathroom.

She patted my arm. "Lexi, calm down. I know you don't have to go to the bathroom."

"You want to discuss my bladder, too?"

"You're going to hide."

"Of course, I'm going to hide. Are you paying attention to what's going on out there?"

"You're doing great."

I stopped, unhooked my arm. "No, I'm not. I can't do it anymore. I really can't. Not even to catch the hacker. I'm ready to throw in the towel. I surrender. He wins."

"Stop. You don't mean that."

"I do mean it. Eldrick wears his freaking underwear in the shower. Truman makes out with topless dolls. How much more am I supposed to make them reveal? Cartwright knows how badly we suck at this, which is exactly why he is forcing us into doing it."

Basia put her hands on her hips. "Yes, they're manipulating you. But let me tell you something, Lexi. Watching really smart people muck up something that comes easily to most of us is entertaining. No one wants to watch perfect people interact perfectly with each other. We want to be able to relate to you, to understand you. People with flaws are real and genuine—and hey, guess what? Smart people have problems just like we do. But it doesn't mean we're laughing at you. We are actually pulling *for* you and the guys to get it right. To find love. To figure it all out."

"It's ridiculous."

"Of course, it's ridiculous. It's Hollywood, so it *must* be dramatic, exaggerated and over the top. Lots of geeks have perfectly fine social skills. Cartwright's team picked the most extreme guys on the planet *on purpose*. The show operates with a specific allotted amount of time and a small window of opportunity. Cartwright has to keep the interactions short, sweet, and exaggerated in order to fill the time slot. The guys knew that when they signed up. Despite their social shortcomings, they aren't stupid. Keep in mind that this show serves a different purpose for every person who watches or is involved in it. Cartwright and the studio need to make money, the guys want some practice and instruction on interaction with girls, and the television audience wants to be amused and entertained for a short period of time. You have the most unique purpose here, which is to catch a hacker. The show has to continue in order for you to do that. Remember, you have only to play along for as long as it takes to catch the hacker. Then it's over. You'll have your hacker, the audience will have had its break from the grind of daily life, the studio will have its money, and your new friends will have had the distinct pleasure of interacting with a woman who is as genuine as they are."

"You sound like you're defending the show."

"I'm putting it in perspective. No one's life is at stake here. It's entertainment."

"It's perpetuating a stereotype."

"Yes and no. Yes, because this is a popular perception of geeks today, despite the obvious exaggeration. No, because at the same time, it also creates a newfound sympathy and understanding of the difficult and painful challenges people like you experience in social situations. It makes what you have to endure in order to form and maintain relationships authentic and real. It thereby fosters a climate of improved acceptance and tolerance, whereas before people might have just considered it rude and annoying behavior."

"I'm not on board with this theory."

"It's okay. You don't have to be on board. Just do what you need to do to catch the hacker and we'll go home."

I closed my eyes. "Why is it so painful?"

"It's painful, yet oddly poignant, because all of you are way out of your comfort zone. Explain to me how is that a bad thing. Don't we all grow and expand as individuals when we try new things in life?"

"I like my life when it's quiet, safe and alone."

"Not true. You like your life because you have friends, family and people who love you. Yes, they complicate it, but you are *not* alone. It's called relationships and as much as you profess to abhor them, without them in any form, you would be a lonely, unhappy person."

I sighed. "I hate it when you're right."

She hugged me. "No, you love me for it. Look, all of you on the show are beyond a-dork-able. Honestly, I can see why this show is popular. The audience will love you as much as they love the guys. Everyone wants you guys to find happiness. So, do your best, roll with the punches, and let's trap this hacker. Okay?"

I considered. Blew out a breath. "Okay."

"Good. No more hiding. Finish this and let's go home."

I straightened. "You're right. I can do this."

"Of course, you can. Now, go get 'em."

Chapter Twenty-Six

The final two interactions with Anson and Ray weren't as bad as I'd anticipated. Other than discovering that Anson still lived with his folks, slept in the closet during thunderstorms, and liked to smell books in private, it went well.

The discussion with Ray was easily the best of the evening, mostly because we didn't talk much. Instead, I insisted on him playing several songs for me on his guitar, which he happily retrieved from his room. He also talked about his love for music, songwriting, and the challenges of breaking into the music business. Cartwright didn't seem overly happy that the conversation was normal, but considering I had actually returned from the bathroom and wasn't putting anyone in danger, he kept quiet.

After one final song from Ray, I stood and clapped (maybe a bit too enthusiastically), thinking the night was finally over. However, before we could leave the patio, Stone strolled out, a smug look on his face. I tensed.

Stone clapped Ray on the shoulder. "Good show, my man. You're quite talented. Thank you for gracing all of us, especially Lexi, with your considerable musical ability." Before Ray could respond, Stone practically pushed him toward the French doors of the living room. "See you later."

Ray stumbled a step and threw me a questioning look over his shoulder. I lifted an eyebrow as Stone faced me, his smirk widening. "Sit down, Lexi. The night is not over."

"But Ray is the last guy."

"Not exactly."

Confused, I glanced over at Basia and Ace, both of whom looked as baffled as me. Basia lifted her hands in an I-don't-know-what's-going-on gesture.

I returned my gaze to Stone's face. "What do you mean, 'not exactly'?"

"It means that we are throwing you a bit of a curve ball, livening things up, so to say."

"I don't want things to be lively."

He laughed. "Of course, you do. You just don't realize it yet."

I narrowed my eyes. I was definitely going to have words with Cartwright. "Get to your point."

The guys, backlit by the bright lights of the mansion, jostled at the doors, trying to get a better look at what was happening on the patio. I caught a glimpse of Barnaby and Gregg, both apparently having joined the group. Barnaby had a white adhesive strip across his nose and sported two black eyes, while Gregg appeared in good—as opposed to twitchy—health, at least from my vantage point.

"My point, my dear lady, is that we've added a new suitor to the mix."

My mouth dropped open. *"What?"*

The guys expressed their surprise with a series of

choice words and phrases. I looked over at Cartwright, whose face was shadowed and impassive, then turned my attention back to Stone.

"Why?"

"Why?" Stone chuckled. "Why do you think?"

"Because you want to heighten the drama. Or because you enjoy being a jerk."

Stone glared at me and one of the cameramen snickered so loudly that Cartwright glared at him across the patio.

Stone narrowed his eyes. "I'll tell you why. We wanted to catch you with your guard down, with no opportunity to prepare or think before a date. Lexi Carmichael, raw and exposed. No chance to prepare herself. How will she manage with a surprise guest? Will she be adept enough to juggle the remaining guys? More importantly, how will our surprise suitor woo the lady? Will the current group of guys be able to deal or compete with him? It's all quite exciting. So, everyone, sit back in your seat and enjoy the experience."

He stepped to his side and swept out his arm in a grand gesture. "Lexi Carmichael, I present to you, Nelson Soddenbag, one of America's youngest multimillionaires and the reclusive owner of Frisson International, LLC in New York City."

A shadowy figure stepped out onto the patio. He was tall, but his posture was hunched as he walked. He seemed to have a limp of some kind. Despite his strange shuffle, something seemed familiar about the way he moved. He stepped up next to Stone and raised his head to look directly at me.

A gasp escaped my mouth.

Slash was nearly unrecognizable with what had to be

a black wig, long sideburns, and a fake goatee. He wore some kind of retainer that made his teeth stick out. But I recognized those eyes. They sparkled with mischief, amusement and a warning. I had no idea what game he was playing, but I couldn't call him out on it here.

Stone, most likely mistaking my surprise for revulsion, clapped his hand on my shoulder, moving me closer. "Say hello to Nelson, Lexi."

I held out a hand. "Uh, nice to meet you, *Nelson*." I hoped my tone was more polite than shocked.

"Likewise, but the pleasure is all mine." Slash had changed his accent to a more nasal New York one. He shook my hand and gave it a quick squeeze before releasing it. I fell, more than sat, in my chair.

Slash took the chair across from me and smiled at Stone.

Stone's glee was almost palpable. "Well, I'll let the two of you get acquainted. Have fun."

The ghostly waiter abruptly appeared, bringing a new already-opened bottle of champagne and two clean flutes. The cameramen quietly maneuvered in closer while I clasped my hands in my lap, not sure what to say.

Thankfully, Slash took control of the conversation. "It's a pleasure to meet you. How do you like being on the show?"

"Honestly?"

"Of course."

"Not much. The guys are nice though, and they put up with me, so there's that."

"I can't see how that's a hardship on their part."

I glanced over and saw Basia and Ace had their heads together, talking softly. Basia seemed upset. Ace had his arm around her as he explained something in an animated fashion. I suspected Cartwright hadn't told anyone about the surprise guest. I sincerely doubted Basia had been in the loop. She would have told me if she'd known.

"Lexi?"

"Huh? Ah, sorry. Did you say something?"

"I said I'm glad to have this opportunity to meet you."

"Oh. Well, I'll admit it is a *big* surprise to see you here."

"I'm sure it is." He removed the champagne bottle from the ice bucket and filled our flutes. He handed me mine and then lifted his. "Let's toast to surprises then."

"To surprises." I held up my glass and we clinked them together.

Slash took a sip. "I'm actually a big fan of the show."

I studied him, doubtful. "Really?"

"Really. Never more so than when you were unanimously selected by your peers to be on the show. It was quite an interesting development."

"*Interesting* being the key word here."

"Indeed." He smiled and sipped his champagne.

I looked to Basia for help, but she was still busy talking to Ace. So I turned back to Slash and took a deep breath. "So, tell me how you were selected to be the mystery suitor this week."

His eyes sparkled. "Ah, yes, that. I thought you might be curious. I'd actually been approached several times before about appearing on the show, but declined for a variety of reasons."

"No way."

"Way."

I set my glass down. "So, why appear now in the middle of the show?"

"I saw you last week and was instantly smitten. I knew I just had to have the opportunity to see you in person. I had my people contact the show and fortunately for me, it worked out. Simple as that."

I narrowed my eyes. "Somehow, I don't think it's that simple."

He laughed. "I sense you suspect ulterior motives."

"I do."

"I assure you, I'll be as transparent as you require."

"I require a lot."

He leaned back in his chair. "Excellent. I enjoy a challenge."

I caught a movement from the corner of my eye and saw Basia waving the dry-erase board.

Ask him about his company.

Who is he?

Jeez, if she only knew.

My mind raced. How and where to take this conversation?

"So, Stone mentioned you are from New York. What exactly does your company, Frisson, do?"

"Data integration, tactical computing, sensor management, simulation-based training, and fusion analysis. Among other things."

"You're the CEO?"

"Of course."

"Tell me what you mean by simulation-based training."

He raised an eyebrow. "Testing me, are you?"

"We've had some past frauds on the show. I'm just making sure you are the real deal."

"Ah, I assure you I am. I assume you already know what simulation-based training is. Otherwise, I could just make it up and you wouldn't know the difference."

"I know what simulation-based training is."

He steepled his fingers together over the champagne flute. "Well, my company, Frisson, is developing and deploying a new generation of cryptologic simulation and training systems for the U.S. government. We have a unique approach to training, focusing on real-time operational simulations and training scenarios. Unfortunately, due to the sensitive nature of our work, I can't say much more. Is that clear enough for you?"

"Close enough."

"Did I pass the test?"

"So far."

"I'm glad to hear that. I'm enjoying talking to you."

I was, too, but wasn't sure if I should acknowledge it. I hadn't even had a chance to decide how mad I was at him for his comments about the video of me in the shower. So, for now, I took a drink of my champagne and tried to figure what he was plotting by coming on the show.

"Are you sure you don't have any other motives for coming on this show?"

He seemed to be having fun with the whole thing, the cad. "A man often has many hidden motives. But for you, I will be an open book. What would you like to know about me?"

I considered a moment. "Are you based in New York?"

"The company is. I'm more of a man on the move, you could say. In fact, I just recently returned from a trip to Europe." His smile widened. "I was in Rome."

I nearly choked on the champagne. I coughed and

then pressed a hand to my chest. "Ah, I... I guess that means you travel a lot."

"I go wherever the business takes me." He played with the stem of his champagne glass. "Now, am I permitted to ask you a question?"

I considered a moment. "Maybe. It depends on the question."

He set his glass down and leaned forward. "I'd like to know what you want in a boyfriend."

"*What*?"

He leaned back in his chair, studied me. "I realize you came on this show unexpectedly. You didn't exactly sign up. You were—more or less—voted in. You've had the chance to ask some of the contestants what they would like in a woman, and now I'd like to know what you'd like from a man and a relationship."

I heard some noise at the French doors where the guys were jostling for a better view at one of the monitors, and hanging on to every word we said. I saw the cameras swivel in their direction. They looked confused, anxious, and...oddly, interested.

The cameras swiveled back to me. Slash waited patiently for my answer. I started to stammer. "I, ah, um..."

"Well?"

I let out a breath. "I... I'm not sure. I guess I'd like to have a relationship with a man that I could be really comfortable with. He'd have to be someone I could trust, someone who understands my quirks. A friend. No, not just a friend, a *best* friend, a person I could count on in any situation. But most importantly, it would have to be someone I could feel at peace with...a meeting of the minds and heart, so to say. That's probably too much to expect from a boyfriend."

"Ah, but if you expect nothing, you get nothing in return."

He had a point. "True. No investment, no return."

I picked up my glass, swirled the champagne. "You know, I recently asked one of the guys on this show why he had put himself out in the public arena to do something as private as find a relationship. He told me there are benefits to being loved by someone else, no matter what. What do you think?"

"I happen to be in agreement."

I sighed. "I wasn't sure at first, but after thinking about it, I believe I am, too." I folded my hands in my lap. "That being said, *Nelson*, I would also value a man who knew how to make amends if he messed up in some way. A man who knew how to eat humble pie if it were warranted."

"Humble pie?" Slash raised an eyebrow.

Basia frowned and started whispering something to Ace, probably wondering what the heck was going on.

"Yes, humble pie. A man who could admit he was wrong and be better for it."

"That can be a hard pie to swallow."

"Yes it can."

I realized my palms were sweaty, so I wiped them under the table on the tablecloth. As far as I could remember, this was the first time Slash and I had ever been so openly at odds. To have our discussion on this very topic broadcast on national television didn't help matters much. But it was important to me. Slash had hurt my feelings and I still wasn't sure how I felt about him after it.

Perhaps disconcerted by the strange veering off of our conversation, Stone abruptly materialized at our table, waving an arm at the guys in the house. "Well, come on out, contestants, and meet the new mystery suitor."

Slash pushed back from the table. I marveled at how he stayed in character.

Gregg reached us first and eyed Slash with mistrust. "You'd better not get in my way, bud. It's obvious to everyone that Lexi has the hots for me. She kissed me."

"I did *not* kiss you."

"So she says. It was her plan all along to get me flat on my back. Baby, you could have just asked me instead of stunning me into it."

"I didn't stun you either."

"Oh, but you did with your beauty and wit."

"For the love of God, shut up, Gregg." Eldrick pushed his way past Gregg and held out a hand to Slash. "I'm Eldrick. Welcome to the nut house. May the best guy win."

I made the time-out signal. "Whoa. Hold it right there. Lest we all forget, I am not a prize, nor am I proposing *anything* to *any* of you. We're here to get to know each other and that's all. Are we all clear on that?"

Truman shrugged. "Sure, but you've got to eliminate us one by one until your favorite is left."

"You all are pretty great guys. It won't be easy to see anyone go."

Stone walked up to me smiling and put his arm around me, yanking me hard against him. I tried not to shudder.

"Okay, audience, it's up to you to help Lexi decide which guys stay and which one should be ejected. Vote for your favorite. Don't let it slide. One vote might make all the difference. Don't forget Nelson, our surprise guest, is now in the running, as well. Will the new suitor be the first off or will he be the new favorite? Vote now and tune in tomorrow for our results show."

I let out a sigh of relief just as Cartwright called out, "That's a wrap. Now team, get to work putting the show together."

Chapter Twenty-Seven

Ace drove Basia and me to the studio. The two of them kept up a light chatter, but I was silent, thinking.

Ace adjusted the rear view mirror. "Are you sure you don't want to go to the hotel instead of the studio? You've got to be exhausted."

"No. I want to go to the IT room. I want to check something."

"How are you going to get to the hotel?"

"Probably Kyle. We're all working late tonight. Tony also said he'd be here tonight to do some work. Someone should be able to give me a ride. Don't worry, Ace. I'll be okay, really."

Ace sighed. "You're the boss."

Basia twisted in the front passenger seat to look at me. "Are you sure you're feeling okay?"

"You've already asked me four times. I'm fine. I'm just thinking."

"I swear neither Ace nor I knew about the surprise suitor."

"I know. I believe you."

Ace pulled up in front of the studio and I quickly hopped out.

Basia climbed out, as well. "Ace, can you wait a minute for me?"

"Sure."

Basia ran after me, trying hard to keep up with my long stride. "Lexi, you know I would have told you if I'd known. Cartwright must have arranged it in secret."

"Basia, I totally believe you. Really. It's okay. It's just that Nelson is Slash."

"*What?*" Basia grabbed my arm, whirling me to a stop. "Slash? What are you talking about?"

"Slash is Nelson Soddenbag. I don't know what he's doing here or what's going on, but I don't have time to worry about it now."

Her eyes were wide. "How did Slash get mixed up in this?"

"How does Slash do anything? He's anyone and anywhere he wants."

"Are you sure it was him?"

"Of course, I'm sure. I almost didn't recognize him. But the eyes...they were all Slash."

"Lexi, are you sure? It was dark and you might have been mistaken."

"I am *not* mistaken. It was definitely Slash."

Basia ran her fingers through her short dark bob, looking agitated. "I believe you *think* it was Slash. But you've been under a lot of pressure these past few days. It could be your mind paying tricks on you."

"You're just going to have to take my word for it. It was him."

She nodded. "Okay. I do. I'm so tired, I can hardly think myself. I don't think I've recovered from Rome yet."

"Go back to the hotel and get some sleep. My real work is just beginning. I'll see you tomorrow."

"What time do you need me here at the studio?"

"Whenever you want. There's no more filming, just editing and putting it all together for the show tomorrow. Thankfully, it's not live, so I don't have to be dressed, present or otherwise. That's good for me because I can be in the IT room as the actual voting starts and finishes. I'm going to catch this guy tomorrow night, Basia. Then we'll have the real wrap."

"Yes, you will." She smiled and gave me a hug. "You did a great job tonight, Lexi. You kept it together under difficult circumstances. I'm proud of you."

"Thanks for helping me, Basia. I mean that. Having you near always makes me feel better."

"That's what best friends are for."

"As usual, you're right."

She patted my cheek. "Good luck catching the hacker."

"Appreciate it. I'm going to need some of that luck."

We parted ways. The studio guard let me in and I walked down the hallway. It was fairly busy with much of the editing staff on hand. I was just outside the IT room when someone grabbed me from behind, slapping a hand over my mouth. Before I could blink, I had been dragged into the nearby employee bathroom with the door closed and locked. I struggled as the light flicked on and the hand lifted from my mouth.

"*Slash!*"

"Sorry, *cara*. I couldn't afford to have anyone see us talking."

He was still dressed as Nelson Soddenbag. He leaned over the sink, pulled the retainer from his mouth, grabbed a case from his pocket and then dropped the retainer in. "That feels much better. Why is it that somehow we are always meeting in the bathroom?"

My heart was still doing the tango from his grab and drag. "You just scared me half to death. What are you doing in California? No, more importantly, what are you doing on the set, masquerading as some geeky CEO?"

He stood and closed the small distance between us. Before I could say another word, he pulled me into his arms and gave me a soft kiss on the mouth.

"I've missed you," he murmured against my mouth. "So much."

It was such an amazing kiss I almost forgot I was mad at him. I blinked and then pushed against his chest. "Don't try to distract me. Seriously. What are you doing here?"

"We need to talk."

"We just had a talk, *Nelson*."

"Ah, but now I want you to talk to me, not Nelson."

I narrowed my eyes. "There is something called a phone, you know. You don't have to show up on a dating show just to talk to me."

"Perhaps, but this needed to be handled in person. Not to mention you haven't been answering your phone."

"I haven't decided how mad I am at you yet. How did you get into the studio?"

"I rode over with Tony. Told him I wanted a tour... after I went to the bathroom." He fingered a tendril of my hair. "I figured you'd come to the studio to work and I was right. How are you?"

I crossed my arms against my chest. "I've been better."

"What on earth made you decide to go on the show?"

I sighed. "It wasn't an easy decision. I wanted to keep the cracker engaged. He's been inconsistent in his goals in regards to the show. At first I think he just wanted to have the power to control it. Then he wanted it shut down. After the guys banded together and threw the fake girl off the show, he did a one eighty. He decided instead of shutting down the show, he wanted *me* to stay as the new girl. I balked at first, but Cartwright threatened to fire the IT staff and members of his own staff if I didn't comply. Plus, I wasn't going to walk away and let the cracker go free because I didn't have the guts to talk to a bunch of guys on television."

Slash frowned. "Regardless, it's not like you to give in to blackmail."

"No, it's not. This is something personal between the cracker and me. How did you find out I had agreed to star on the show?"

"I talked to Elvis. In a bizarre twist of coincidence, I had been approached several months ago about appearing on this show. Well, not exactly me, but my alter-ego, Nelson Soddenbag."

"Seriously? You made up a fake identity to come on this show?"

"The identity is fake, but my company is real."

"What's with the name Soddenbag?"

He chuckled. "I wanted a name that would project a certain sort of image. I really do own Frisson LLC of New York. I set up the company under a pseudonym. I created the persona of a reclusive scientist who had no interest in mingling in New York circles. I'm helping the government with exactly the things I told you about on the patio tonight. However, because I'm never seen, I've become gossip fodder in New York high society circles. People believe I'm a rich, clueless bachelor, a perfect target for many society types I don't have time for. They've been trying to figure out who I am since I started the company two years ago. Naturally I'm reclusive because no one can know who I really am."

I frowned. "So, you're like some gazillionaire businessman on top of everything else you do?"

He shrugged. "The company has done better than I expected."

"So why in the world would you risk that anonymity on national television?"

"Why else, *cara?* I wanted a chance to win the heart of the girl. I really did have my people call the studio. It was arranged in less than an hour. Mr. Cartwright was almost delirious."

I studied his face. "You do realize you didn't have to do this to win my heart."

"Perhaps not. But it isn't beneath me to try to impress you, especially after I completely mishandled our earlier conversation about the video. I'm sorry, *cara.* I said everything wrong."

I closed my eyes. "You hurt my feelings."

He took my hand. "I know. I apologize. I had no intention of doing so. The truth is I watched the video because I wanted to know what kind of camera he used and if I could figure out to trace it. The fact that he hurt you—embarrassed you like that—it made me crazy. I didn't know how to best help you."

I opened my eyes. "Really?"

"Really."

"Is that part of the reason why you came out here?"

He exhaled. "Yes, I needed to see you, to convince you I'm sincere in my apology."

"He filmed me naked in the shower."

"I wish you would let me go after him."

"This is my deal."

He clenched his fists. "Can't you see how hard this is for me? I understand that this is your operation, not mine. I get that, despite my protective tendencies when it comes to you. But don't tie my hands completely."

I considered his words. "Hmmm. You know what I think?"

"I'm almost afraid to ask."

"I still think you came here because you don't think I can handle it."

"Not true. I *know* you can handle it. But I'm also here to help. If you so wish it."

"Help? How?"

"Well, I figured you considered it an inside job, which is part of the reason why you agreed to go on the show. By extension, that makes the contestants suspect. So, what better way to keep an eye on the suspects than to become one and move in with them?"

My mouth dropped open. "You're living in the mansion?"

"I am now. But I'm out of there if you wish it."

"No, that's...that's actually great. Clever idea, Slash."

"I'm relieved you approve. I toyed with letting you know ahead of time, but I wasn't sure I'd be able to pull it off. When it finally worked out, things went down to the wire in terms of logistics and time. In addition, I thought your reaction would be more genuine on film if I didn't tell you I was coming. There was little time to prepare as it was."

"That outfit...your walk, the teeth. I understand the shuffle, given the cast, but it's really prime. I *was* surprised tonight. You truly are a master of disguise."

He grinned. "I do want to remain as anonymous as possible. I was afraid you wouldn't recognize me."

"You're wrong, Slash. I'd know you anywhere."

"That's my girl."

"You think I'm your girl?"

"Well, I'm working on it. Eating humble pie is not an easy task for me, but I'm learning."

I smiled just a little and then leaned forward. A million thoughts went through my head, but I tried to focus on the important ones—lips soft and slightly parted, eye contact, a slightly tilted head, and breathe. I cupped his cheeks with my hands, touching my lips to his, trying to remember the precise calculation for mouth pressure.

He stilled as my lips touched his and then he sighed, his arms sliding around my back, pressing me closer. "Ah, *cara*, does that mean you're not mad at me anymore?"

"It means you are on the right road."

He nibbled at my ear. "I didn't think it would be that easy."

"Good."

My thoughts started to drift as his lips made his way down my neck. I snapped myself back to focus. "Okay, you can stop now. I'm trying to think. When you do that, I can't hold a rational thought."

"Mmm…"

I pushed him again. "Slash, seriously. Your presence at the mansion changes things. It's given me an idea…"

He lifted his head, his eyes gleaming. "What do you have in mind?"

I gave him a quick run down. He listened intently, nodded, and offered a few refinements. Finally he nodded.

"It's doable, *cara*, and better than that, it's good."

Someone knocked on the bathroom door.

"Taken!" I yelled.

Someone said something and I heard footsteps walking away.

"Slash, I've really got to go."

Slash braced an arm on either side of me against the door and leaned in for one more kiss. "I know. I just want to say you look beautiful tonight, *cara*. You turned every head in that room, mine included."

"You're just saying that. They put all these fancy clothes and makeup on me. I didn't do anything."

"Except be yourself, which makes you more beautiful and desirable than ever. Be careful tonight."

"He's a misguided hacker, not a psychopath. Well, at least, I hope not."

"He might be dangerous if you box him in. And *that* worries me."

"I can take care of myself."

He sighed. "*Si*, I know that well, and yet it doesn't quite ease my concern."

I opened the bathroom door a crack and peeked out. The hallway was empty. I started leave, but instead, I stopped. I took a breath and turned to face Slash.

"By the way, I talked to Finn. We're not dating. I clarified things. I like him, quite a lot, but I'm not sure things were ever aligned in the right way for us in terms of dating. Most importantly, I can't manage the boss-employee-potential boyfriend angle. So, I told him that."

"I see. How did he take it?"

"He seemed kind of surprised. Maybe disappointed. I can't be sure. But he said he understood and he still wants to be my friend. Most importantly, I can keep my job."

He kissed my cheek. "I appreciate you clearing that up for me."

"Slash, would it…have made a difference to you if I had been dating him?"

Slash didn't answer right away. Then he smiled. "It doesn't really matter now, does it?"

"I guess not. So, what does that clarification mean in terms of our situation?"

He ran his fingers down my bare arm. "It's up to you. You know where I stand. You'll figure it out." He gave me a little push out the door. "Go catch that hacker, *cara.* I've got my own work to do."

Slipping out, I closed the door behind me. I smoothed down my hair. I hoped I didn't look guilty from the kissing as I opened the door to the IT room.

The entire IT staff was present and accounted for. Noah whistled as I walked in. "Wow, you clean up well, girl boss."

I shrugged. "It's just an illusion. Don't get used to it." I sat down in front of my monitor, slid my computer glasses on my nose and wound my hair back into a ponytail. "Anyone got a rubber band?"

Melinda dug in her purse. "Use a scrunchie. A rubber band will break your hair." She tossed me a black one.

I caught it with one hand and tied my hair back. "Anything new?"

Kyle shook his head. "He's been awfully quiet. No manifestos, no systemic or careless attacks on our system, no nothing."

I nodded. "That's okay. Hopefully, I've given him something to vote on tomorrow after the show."

Carlos perched on the desk next to me. "So, how'd it go with the guys tonight?"

"Really? You have to ask?"

He looked delighted. "I most certainly do."

"Well, if you must know, it was beyond hellish. But I managed it in a weird sort of way. At least I was one of the lucky ones who didn't get hurt."

Carlos laughed and rubbed his hands together. "Oh, man. I can't wait. It's hard to believe I'm looking forward to watching the show."

"Forget it. You're going to be watching your screen."

He pointed to the television hanging from the wall. "I can do both."

"Not if you're going to be distracted."

Carlos held out his hands. "Hey, as soon as the voting starts, it's eyes on my screen only. I promise. Until then, I'm planning on being entertained by you and that screen up there."

I still hadn't got used to the idea that I would be appearing on television. It gave me the heebie-jeebies.

"Fine but now it's work time. We need to finish the final preparations for the voting tomorrow. Everyone knows their assignments."

"Slave driver," Noah mumbled, but everyone settled down in front of their respective computers.

Tony and Nelson came by about a half hour later, but I sent them on their way after Kyle said he'd drop me by the hotel when we were done.

We all worked until about eleven o'clock until Kyle sent everyone home. He and I worked for another hour until he pulled my chair away from the computer.

"C'mon, Lexi. Let's go home. We've got to get some sleep. We're as ready as we're ever going to be. We've got a long day tomorrow."

"I know. I just want to double-check everything."

"You've double—and triple-checked and so have I. The bases are all covered. We're both dead tired and we're going to make a mistake if we keep on going in this condition."

I rubbed my eyes. He was right. I pushed back from the terminal. "Okay. I'm done."

We locked everything down and left the studio. When I got to the hotel, I dragged myself to my room, undressed, and spent a good fifteen minutes scrubbing every bit of gunk off my face. I fell face-first on top of the bed and was out before I could even climb under the covers.

The perfect end to a not-so-perfect day.

Chapter Twenty-Eight

I dreamt of birds.

Beautiful rainbow-colored birds that flew among the lush jungle foliage of the Amazon. Birds that twittered, chattered and chirped. And chirped some more.

I sat up in my bed. Sun streamed into the room from a small part in the curtain. I glanced over at the clock. Ten thirty in the morning. Crap.

I stumbled to my purse and dug out my phone. It wasn't chirping anymore. I checked my phone. Low battery and I had eighteen messages.

"Jeez."

I pulled up the call log first. Seven calls were from my mother, one from my brother, Rock, one from my dad, three from Finn, one from Ken, my assistant at X-Corp, three from a series of unknown numbers (probably Slash), two from Cartwright and six from Kyle. All were from this morning.

I called Kyle. He answered the phone on the first ring.

"Where have you been?"

"The hotel. I overslept."

"You'd better get down here."

I pushed my hair out of my face and tried to get my brain to focus. "Why? What happened?"

"We've got another note. This one is for you specifically."

"I'm on my way."

It took me five minutes to get ready and five more to jog to the studio. When I got there, Kyle waved me into his office and closed the door once I got there.

"What do you have?" I said dropping into a chair.

"An email. It came to your account, but I was checking all incoming messages and I flagged it."

"What did he say?"

"He warned you to let his votes stand or else."

"Or else what?"

Kyle handed me a piece of paper.

I admire your tenacity and persistence, Lexi. You are making an admirable effort. But you cannot and will not catch me. It's elementary, my dear Watson. If you try to catch me again or alter the outcome I expect, be warned that I will not hesitate to show my displeasure. I am in full control of your destiny.

"Sherlock Holmes." I handed the paper back to Kyle. "Has Cartwright seen it?"

"Not yet. Should I forward it to him?"

"Yes, and tell him I'm on it."

Kyle shook his head. "Cartwright is going to crap his pants. Our cracker is escalating."

"Good."

"Aren't you worried?"

"I know what I'm doing, Kyle."

"Okay. I trust you."

"We just have to sit tight until the voting this evening. But let me give you one tip. No matter what happens tonight, you need to stay neutral. I might do things that don't seem logical to you, but I'm doing them for a very specific reason. Don't countermand me or draw attention to anything I do that may seem out of the ordinary. Most importantly, remember that appearances aren't always what they seem."

"Wow. That couldn't have been any more cryptic."

I smiled. "You're an extraordinarily sharp guy, Kyle, so I just want to make sure I don't underestimate you. Follow my lead, okay?"

"Okay, Lexi. You can count on me."

When the canned episode of *Geeks Get Some* finally began to air, the staff and I were locked up tight in the IT room. Everyone—myself excluded—was watching the show. Carlos and Noah were laughing hysterically and even Kyle and Melinda were giggling. I put earbuds in, cranked up my music, then turned my back to the screens, refusing to watch or hear myself on the television.

About five minutes before the show ended and the voting opened, I glanced up at the television. Gregg was twitching on the floor with me bent over him. Carlos and Noah were howling. I winced. Even I had to admit it didn't look good.

I took my earbuds out and clapped my hands. "Okay, everyone, show time is over. I'm glad you're all so amused. Get to work."

Carlos grinned. "Come on, Lexi. It was just getting to the good part."

"There is *no* good part. Trust me, I was there. Now let's get to work."

Chuckling, everyone headed toward their desks.

I was just about to sit down at mine when Melinda put her hand on my arm.

"Just to add my two cents. Lexi… I like Nelson the best." She smiled shyly. "He's not very attractive, but there's something really sexy about him all the same. He's got some kind of mysterious vibe to him."

"Really? You think so?"

"Totally. There's just something about him. I think he'd be your best choice."

"Thanks. I'll keep it in mind."

Kyle monitored the countdown until the voting opened. "Three…two…one. And, we're open. Incoming now."

The votes began to pour in. The sheer volume surprised me.

Kyle walked back and forth between his monitors and mine. "If he adds his votes now, we'll never find him. We'll have no surge evidence."

"We'll get him. Don't worry."

Carlos sounded agitated. "But the votes are pouring in. It's unbelievable. We've never had this volume before. The show must be pulling in a record number of viewers."

Melinda's fingers tapped on the keys. "But how do we find him? Lexi, he could be adding votes anywhere."

I kept my voice calm. "We're going to get him."

Noah laughed. "Seriously? We've logged over four million votes in less than thirty minutes. The show hasn't even opened yet for voting in the Midwest or the West Coast. Either our hacker is hiding, waiting, or blending perfectly. Or this show has suddenly become crazy popular."

I shrugged. "It could be a combination. Doesn't matter. Either way, we're covered."

"I hope you know what you're doing, girl boss. You seem pretty relaxed."

"I do and I am. Any obvious sign of our friend?"

Kyle shook his head. "Not a thing."

Melinda leaned forward. "No anomalies on the network either. All seems in order."

"Hardware is secure," Carlos added.

"No blips on my end either." Noah glanced my way. "Come on, Lexi, aren't you going to share what traps you've set so we can keep a lookout?"

"Not yet, but soon."

"Any reason you feel you have to be so cryptic?" Noah frowned.

"Yeah, there's a reason, but you're just going to have to trust me for now."

"Okay, girl boss. Just hope you've got it under control."

"I do and I'm glad you're on board. I'll let you all know what I did when the time is right."

Four hours later the voting closed with no obvious sign that the cracker had come and gone. But I knew he had.

The IT staff looked at me questioningly.

"Now what?" Kyle asked.

I stretched my arms over my head. "Now we nab the cracker."

Chapter Twenty-Nine

Everyone's mouth dropped open.

Carlos snapped the pencil he was holding in two. "Huh? Is this some kind of joke?"

Kyle frowned. "Just how are we going to do that?"

"Yeah, and when?" asked Melinda. "Didn't our window just pass?"

I smiled. "Not really. Look, our cracker is an inside threat. He's been inside all along. Truthfully, it didn't matter how good any of our outward preparations were, he was never going to come at us that way. So, I only opened one door on the inside. My door. Everyone from SWM, or who is using SWM's internal connection to vote, came through me. I tagged everyone who came in with a tracking device on their way out. Our cracker is toast now. We'll be able to follow him from the inside out. His trail and actions are burned on those logs. But the best part is, we don't even have to hurry to catch him."

"B-but how?" Noah stammered. "A tracking device? Girl boss, is that even possible?"

I nodded, my smile widening. "Yep. It's the latest and greatest in cybersecurity technology. I've got two personal friends who just finished the prototype. From the initial results, I would estimate it should take us about two hours or less to sort through the webserver logs and nail him."

Carlos's mouth dropped open. "All of that from the webserver logs?"

"Yep." I glanced over at Kyle. "It's pretty simple, actually. I could have done it instantaneously except it will take me a bit of time to sort through the…ah, how many votes did we get tonight, Kyle?"

"One hundred and sixty-seven million."

"One hundred and sixty-seven million votes. But the bottom line is that the trail to our cracker is right in our very own webserver logs. It's a done deal."

Carlos plopped in his chair. "Wow. It almost feels anti-climactic."

I shrugged. "A lot of people don't understand that cybersecurity is really a combination of patience and persistence. Our cracker was so worried about coming *in* undetected, he didn't pay a lot of attention to how he got *out*. He never saw my tag or even knew it was possible, and therefore, I've nabbed him. So, tomorrow we end this standoff."

I stood up, did a full body stretch and then bent down to touch my toes. "We could examine the logs tonight, but we're all tired and it doesn't matter whether we tell Cartwright who the cracker is tonight or tomorrow. The server is shut down and locked up tight. No one in the company, except for us, can get in here. So tonight we rest, and tomorrow morning, after an hour or two, we celebrate and give Cartwright the good news."

Melinda yawned. "Fine with me."

Carlos gave a thumbs-up. "Whatever you say."

We gathered our stuff and Kyle locked up the room behind us. When we got in the car, Kyle turned to me.

"Bull."

I grinned. "I knew you were sharp. But I also told you to trust me."

"I do trust you. I just don't understand your game."

"It's not a game. I'm deadly serious. But it's okay to be skeptical. I'd be the same way if I was in your place."

"Look, I'm not a cybersecurity expert, but I've never heard of any such tracking device."

"Stay with me, Kyle. I've got him, okay? Just trust me."

He let out a sigh. "I sure hope you know what you're doing."

"It's already a done deal. Okay?"

"Okay."

After he dropped me off at the hotel, I took the elevator to my room—completely exhausted. I keyed open the door and literally jumped two feet in the air, my heart racing.

Slash sat in the chair at my desk. He was no longer dressed like Nelson Soddenbag. Instead he wore a long-sleeved black T-shirt and jeans.

"*Aaagh!* How did you get in here?"

He raised an eyebrow.

I pressed a hand to my chest. "Okay, never mind. I retract that question. How did it go at the mansion?"

"Your plan went off without a hitch."

"Were all the guys in the mansion accounted for?"

He stretched out his legs. "*Si*. Every single one. No one departed the premises. It was quite unfortunate too, as the electricity in the mansion went out for just over two hours. We didn't know what to do with ourselves."

I grinned. "Wow, you are good. What about the wireless? Were you able to pull that off, too?"

"What's the point of being a gazillionaire if you don't have access to a satellite or two?"

"Way to go, Nelson. The guys were completely off the grid. You're amazing. Well, that only confirms my suspicions."

Interest lit his eyes. "Which are?"

"I know who did it. I think I've known all along."

"I take it the voting was compromised again."

"It sure was. He took my bait, hook, line and sinker."

"I had no doubt."

I walked over to my laptop, opened it up and logged on. "He's going to come back tonight to try to wipe the webserver logs. He has to. But what he won't know is that he'll be wiping dummy logs and tripping an alarm that leads to my computer. Now, I just have to be patient."

My phone chirped. I unplugged it from the dock, checked who was calling, and then answered it. "Hey, Dad. What's up? Why are you calling me so late?"

"It's not your father. I called on his phone because I *knew* you wouldn't answer if I called you."

"*Mom!*"

"Are you starring in a dating show? Don't you dare lie to me."

My thoughts raced. What in the world could I say that would explain this in a way that would make sense to my mother? "Ah…"

"Karen Culpepper just called. She said she saw you on a dating show and that you stunned a man."

"Mom, I did *not* stun him!"

She gasped. "So, it's true? Lexi, if you needed help

with dating, why didn't you just ask me? For the love of God, I'm your mother. You don't know how deeply this wounds me."

I turned my back toward Slash and tried to speak softly. "Mom, look, I don't need help with my love life."

"No, of course not." Her voice raised to a near shriek. "That's why you have to go on national television to meet men. Karen said you stunned one man and knocked out another. She said she'd never laughed so hard. Dare I even ask what happened to the rest of them?"

"I did *not* knock anyone out. One guy tripped and hit his nose on the table. Another one accidentally stunned himself with my stun gun. The rest of the guys are fine. I think."

She moaned so loudly, I held my phone away from my ear. "I can't believe this is happening. Karen's daughter is two years younger than you and she's already engaged. To an attorney. Why can't you do that? What normal man is going to want to go out with you after this mockery? First you nearly get yourself killed in Rome and then you run off to Hollywood to meet men. Do you realize what you are doing to your reputation?"

"Mom, I appreciate your concern, but I've got everything under control."

"You stunned a man. How is that under control?"

"Oh, I'm sorry, Mom, you're breaking up. It must be a bad connection. I'll talk to you later. Love you."

I punched the button on my phone, tossed it on the desk and turned to face Slash. "That was my mom. Are you trying not to laugh?"

"Guilty." He chuckled. "She see the show tonight?"

"Worse. Her best friend saw it."

"You okay?"

"Not really. My mother always makes me feel like breaking something."

"Mothers. It can be a delicate relationship."

"You have no idea. She may look fragile, but she rolls over me like a steamroller."

"Sounds like you handled her just fine."

"I wish."

Slash stood. "Come sit next to me, *cara*." He sat on the bed and patted the spot beside him.

I stared at him. "You want me to sit with you on the bed?"

"Unless you'd rather do something else. I'm open to suggestions."

"That was a sexual innuendo, right?"

He smiled. "Right."

I considered it. Sex with Slash, that is. I was confident that sex with him would be interesting, enlightening, and…fun. I'd read enough books, including those with illustrations, to realize that there was a high statistical probability of significant pleasure with him. I also knew from a biological standpoint that sex was good for relieving tension, reducing stress, and releasing relaxing hormones. It sounded like exactly what the doctor would order—except sex with Slash also carried an emotional component. I wasn't sure I was ready for that. Certainly not tonight when I was exhausted and needed to stay focused on catching my cracker.

I decided to clarify. "We can just sit and relax without the sex, right? I need to keep sharp."

"Whatever feels right to you, *cara*. If you want to sit and relax, that's what we'll do."

I joined him and he put his arm around me.

"Now, about your mother. She loves you. Love can bring out the best and worst in people."

"I guess. Maybe I'm just tired."

"*Si,* you need to rest."

"I wish. I have to concentrate on the matters at hand."

"Like the results of the vote, as skewed as they may be?"

"Oh, I already know who will get voted off once I adjust the votes. But that's a moot point at this stage of the game."

"As one of the contestants vying for your heart, I take exception to the dismissive tone of your voice."

I rolled my eyes. "Oh, so *that's* why you want to know? Okay, I'll tell you. Nelson is still in. Strangely enough, you garnered the second most votes. You're a popular guy. Even Melinda said you were sexy. Plus, I'll throw in my vote for you. That should keep you safe."

"Lucky me, and I mean that sincerely. So, how am I doing really?"

"At what?"

"Winning the heart of the girl, of course."

I laughed. How was it that he usually knew just what to say?

"Ah, well, truthfully, Nelson is light years ahead of the others."

"Excellent news. My plan is right on schedule then."

"You have a plan?"

"*Cara*, I *always* have a plan. Not that things *ever* go according to plan with you, but I'm rarely without one." He grinned. "So now we wait?"

"Yes. He knows he has to destroy the evidence that will lead me to him. Even better, he has to physically go to the office to do it. Once he starts trying to wipe the dummy logs, he'll trip my alarm. I should have plenty of time to go to the studio and confront him."

Slash held up a hand. "Stop right there. You're going to *confront* him?"

"Well, yes. How else would I do it?"

"And you were planning on doing this alone?"

"Well, we're talking about a cracker, not a murderer. I sincerely doubt he'd get violent."

"He certainly will not with me around."

"Slash, you don't have to come."

"Now you're insulting me. What would you do if he did turn violent? Do you have a plan for that?"

"I can handle myself."

"On a keyboard, yes. Now, you're so physically exhausted, you're about to drop. Which is why I'm excusing your apparent lapse of good judgment."

I sighed. "You're not going to budge on this, are you?"

"No."

"Okay, then you can come."

"Glad that's settled." He shook his head. "Now, Madame Chuck Norris, come and let's have a rest."

"Ha ha. Very funny."

"Exhaustion is not funny. You need to keep sharp. I mean that. A little rest can go a long way."

He was right, so we adjusted our position so that we were sitting together on the bed, our backs padded with pillows up against the headboard. He kept his arm around me and I enjoyed his warmth.

"You know, I'm not tired from trying to catch the hacker, believe me. It's all this other social crap that's wearing me out."

"Ah, yes. The indignity of suffering through meaningless conversation and fending off male advances."

I leaned my head on his shoulder, closed my eyes. "Fine. Go ahead and make fun of me."

He kissed my head. "That's difficult to do when I adore you so."

"Hmm."

"You haven't even had time to heal properly from Rome. Your body, your soul, they both need nourishing." He began to stroke my hair. His hands were so gentle and soft, I almost purred.

"That feels really nice."

"I'm glad."

He shifted behind me on the bed, cradling me between his legs and moving his hands down to my neck and shoulders to massage a knot in my right shoulder. As he worked the knot out, the tension of the night begin to slip away.

"Slash, can I ask you something?"

"Of course."

"Why is it that you've always been so…patient with me in terms of a physical relationship?"

His hands stilled. "What do you mean?"

"I mean you've been restrained for lack of a better word. There were opportunities you could have pushed to advance that part of the picture, for example now, but you never did. Well, sometimes, in the past, there were moments, but you mostly held back. I think. Why?"

He took me by the shoulders and pulled my back against his chest, slipping his arms around me. He rested his chin against the top of my head.

"Ah, *cara*. You have been a dilemma for me from

the start. I'm not even sure how to say it. I suppose you could say I've tried very hard to honor your boundaries."

"I have boundaries?"

He nodded. "*Si*. I've watched you for some time to see if you were ready, until I finally realized that when you were, you'd let me know. Pushing against those boundaries would only push you away."

"I'm mystified. I somehow exude a boundary?"

"You do."

"Well, how do I adjust it?"

He kissed my hair. "I cannot say. When you are ready, you just will. Then I will know."

There he was being all cryptic again, saying how I would just *know* when I'd be ready for sex, a relationship, or both. He offered no criteria, standard or variables. Just a feeling. Ugh.

I tried to fight the heaviness of my eyelids, knowing I had to stay up to listen for the alarm. "By the way, you can stop eating humble pie now. You did a good job of making up."

"Ah, but I haven't even used all the forks in my disposal."

I smiled. "Save them. You might need them again."

"Excellent point."

I shifted and curled into him. "I'm just going to stay here for a minute or two. Okay?"

"Okay. Close your eyes, *cara*, and rest. I'll listen for your alarm."

Chapter Thirty

I wasn't sure how much time had passed when Slash gently shook me. "Time to wake up. The alarm is sounding."

My eyes flew open and I scrambled off the bed. "I fell asleep? What time is it?"

"Three-twenty."

"I was asleep for that long?"

"Don't worry. The alarm just tripped."

"Thanks." I staggered to my computer. I sat at the desk and blinked a couple of times to bring the screen into focus before typing in some commands.

Slash leaned over me. "Is it him?"

"Yes. I *knew* it! He's in. Let's go."

"I'll drive. It'll be faster."

I didn't waste time arguing. We arrived at the studio in about five minutes and the night guard let us through. I parked away from the studio and we headed over on foot. Slash took my hand and held it. It felt right. I was glad he came with me.

There was no guard at the front door, but Tony had given me the code. I punched it in, and Slash went in first, holding his finger to his lips.

The hallway was dark and deserted, except for emer-

gency lighting along the floor. We crept down the hallway. I keyed in the code on the IT door and Slash pulled
it open quietly. The room was dark, but a light from a
screen glowed in one corner of the room. A dark figure
with its back to us hunched over the keyboard.

Slash let the door close with a bang just as he snapped
on the lights. Noah whirled around and jumped up from
his chair.

"Good God in heaven, girl boss. You scared the hell
out of me. What are doing here?"

I frowned. "I could ask the same of you, Noah."

Slash leaned back against the door, crossing arms
loosely across his chest. He looked mean and lean, even
with a walking cast on one foot. I was glad he'd come
with me after all.

Noah's eyes darted nervously between the two of
us. "I, uh, couldn't wait to see who was the cracker."

"Really? So you decided to come back in the middle
of the night to find him? In the dark?"

"Why not? I couldn't sleep."

I walked past him, examined his monitor. "So, your
investigation involves wiping the webserver logs?"

"I wasn't wiping them. I was examining them."

"That's not what I see."

"Oops. My bad. I just got really excited when you
said we could trace the hacker this way. I couldn't wait
until tomorrow to find out who it was. I admit I got a
little overenthusiastic. I should have called you. I apologize."

"Noah, you were wiping the logs."

He started breathing faster. "No, no. It's a mix-up."

"No it isn't." I pulled out a chair and sat backward

on it, facing him. "Okay, let's talk. Why did you do it, Noah?"

"Do what?"

"Manipulate the votes. Threaten Cartwright. Write the manifestos."

He started to look panicked. "I didn't. You've got this all wrong. I swear. It's probably one of the contestants."

"The contestants were effectively ruled out this evening with a surprise power and wireless failure at the mansion."

"What? That's impossible."

"Not really. Not if you have the right people on your team, at least."

His eyes widened and nostrils flared. "Then it must be someone else."

I crossed my arms against my chest, decided how best to approach this. "So, Noah, if I were to review the webservers, none of it would trace back to you?"

"I... I..."

I waved a hand. "Come on, let's just skip this part and cut to the chase. I trapped you. I already knew our so-called hacker was an insider. I even suspected it was someone among the IT staff. I've been pretty sure it was you for some time and for a number of reasons, which is why I *let* you manipulate those votes tonight. I also knew you'd return to wipe the logs clean. In your defense, it really was the smart thing to do. So, let's take a look at the big picture. I set a trap, you took the bait, and here we are. Why, Noah? That's what matters to me now."

"You've got this all wrong. It's not me. You're just fishing."

"Wrong. I've got the proof in the ancillary evidence

that I've safely stored away. These are dummy logs you are fiddling in, Noah. I would never have left them unprotected. The trail leads to you and we both know it. So, let's not waste time on denial. I want to know why you did it."

"I... I..."

"The truth. You owe it to me."

His lips began to tremble. "Look, I didn't plan on hurting anyone, Lexi. Really. I just wanted the studio to know that the portrayal of people like me on *Geeks Get Some* was really mean and insulting. I thought fooling around with the votes would be enough to scare them."

"It was a power trip."

"No, I was making a *statement*. A *political* statement. I was standing up to them for people like you and me. You understand that, right?"

"No, I don't. A manifesto and some threatening notes with veiled threats couched in Hollywood movie references? That does *not* equal a political statement."

"Yes it does. I was trying to talk to them in their own words. Don't you get it? Hollywood movies seemed the best way to catch their attention, to mock them the way they were mocking me."

"For God's sake, can't you see how seriously immature that is? You could have cost everyone their jobs, Noah, including your own. We're talking livelihoods here. Cartwright was ready to fire the entire IT staff and most of his personal staff as well."

"I didn't really think he'd do it, and so what if he did? I'm smart. I'm not worried about finding a new job."

"That makes you not only arrogant and immature, but really stupid as well. I wouldn't be so certain about finding a new job. I assure you, getting fired right out of the gate isn't something so easy to overcome in a career."

"I guess I didn't consider that. I... I'm sorry."

"That's not enough." I scooted my chair closer, leaned into him. "This is how I see it. You got sucked into the power of the crack. Thought it was cool to be a bully, to lord that power over everyone else."

"No, it wasn't like that. I just wanted them to stop."

"So, instead of using your brain, you became a guy who used intimidation to get his way. Sounds like a bully to me."

Noah shook his head vigorously. "No. That's not what I intended. It's not. It's just you can't fathom the intimidation, the ridicule, the jokes and cruelty I've gotten."

"Oh, really? What makes you think you're so special, Noah? Do you truly think I haven't experienced that same kind of bullying? Except you forgot to add blatant sexism, jokes about my clothes, taunts for ruining the grading curve, never getting asked to dances or out on dates, and never *ever* getting invited to parties, not that I would have gone even if I had been invited. Still, I assure you, girls can be far more cruel and catty when it comes to bullying other girls. You men get off easy, trust me."

His eyes began to water. "You got bullied?"

"I can't believe you just asked me that."

"I guess... I didn't think."

"No, you haven't thought at all, which is why we're sitting here right now."

Tears spilled down his cheeks. "I added to that, didn't I? I bullied you about being a female tech head. I... I posted the video of you in the shower online."

I heard Slash growl low in his throat and wondered what I'd do if he strode past me and beat the crap out of Noah. Maybe I'd let him.

But just thinking of the video made me sick to my stomach again. "Yes, you did, Noah. That video…it hurt me a lot. It's the worst I've ever been bullied in my life. The boy who got bullied turned into a master at the very thing he despised. But I didn't let it knock me down, no matter how much it hurt. You know why, Noah? Because the power of a bully—any bully—is just an illusion. You alone hold the power of your identity. Get comfortable in your skin or you aren't going anywhere but down."

He started to sob. "Oh, my God. I totally screwed up. I wasn't going to hurt anyone."

"Yes you were. You're a cracker. It's illegal, it's wrong, and you did it with a specific threat of economic ruin and misfortune. You *violated* me. What's worse is that you *knew* better. You have wicked skill. You're way smarter than that, and yet you dumbed yourself down in a stupid attempt to hurt others. You lashed out at others and end up hurting only yourselves and others who have endured the same bullying as you."

He took off his glasses, tears smearing the lenses. "I can't tell you how sorry I am, Lexi. I can't believe how much I messed up. Please, I'm so, so sorry."

"Sorry isn't going to cut it, Noah. You do realize your actions will likely add up to ten to fifteen years in prison. White collar crime is still a serious crime and punishable by significant jail time."

He paled drastically. "Jail? I can't go to jail. Oh, God, no." He cried in earnest now, fat tears streaming down his cheeks.

"Cracking equals jail. You did this to yourself."

He moaned. "No, no, no. I never meant it to go this far."

"Even worse, you took the crack directly to *me*. To *my* family. To *my* friends. You called *me* out, Noah. You made it personal, so now you suffer the consequences."

He covered his face and sobbed so hard, water leaked between his fingers. "I just wanted you to stop. I was scared you'd catch me and you did. I thought if you were busy with the contestants, you wouldn't have time to look for me. I wouldn't have done anything to the studio. It was all just fake bravado. I swear."

"You threatened them. You threatened me."

"No." He wailed. "I would never have hurt you or them. I swear. I just wanted to make the studio pay for the way they were portraying geeks. It was a game, that's all. I was going to scare them into shutting down the show."

"Cracking is *never* a game, which is why it carries harsh legal penalties."

"I… I didn't consider that. Oh, God."

The room was silent except for his rasping sobs. After a minute, I snapped my fingers.

"Stop crying, Noah. Turn it off and listen to me."

He kept weeping into his hands, his whole body quivering. He gulped a few mouthfuls of air, looked at me and then started bawling again.

"Noah." I raised my voice. "Jeez, Noah. Look at me."

He lifted his tear-stained face. His skin was red and blotched, his eyes still leaking tears, and his expression miserable.

"Listen to me. Okay?"

He nodded, drew an unsteady breath, and wiped his nose with the back of his hand.

"You *will* stop cracking. You will never *ever* crack again. You're a smart, capable guy and you have an enormous amount of potential. Do me a favor and grow up already. You're not that abused little boy any more. You're a man fully capable of controlling his own destiny. Take a cue from the guys in the show. They may not have it all together, but at least they're trying. Me too, actually. Take charge of your life, but don't do it by hurting others, no matter how much they may deserve it. Do it by being smarter, and by being kinder. What you did was really, really dumb."

He nodded, fresh tears spilling down his cheeks. "I know. Oh, God, I know. I'm sorry. So sorry. And now I'm going to jail. What will my mother say?" His lower lip quivered and then he blubbered and started wailing into his hands again.

I glanced over at Slash and saw the question in his eyes. He was wondering where I was going with this. I was wondering it myself. I took a deep breath and turned back to Noah.

I said quietly, "You're not going to jail, Noah."

He lifted his tear-streaked face from his hands. "What? I'm not? But you know what I did. You have the evidence."

"Yes, I do, and I fully intend to keep it as insurance. Insurance against you *ever* doing *anything* like this again. What I am asking for is your word that you'll stop cracking and leave SWM, the show and everyone connected with it alone."

"But…but what about Cartwright?"

"I'll tell Cartwright I found the hole. I shut you down

and closed you out, even if I was never able to catch you properly. I effectively plugged the hole. I'm going to give him my guarantee, and I don't give my word lightly. But if you ever come back in any way, shape or form to harass Cartwright, the show, or anyone else at SWM, I'll hunt you down. It won't be pretty and there won't be any second chances. I'll catch you, fry you, and enjoy doing it. Do you understand me?"

He stared at me, disbelief blooming across his face. "You'll...you'll just let me go?"

"You'll have to keep your job here, at least for a while, to avoid suspicion. But my advice to you is to get out of Hollywood and do it soon. If you're looking for respect and sincerity, you're *not* going to find it in Hollywood. Find your niche and passion, but for God's sake, keep it legal."

Noah's eyes shimmered with tears and shock. "You'd...you'd do that for me?"

"Only if I have your word. Swear it. Hacker to hacker. Geek to geek. When I leave here, you'll still have access to the system, so I'm taking a big professional and personal risk doing this. Don't make me sorry."

"Oh, my God. I won't. I won't, Lexi. I swear it."

"You *will* leave cracking behind you. Forever. From this moment on."

"Yes. Forever." Noah kept his eyes on me as he held out a trembling hand. I took it and we shook. "I swear to you, Lexi Carmichael. Geek to geek. I swear I'll never crack again."

He dropped my hand and started a fresh burst of crying. "I can't believe it. No one has ever done anything this nice for me. *Ever.*" He started blubbering. "I'm going to pay it forward. I really will."

"I know and I sincerely believe that or I wouldn't be doing this. Now get out of here. Go home, get some sleep, and show up here in the morning, acting as if nothing happened tonight. I'm going to fix the real logs. You'd better do a good job of acting or else you're toast."

"I will. I really will." He scrambled to his feet. "Thank you, Lexi. Oh, my God, thank you so much."

He ran to the door, but Slash still blocked it. He was frowning and had pushed his leather jacket aside so his gun clearly showed. His arms were crossed against his chest and he looked mad and dangerous. Noah noticed the gun and started shaking.

He looked nervously between Slash and me. "Um, who exactly is he?"

My gaze met Slash's across the room. Suddenly I knew. Of all the times in the world for it to happen, in that crazy instant in time, my boundaries shifted.

I knew.

"That's…my boyfriend."

Noah gasped. "What? *He's* your boyfriend?"

My eyes didn't leave Slash's. "I guess so."

Slash's smile spread across his face slow and easy. Then he leaned down close to Noah and spoke in a low voice. "You are lucky. If it were up to me, I'd snap your neck for that shower stunt. Let's make one thing clear. If you betray her trust in you, she won't be the only one hunting you. Do you understand me?"

Noah gulped. "Y-yes, sir."

Slash stared at him for a tad longer than necessary. Noah's legs were trembling so badly and I thought he might collapse. Slash gave him one last menacing look and then stepped aside.

Uttering a small cry, Noah threw open the door and

ran out. His footsteps echoed down the hallway. After a moment, I heard the main door to the studio slam shut.

"You scared the living crap out of him," I said.

"Good."

I blew out a breath and walked over to Noah's terminal. I sat down and started working on his computer. Slash pulled up a chair and sat beside me, but said nothing while I worked. I had no idea how much time passed until I was finished. When I was done, I leaned back and swiveled my chair toward him. I felt old and really, really tired.

Slash reached out and took my injured hand, capturing it between his. His thumb gently rubbed the sore spot in the center of my palm. "Tell me. Why did you do it, *cara?* Why did you let him go?"

I looked down at my hand, caught between his. "I'm not sure. I did it because…he's me. No, I'm him. What I mean to say is that I understand him. Don't misunderstand me. What he did was wrong. I'm not in any way condoning that. All the same, I believed him. I don't think he intended any actual harm. Besides, his crack backfired. SWM didn't suffer economically and, in fact, he probably made the studio more money than they might have ever expected from an inane show like this. The guys on the show got a kinder, albeit inept, girl to interact with. And maybe, just maybe, I'm feeling benevolent because somehow in the midst of this insanity, I found a boyfriend."

He smiled. "It looks like I arrived on the show just in time."

"Looks like it."

I tried to ignore the pounding headache that had started behind my eyes. "You know, I meant it, Slash, when I said I'd fry him if he ever came back. I know him now. I know his methods, his style, and his signature. I'd find him again, and he's smart enough to know it. I don't think he'll ever crack again."

"Agreed. Still, I would have tossed him in jail. He was arrogant and stupid. A dangerous combination. But you have a tender heart."

"You could have stopped him, you know. Stopped me from doing it."

"*Si*, I could have, but it wasn't my call. It was yours. While I might not agree that the punishment fits the crime, I still think you did the right thing." He stroked my cheek with the pads of his fingertips. "You did some fine acting yourself tonight."

"You liked that bit about the prototype?"

"It was risky. He might have known there is no such thing."

"Maybe, but it was doubtful. I didn't lie when I said he has wicked skill, but he isn't my caliber. Not yet anyway. All the same, I think he needed that last push to believe I had him."

Slash leaned forward and pressed a soft kiss on my mouth. "You are, by far, the most extraordinary woman I've ever met."

I sighed as he cupped my face with his hands.

This time he kissed me longer and more thoroughly. He was so gentle and tender, it nearly brought tears to my eyes.

"Mine," he murmured against my lips.

We stayed there for a moment in silence. He finally pulled me to my feet. "Let's get you back to the hotel and to bed. You are about to drop."

I didn't have it in me to argue. "I'm going to need all

my strength to face Cartwright in the morning and tell him I've caught the hacker and I'm leaving the show."

Slash put his arm around me as we headed out of the IT room. "He's not going to be happy to hear that."

"I know."

"But you'll handle him."

"Yes. I've got an idea I think will make everyone happy."

He grinned. "At least you have no worries about poor Nelson. He's already deliriously happy."

I smiled. "Well, there you have it then. The hardest part is already done."

Chapter Thirty-One

Slash was waiting for me in the parking lot at the studio. He leaned against a black sports car. Dark sunglasses covered his eyes, and he smiled when he saw me.

"How'd it go?" he asked when I reached him.

"It was touch and go for a while. It took me some time to bring Cartwright around, but thankfully everyone else was on board."

"Everyone?"

"Pretty much. Cartwright wasn't exactly happy, but he didn't have a lot of room to maneuver."

He reached out, took my hand. "What was your solution?"

"The show goes on, just without me. In place of me will be Basia. Thank goodness Finn approved. Basia will spend the rest of the series helping the remaining guys truly learn how to interact with girls. The intention is for her to help set them up with real-life young women chosen from online profiles. She'll view the profiles with each of the guys and try to help them find the qualities she thinks will best match their personalities. Then they will go out on dates with the girls they choose. Each episode will be filmed and afterwards, Basia will offer them a gentle critique or pointers to help them improve their skills. All this dumb stuff about hot tubs, marriage proposals and extreme, not to mention uncomfortable, situations is over."

"The contestants agreed?"

"It wasn't too hard to bring them around. After all, it's why they came on the show in the first place. At first they tried to talk me into staying, but technically, this solution was much more appealing to them. Cartwright finally agreed after the studio executives gave it the green light. There wasn't much they could do anyway. The season is near its end anyway, plus Finn had it spelled out in no uncertain terms that I was gone as soon as I caught the hacker. They didn't want to cancel the show, but they couldn't continue as they were. So, they had to make a choice. Right now *Geeks Get Some* is ridiculously popular. I'm sure Cartwright will get his PR team to spin the new development in their favor."

"Of that, I have no doubt. What about the voting?"

"Oh, the voting will continue as well. The audience will decide who has improved the most. The voting system is secure now and I'll bring Kyle up to speed on everything I did, including how to keep an eye out for an insider threat."

"So, your moment in the television spotlight is finished?"

"Pretty much, although I agreed to come back for the final show this season. I balked at first, but it was Basia's idea for a compromise and it did help bring Cartwright and the studio execs to our side. Plus, Cartwright was pretty upset by the abrupt departure of Nelson Soddenbag."

"Ah, yes, that was quite unfortunate."

"He'll probably never ask Nelson to come back."

"I assure you, Nelson considers himself fortunate."

"Also Cartwright got this bright idea to do one whole show on the situation with the cracker. How I got stuck on the show and eventually how I shut him down. It will be part of a two-hour finale. They expect a fantastic ratings night. I have to come back to be interviewed about my role in it. It's all a bunch of crock, but I can manage it, I suppose."

"You'll do just fine. So, you convinced Cartwright the cracker is gone and the holes are plugged?"

I leaned against the car next to Slash. "He really has no choice but to take my word for it. I could explain what I did six ways to Sunday and he still wouldn't have a clue what I was talking about. In some ways Noah was correct in his manifesto. People who control the ins and outs of cyberspace are the new force in the universe. It's looking more like the geeks, and not the meek, shall inherit the Earth."

Slash nodded. "*Si*, it's a new world out there." He lifted his face to the sun. "You ready to go home?"

"You have no idea how much. I already had Glinda make my plane reservations home. I've got to tie up some loose ends here and I should be home by tomorrow evening. How about you? Are you headed back to DC or New York?"

He smiled. "I'll be wherever my girl is."

It was harder than I expected to say goodbye to everyone. I decided to do the guys first. Tony drove me out to the mansion. When I arrived, they were playing "The Elder Scrolls 5: Skyrim." They looked up when I came in.

Eldrick hopped off the floor and approached me first. "Hey, Lexi. How did it go with Cartwright?"

I gave him a fist bump. "It's a done deal. You guys start shooting the new scenes tomorrow with Basia."

Gregg swaggered toward me. "Baby, that's really good news, although I'm sorry you're leaving. I felt as if we were just getting to know each other better. So, how well do you know this Basia woman? Think you could put in a good word for me? She's hot and looks like a smart woman. She might be able to fully appreciate my mojo."

I rolled my eyes. "Listen to me, Gregg. You are *not* going to hit on Basia. She's just going to help you find a woman with whom you might actually be compatible."

Truman slapped Gregg on the shoulder. "Dude, finding that girl for you would be a true miracle."

I shrugged. "If anyone can do it, Basia can."

Gregg frowned. "I think everyone is underestimating the power of my mojo. Need I remind this group that I was the only one who got anywhere near Lexi's lips."

I grinned. "Just a word of advice, Gregg. Stay away from girls with stun guns. It's not a good mix for you."

He crossed his heart. "Okay, baby. It's a deal on that one."

Truman edged Gregg to the side. "So, Lexi, are you going back to the East Coast now?"

"Yep. That's where I live. But the next time I'm out here, I'll look you up. I'm sincerely looking forward to that tour of Black of Night you promised me."

"Great. You know, I sometimes get spooky cases in New England. Wouldn't be too hard for me to make a trip down to the nation's capital sometime to say hello."

"Sure, anytime."

To my surprise, Anson suddenly enveloped me a hug. "I'm going to miss you, Lexi. Can we stay in touch?"

"I don't see why not. Plus, it would be prime if you could pass on a discount or two from any of the excellent Wicked Fish games. Most of the stuff coming out of the company these days is first-rate."

"I can do that and go one better. I'd be happy to give you some hints on getting past the Seismic Sorcerer."

"Sweet." I gave him a high five. "I'd appreciate it."

Ray came next and he gave me a hug, too. "I wanted you to be the first to know—well, after Tanya—that I've been contacted about cutting a demo album. I wouldn't have had that opportunity if it wasn't for you."

"I don't think that's true, but it's great news, Ray. Let me know when your album is out so I can buy it."

"Thanks. I may just write a song for you."

"I hope it's not some sappy thing."

He chuckled. "No, it will be something along the lines of the cheeky, geeky girl who put me on the right path."

I thought about it. "If you put it that way, I say go with the sappy thing."

He laughed and I looked over his shoulder and saw Barnaby. He looked forlorn, standing to the side of the group, watching me and waiting.

I disengaged from Ray and walked over him. "Hey, Barnaby. I came to say goodbye."

"I know."

"Okay, so, goodbye. I wish you luck in all of your endeavors."

He studied me for a moment. "Did you mean it?"

"Yes. I really do wish you luck with your endeavors."

"No, not that. Did you mean it, back at the comic

book convention, when you said you would be interested in talking to the real me?"

"Do I look like a person who goes around saying random nice things to people for no reason?"

He smiled. "No."

"Then I meant it."

"But *why* did you say it? What do you see in me that would give you any indication I would be interesting to talk to?"

I looked at him, considering. "Well, for one, you have a photographic memory like I do. You have an enormous capability to remember and recall facts and information, not to mention quotes. As a result, it's logical to extrapolate that you have a valuable—not to mention fascinating—amount of data stored in that brain of yours. In my experience, vast knowledge usually equals unique and intriguing insights and perspectives. I could easily see us talking for many hours about a wide variety of topics. Plus you are a theoretical physicist, which interests me on a personal level. Therefore, that's why I would be interested in talking to the real you as opposed to Ab'Jona, the sock puppet."

"I'm not good at real conversation."

"I'm not either. But at least I try. I don't hide behind props. What you see is what you get. It doesn't always work, but it moves me forward at the very least."

"Fair enough. Do you really think Basia can help me? I need to learn to interact better with stakeholders to solicit increased funding for my projects."

I nodded. "She can. Truthfully, I've come a long way in regards to interaction with others and a true social life thanks to her. She'll make you go outside your comfort zone, but that's okay. I've found stepping outside the zone is critical to developing all relationships, stake-holders or personal. But whatever you decide, Barnaby, I'm leaving you in capable hands."

"I will consider all you have said. Thank you, Lexi, for many things. You have influenced me more than you may realize."

I patted his shoulder. "I expect great things from you. You've got this."

"I'll keep you posted on my progress."

"I'd like that."

I waited a beat, but it didn't come. No *Repercussions* quote, no Shangra farewell gesture, no nothing. Optimism swept through me and I grinned as he turned back to the television and joined the others in the game.

Tony drove me back to the studio in his convertible. The top was down and despite the fact it was early December, the sun shone brightly and my spirits were high. Tony cranked the music and a screaming guitar howled along with the wind in my ears.

Shortly before we reached the studio, Tony turned down the radio. "Hey, Lexi, it's going to be really boring without you around here."

"I sincerely doubt that. Plus I'll be back for the finale."

"Can't wait." Tony laughed again and stepped on the gas again. I leaned back in the seat and closed my eyes.

When we got back to the studio, I stopped by my old dressing room to wish Basia good luck and say good-bye to Ace, Rena and Mandy.

I was surprised to once again feel a tug at my heart-strings. I'd become rather fond of all of them. I wondered if that meant my emotional intelligence was stretching and growing. Everyone gave me a hug and I didn't mind in the slightest.

The biggest hug came from Basia.

"Look, I *so* owe you for taking my place," I said as I hugged her. "I don't know how to thank you."

"You are so wrong. No owing or thanking is involved. Friends do it for love. Besides, this is a job and I've got it covered. You need to go back to Washington, hunt down some more crackers, and make sure X-Corp stays in business so we can both stay employed."

I smiled. "Deal."

I left the group as soon as they began talking about Basia's wardrobe for the upcoming session. I was so thankful it wasn't me, I had a spring to my step.

When I reached the IT room and went inside, everyone started clapping. A dozen balloons were tied to my swivel chair and a big sign that said *Goodbye, Lexi* hung below one of the giant television screens.

I looked around in astonishment. "What's this?"

Carlos blew a noisemaker in my face. It unfurled and snapped back while Melinda brought me some flowers.

"It's your going-away party," she said.

"A party? For me."

Noah stepped forward, met my eyes evenly, calmly. His eyes were still swollen and puffy, but it could have easily been explained away by exhaustion. More importantly, I saw a gratitude and newfound determination in them, and felt better for it.

Noah nodded. "You stopped the cracker. You saved our jobs and we are beyond thankful for it."

I met Noah's gaze for a moment and then nodded. "Well, you're all welcome. It didn't require a party though."

The team moved aside and Kyle walked toward me, carrying a large platter with a chocolate cake in the shape of a computer monitor. The cake read in green squiggly lines *Thanks, Lexi.*

We'll miss you.

Kyle held out the cake. "Noah is right. It did require a party. You went the extra mile for us. Even if we're not sure exactly how you did it, we're pretty appreciative that you did."

I looked around at their faces and knew they would be okay. Even Noah. No, *especially* Noah.

I held out my hands, took the cake. "Okay, well, in that case, I've got dibs on the piece that says Lexi."

Kyle grinned at me and nodded. "Only fair. It's all yours."

Chapter Thirty-Two

I put away the rest of my clothes in the dresser and shoved the suitcase under my bed. After changing my clothes, I headed into the kitchen in light blue sweatpants and a long-sleeved white T-shirt. My feet were happily bare and I wound my hair up in a ponytail as I walked. It felt nice to be home, even if it meant my mother would likely be coming over in the morning.

A knock sounded just as I stepped into the kitchen. Puzzled, I turned around and opened it.

Slash leaned against the doorjamb. He was dressed in his black leather jacket and jeans, and he smelled amazing, as usual.

My mouth dropped open. "Y-you knocked. You *never* knock."

He smiled. "There's a first time for everything."

"I'm really surprised."

He paused. "Are you going to invite me in?"

I stood in the doorway. "Look, Slash, I've been thinking. I'm not sure this is a good idea. I've never had a boyfriend before."

"I'm honored to be the first."

"You might want to reserve judgment on that."

"That's doubtful. I'm completely captivated by you, *cara*."

"Sure, now at the beginning of our relationship when our hormones are dancing around and we are clueless to our respective bad habits. What if I disappoint you? What if I'm the worst girlfriend in the history of girlfriends? You may be sorry you ever fell for me."

The amusement faded from his face and he sighed. "Falling for you is indeed a danger, but not in the way you think."

I blew out a breath. "I'll be honest. I'm just worried this situation could get really complicated. I don't do well with non-mathematical abstracts, especially feelings. I'm not even sure what love is. Something like that could be a deal breaker in a relationship."

"We've already had this discussion. We will *not* start defining our feelings. You will either feel it…or you won't."

"But you already know you love me. You've accepted it. You're at peace with it. I'm just figuring it all out."

"It's not a race."

I looked down at my feet. "I know. I do feel warm and happy with you, Slash. Sometimes my stomach gets all fluttery when you're around. And when you kiss me…well, it's like some kind of magic, for lack of a better expression."

"Ah, that's good to know."

We stood in silence for a moment before Slash asked, "So, now what?"

"I don't know. That's the problem. I mean what happens next? Do we go out on dates and stuff?"

"*Si*, we will go out on dates and *stuff*. That's usually how relationships work."

"Right. But there are so many other things to consider. I haven't even factored in what a serious disadvantage I have when it comes to your significant experience."

He raised an eyebrow.

"I'm not *just* talking about sexual experience, although you definitely have me at a disadvantage there as well. I would assume that, to a certain extent, sex is a learned skill. I'm pretty good at visualization, so once you show me your preferences, I should have a decent handle on things."

He chuckled. "Ah, *cara*, you are magnificent."

"Are you teasing me again?"

"Of course."

"I'm trying to be serious here. I'm worried about managing our relationship. The emotional give and take, the compromise that is required of having of boyfriend. I don't know if I'm up to the challenge. It's likely to be draining and considerably time consuming."

"Are you done?"

I thought for a moment. "Did I forget something?"

"There might be a mathematical equation you haven't factored in yet."

"Very funny."

His eyes twinkled. He reached out and lifted my chin so I looked directly into his eyes. "So, *cara*, can I come in?"

I gazed into the face I'd come to know so well, the mischievous brown eyes filled with amusement and perhaps even desire. We'd been through a lot and would probably go through a lot more before anything became clear to me. The girl with such a small horizon was taking a really, *really* big step.

"Wait here, Slash. Don't leave, okay?"

I left him at the door, went to the kitchen and rummaged around in one of the lower cabinets. When I found what I was looking for, I stood up and walked back to the door.

I was relieved to see he still waited there with a be-mused expression.

"*Cara?*"

I pulled out a bottle of wine from behind my back. It was the same bottle of wine he'd given me several months earlier while confidently announcing we'd open it on the night we first made love.

From the expression on his face, I'd surprised him, but a slow smile spread across his lips. He leaned forward and kissed me. "We're going to be really good together."

"I hope so."

"I *know* so."

I opened the door wide and stepped to the side. "Please, come in, Slash. But just so you're aware, I'm not going into this situation blind. I have a relationship plan. Sort of."

He stepped across the threshold and put his arm around me. "Ah, now *you* have a relationship plan. You're beginning to sound a lot like me."

"I know. But there's nothing wrong with a little fore-planning, right?"

"Not as long as you figure in extra time for foreplay."

"Yowza!" I said as he laughed and kicked the door shut behind us.

* * * * *

Read on for an excerpt from
No Test For The Wicked, *the next book in the Lexi Carmichael Mystery series from Julie Moffett.*

Acknowledgments

I'd like to acknowledge those people behind the scenes who provided wonderful input, suggestions, and advice while I was writing the book. As always, my Carina Press editor extraordinaire, Alissa Davis, provided amazing insights and suggestions that helped me significantly. She knows Lexi almost as well as I do! I would also like to thank my parents, Bill and Donna Moffett, and my sister—fellow author Sandy Parks—for being the first beta readers and giving me valuable comments on the story arc. Most importantly, I must thank my brilliant nephew, Kyle Moffett, who works at Google, and his lovely girlfriend, Julia Boortz, for their absolutely critical tech brainstorming, details and suggestions. However, any mistakes or poetic license in regards to technology is on me alone!

I would also like to thank the rest of the Carina team from Executive Editor, Angela James, down to the marketing and promotion team that do so much to help get Lexi and her stories out to the world. Your enthusiasm, support and advice are very much appreciated! Lastly, I would like to provide a belated kudos to Carina Editor Deb Nemeth who did a great job editing the novella *No Money Down*, and whom I inadvertently forgot to thank in the acknowledgement. You all rock!

About the Author

Julie Moffett is a bestselling author and writes in the genres of mystery, young adult, historical romance and paranormal romance. She has won numerous awards, including the Mystery & Mayhem Award for Best YA/New Adult Mystery, the prestigious HOLT Award for Best Novel with Romantic Elements, a HOLT Merit Award for Best Novel by a Virginia Author (twice!), the Award of Excellence, a PRISM Award for Best Romantic Time-Travel AND Best of the Best Paranormal Books, the EPIC Award for Best Action/Adventure Novel. She has also garnered additional nominations for the Bookseller's Best Award, Daphne du Maurier Award and the Gayle Wilson Award of Excellence.

Julie is a military brat (Air Force) and has traveled extensively. Her more exciting exploits include attending high school in Okinawa, Japan; backpacking around Europe and Scandinavia for several months; a year-long college graduate study in Warsaw, Poland; and a wonderful trip to Scotland and Ireland where she fell in love with castles, kilts and brogues.

Julie has a B.A. in Political Science and Russian Language from Colorado College, an M.A. in International Affairs from The George Washington University in Washington, DC, and an M.Ed from Liberty University. She has worked as a proposal writer, journalist, teacher, librarian and researcher. Julie speaks Russian and Polish and has two sons.

Visit Julie's website at juliemoffett.com.

Watch the Lexi Carmichael series book trailer at Youtube.com/watch?v=memhgojYeXM.

Join Julie's Facebook Reader Group at Facebook.com/groups/vanessa88.

Follow Julie on Social Media:

Facebook: Facebook.com/JulieMoffettAuthor

Twitter: Twitter.com/JMoffettAuthor

Instagram: Instagram.com/julie_moffett

Pinterest: Pinterest.ca/JMoffettAuthor

How is it possible that even though I graduated with a double degree in Mathematics and Computer Science from Georgetown University, saved the Vatican millions of euros and caught a reality television-obsessed hacker while posing as a dating contestant in Hollywood, I still can't figure out how to tell my mother I have a boyfriend?

I can visualize it now. I'll blurt out the news, she'll hug me and shriek in my ear for a while, and then the analysis will commence. My mother will ask me if he's rich, if he comes from a good family, and if he has a respectable job.

I don't know the details of his bank account and, in terms of his family, I've only met his grandmother. But regarding the job... Would a super-secret hacker spy who may (or may not) work for the Vatican, but is definitely working for the National Security Agency, qualify as respectable? I'm afraid that would be iffy.

Then my mom would want me to tell her all the gory details of how we met, whether or not he's a foreigner (he is, so that may not go over well), and if he has some weird religion. Maybe I shouldn't tell her he's on a first-name basis with the pope.

After I've been forced to give her specifics about my boyfriend's career, ethnicity and religion, she will take my hand and tell me that a June wedding would be just lovely. Besides, if we held it at the ultra-expensive Willard Hotel in Washington, DC, we could invite up to several hundred guests. By that point, I'd be so panicky and nauseated I'd upchuck on her three-hundred-dollar Manolo Blahnik leather pumps.

That's my life. My name is Lexi Carmichael and I'm a twenty-five-year-old hacker, gamer and fangirl who isn't planning on getting within spitting distance of a white dress anytime soon. Normal relationships are murky waters to navigate even if one is emotionally astute and socially capable. For those of us with less than stellar skills on these fronts, entering into a romantic relationship can be exhausting, not to mention terrifying, especially if my mother is involved.

It's hard enough for me to manage the few relationships I have outside of my boyfriend. I can count the number of close friends I have on one hand. Add in the work relationships I have to navigate, and things really get complicated. Now that I'm the Director of Information Security at X-Corp—a cyberintelligence firm right outside of Washington, DC—I have employees to manage and staff to keep busy. It wouldn't be a stretch to say it's all a bit overwhelming.

It didn't used to be that way. I once lived a relatively quiet life working as a tech head for the NSA. Not too long ago, the agency operated in relative obscurity with less than five percent of the American population even knowing that we existed. That anonymity was blown out of the water by the Edward Snowden scandal— he's the guy that filched an enormous amount of top-secret cyber information from the NSA, implicating the agency in questionable privacy actions. Now everyone in the world knows about the NSA. Although I'll be the first to admit my life has been anything *except* quiet since I joined X-Corp, at least I got out of the NSA before the scandal broke. Still, I know several decent people who continue to work at the agency in one capacity or the other, including my new boyfriend. Slash is a master hacker, one of the best I've ever met, and he also supports the NSA in other intelligence efforts, including terrorism and cyberterrorism. He is a man of many, many talents.

My office phone rang and I picked it up.

"Carmichael."

"Buon giorno, cara."

His voice was so sexy it almost made me forget how much I hated talking on the phone.

It weirded me out that my stomach felt all tingly. "Hey, Slash. *Si deframmenta la mia vita.*"

There was silence and then a soft laugh. "You are studying Italian now?"

"Isn't that a practical thing to do when one has an Italian boyfriend?"

"Not necessarily, but I'm pleased. Did you mean to say that I defragment your life?"

"Yes. Is that inappropriate?"

"No. It's perfect."

"Okay. Good. I know I have to work on the accent. I'd like to be able to say at least a few words to your grandmother in Italian the next time we meet."

"She'd love that. That reminds me, I owe you another trip to Italy, this time for pleasure. Perhaps you can meet some more of my family."

He said it casually, but my stomach flipped. He wanted me to meet more of his family.

Intellectually I knew this was part of the boyfriend-girlfriend dynamic, but it scared the heck out of me. I mean, Slash had a mother. He'd mentioned her when we were in Rome. What would I say to her? What if she couldn't speak English? And how could I look her in the eye after having engaged in sexual intercourse with her son? Oh jeez, who knew what would come out of my mouth!

Even worse, it was logical to extrapolate that if I met Slash's family, it meant he would have to meet *my* family. And that brought me back to the fact that I hadn't even *told* my family I was dating anyone. The mere thought of it made me so unnerved that I had to recite the first three lines of Fermat's Last Theorem in order to calm down. My mother had been planning my wedding since the day I was born. If I brought Slash home for dinner, there was a statistically significant chance she'd have him measured for his tuxedo before we finished the first course. Or worse, she'd pull me aside at dessert and give me the dreaded sex talk.

I started to hyperventilate. "Um, sure, Slash. That would be great someday."

He chuckled. "I didn't mean to scare you."

"Why do you think I'm scared?"

"You paused for a bit too long and then your voice quavered. Don't worry, I'm teasing you again."

"I knew that."

But I hadn't really. Slash was a geek, but he was able to read people in ways I never could. He was pretty clever and talented, that boyfriend of mine.

I heard an electronic beeping sound in the background over the phone. Where was he? Before I could ask, he spoke.

"I just called to say good morning and that I miss you. I'm not sure how my day will shape up, but I'm going to figure out a way to make sure it ends with you. Are you available?"

"Yes."

"That's my girl."

"Slash?"

"Si?"

"I like being your girl."

"Ah, that makes me so very happy." I could hear the smile in his voice. "See you soon."

"Okay. Bye."

I hung up the phone and stared at it. I'd just made casual plans with my boyfriend. This was going to take some getting used to. I'd never had a boyfriend before. Not even in high school. In fact, I'd never even had a *date* in high school. Slash has been my significant other for just a few days. A couple of wow-I-can't believe-he-can-do-that days, mind you, but I still haven't adjusted to our relationship yet. It may take me some time to get used to it. Maybe forever. That's hard to calculate in real-time terms.

While our relationship is still new, I couldn't spend all day thinking about it. Especially since I was on the clock. So, I took one more sip of my coffee, straightened the glasses on my nose and hunched over my keyboard, hoping today would be a quiet day in the office so that I could catch up on paperwork. A glance out the window confirmed the December weather in the nation's capital remained crappy—snow, ice and freezing rain. Most of the area schools had closed and more than a few X-Corp employees had called in. But hackers don't take snow days, so neither do I. Somehow I skidded and slid my red Miata all the way to Crystal City, Virginia, about a forty-five-minute drive from my apartment in Jessup, Maryland, to show up for work. I was a bit disappointed to see the continued snowfall because I had hoped the weather would ease up a bit so I could go for a late-morning donut and coffee run. Unfortunately, it would have to wait.

It was nearly noon and my stomach had started to growl when the phone rang. Internal number.

I picked up the phone and jammed it between my shoulder and ear while I continued to type. "Carmichael."

"Lexi, we have a client here. Can you meet me in conference room two?"

I stopped typing. It was Finn, my boss and onetime romantic interest. I liked Finn a lot and he liked me, but the possibility of a romantic liaison had come to a screeching halt because I couldn't handle the boss/employee aspect of our relationship. Luckily for me, Finn had been taking it well, although I wasn't sure what he'd think about me and Slash. Not that I intended to tell him about it any time soon.

"Sure, Finn. Be right there."

I logged out, then snatched my laptop in one hand and my coffee mug in the other. I swung by the kitchen, poured exactly three-fourths of a cup of coffee, added two teaspoons of creamer and one-and-a-half teaspoons of sugar in the mug and stirred it four times counterclockwise. Then I snatched a couple of Christmas cookies off a tray. Stuffing the cookies in my mouth, I walked toward the conference room.

As I passed through the outer office, where white

lights twinkled on a lovely floor-to-ceiling Christmas tree, I could hear the strains of "Joy to the World" playing softly over the loudspeaker. It made me feel warm and cozy.

I walked into the conference room. Finn sat across the table from a pretty young woman in a red suit. She had shoulder-length blond hair that curled around her chin. Her face was perfectly made-up, with just the hint of a rosy glow to her cheeks. Her hands rested atop the table and, although they were devoid of any jewelry, they were perfectly manicured with red nail polish. Next to her sat a very distinguished-looking man with gray hair and sideburns, dressed in a three-piece suit and steel-blue tie. I felt like an outlier in my purple sweater, black slacks and ponytail.

I set my laptop down on the table as both men rose. Finn swept out his hand. "Glad you could make it. Lexi, I'd like you to meet the Honorable Percival O'Neill, Ambassador of Ireland to the United States."

Jeez, I *was* underdressed. An ambassador? I hoped I'd brushed the cookie crumbs off my sweater.

The older gentleman extended a hand and I shook it firmly.

Finn nodded to the young woman, who remained seated. "This is Bonnie Swanson, Headmistress of the Excalibur Academy for the Technologically Gifted in Washington, DC."

I leaned across the table to shake her hand and she smiled at me.

"Glad to meet you." Although she looked young, she had a firm grip and a no-nonsense look to her.

After the introductions were finished, we all sat

down. Finn leaned forward, consulting what looked like several pages of notes.

He shuffled them around and then placed his hands atop the small stack. "Ambassador O'Neill and I have been talking over the phone for a couple of days. In the spirit of full disclosure, our families have been close friends for years in Ireland. He recommended X-Corp to Ms. Swanson to see if we can assist with her current situation."

I looked between the ambassador and the headmistress, wondering what kind of situation would bring the two of them together via X-Corp.

Finn leaned back in his chair and pressed his fingertips together. "I'll go ahead and let Ms. Swanson explain her situation to us."

Bonnie smiled at us around the table. "I greatly appreciate the ambassador's assistance in bringing me here to discuss this confidential matter. His daughter, Piper, is a junior at our academy, so it goes without saying that he is personally invested in helping us come to a satisfactory solution. Actually, I'm not sure whether to be embarrassed or proud of our problem, but…" She paused. "There is no easy way to say this. We can't seem to keep our students out of the school's computer system."

I grinned before quickly fashioning my face into a somber expression. Bonnie caught my smile, but to my surprise, I didn't see disapproval in her eyes, only amusement.

She looked at Finn. "So, do you think X-Corp can help us?"

Finn glanced down the table at me. "I'm sure of it. This kind of situation is Lexi's specialty."

I hadn't realized I had a specialty, but if Finn said so I wasn't going to contradict him.

Bonnie studied me. "I've seen you before."

"I'm pretty ordinary looking. A lot of people say that."

She stared at me a moment more. "No, I'm sure of it. Have you ever been on television?"

I cleared my throat. "Ah, briefly. Very briefly."

"I *knew* I'd seen you before. I rarely forget a face. Well, glad to make your acquaintance."

I mumbled and looked down at my laptop, pretending to search the web for something.

Finn spoke. "Well, if we are in agreement, we can have Lexi accompany you back to the school or come at your convenience to determine a solution to the problem."

Bonnie nodded. "Actually, today would be excellent if she is available. There are no students there now because of the weather. I'll be happy to sign the paperwork as soon as it's ready."

"Of course." Finn reached into his briefcase and pulled out a sheaf of papers. "It will take me just a few minutes to prepare them."

I stood. Both men rose to their feet.

"I, ah, thought I'd just get my things together so I'm ready to go when Ms. Swanson is."

"Call me Bonnie, please."

"Sure, Bonnie. Then you should call me Lexi."

I left the room and went to get my laptop case, a notepad, my coat and purse. The rest of my tools were either in my head or at my fingertips online.

I returned to the conference room as Finn and Bonnie were signing papers. The ambassador stood at one of the windows looking out at the city below. I walked up and stood beside him.

"It looks festive with the snow," he said.

"People around here can't drive for beans in weather like this. Adverse weather conditions, such as snow and ice, are present in nearly thirty-four percent of total vehicular crashes and nearly twenty-eight percent of highway fatalities in America. Or in other words, Americans can't drive in such conditions."

He chuckled and glanced at me sideways. "Bloody truer words I've never heard. None of them has ever seen an Irish snow. Have you ever been to Ireland?"

"No, but Finn speaks quite fondly of it."

We stood in silence for a bit before he spoke again. "So, Ms. Carmichael, did you go to a school like that?"

"Excuse me?"

"The Excalibur Academy. Did you attend a school like that?"

"No. I attended public school. My parents thought it important I get the full experience of a diverse student population."

"Did they make the right decision?"

I sighed. "Probably not. It was a waste of my time, academically speaking. But I survived."

"You look quite young. Have you been out of school long?"

I bristled, ready to snap out my list of academic and workplace accomplishments. *Wait.* I paused, then watched him. He looked curious, so maybe he hadn't meant it disparagingly. Per Basia's advice, I'd started trying to assess my conversational partner's facial expressions before I responded to any remark that seemed contentious.

I kept my tone neutral. "I graduated from Georgetown a couple of years ago. But age is not an indicator of ability. I am fully capable of handling this assignment."

He smiled. "I don't doubt that and I certainly didn't

mean to imply otherwise. I've known Finn for a long time and he has impeccable taste in people. I just wondered how long you've been into computers."

I stared at him for a moment. Where was he going with these questions?

"Truthfully? I've been into computers since I could type on the keyboard. I also had an early aptitude for math. The two subjects meshed quite well for me."

He nodded. "It's been the same for my daughter. She is obsessed with math, code and computers. Her mother and I are worried. She has no outside interests, including friends or boys."

I stiffened, feeling an immediate kinship with Piper even though I'd never met her. I wanted to leap to her defense, but didn't have a clue what to say.

Before I could say anything, Finn and Bonnie stood up and shook hands. Bonnie walked over to me. "Are you ready, Lexi?"

"Sure. Give me the address so I can plug it into my GPS."

She handed me her business card. "Here you go. See you there."

"Okay."

Just like that, I was on my way back to high school.

Don't miss No Test For The Wicked, *the next book in the Lexi Carmichael Mystery series from Julie Moffett.*

www.CarinaPress.com